HEATHER JUSTESEN

HEATHER JUSTESEN

CFI
Springville, Utah

The views expressed within this work are the sole responsibility of the author and do not necessarily reflect the position of Cedar Fort, Inc., or any other entity.

This is a work of fiction. The characters, names, incidents, places, and dialogue are products of the author's imagination, and are not to be construed as real.

ISBN 13: 978-1-59955-234-7

Published by CFI, an imprint of Cedar Fort, Inc., 2373 W. 700 S., Springville, UT 84663
Distributed by Cedar Fort, Inc. www.cedarfort.com

LIBRARY OF CONGRESS CATALOGING-IN-PUBLICATION DATA

Justesen, Heather, 1976-
  The ball's in her court / Heather Justesen.
    p. cm.
  ISBN 978-1-59955-234-7 (acid-free paper)
  1. Adoptees--Fiction. 2. Women basketball players--Fiction. 3. Adult
children of drug addicts--Fiction. 4. Mormon--Fiction. I. Title.
  PS3610.U883B35 2009
  813'.6--dc22

                         2009008910

Cover design by Angela D. Olsen
Cover design © 2009 by Lyle Mortimer
Edited and typeset by Heidi Doxey

Printed in the United States of America

10 9 8 7 6 5 4 3 2 1

Printed on acid-free paper

This story is dedicated to the foster kids who lived with us, to their struggles and triumphs despite difficult situations. I still joy in their triumphs, cry for their struggles, and think of them all regularly.

CHAPTER ONE

Red and blue lights flashed in the apartment parking lot as Denise DeWalt pulled in. She watched some officers lead a handcuffed man to a squad car. A police car parked at an angle across the driveway forced her to stop. "What's going on?" she muttered. She considered backing up, but a red Jeep Cherokee had pulled in behind her and blocked her escape. She had driven up to her complex still feeling the endorphins from two hours of playing basketball, but that high was now disintegrating quickly.

A well-dressed woman led two little girls to a state vehicle. The younger of the two elementary-school-aged girls was crying and clutching a stuffed animal. The older girl adjusted a green backpack over her shoulder. The sight brought back memories so vivid that Denise could hardly breathe.

Her stomach ached as all the muscles in her body tensed up and her lungs fought to draw breath. Unable to move and surrounded by strangers, Denise fought the urge to escape her car. Her hands clamped on the steering wheel, turning her knuckles white as she was swamped with memories that refused to go away.

She relived the terror of not knowing what was going to happen next. Where would she stay when the doctors sent her home? Was she in trouble? In her mind, she heard the commotion of her mother being handcuffed and carted away.

Her stomach rolled, and Denise lowered her window partway, desperate for fresh, cool air. The tepid September breeze barely took the edge off, but she pulled her chin-length brown hair back from her face and gulped in gratefully, her blue eyes sealed shut as she tried to push the emotions away.

She was surprised when she heard a knock on her window and looked up to see an officer peering through the opening. "Are you okay, ma'am?" She had been too wrapped up in memories to notice the police car in front of her move out of the way.

"Yes, fine. No problem." *Just falling apart here.*

The young officer looked as though he didn't believe her. "You don't look well. Are you sure you don't need some help?"

She shook her head. "I'm fine, really. I just need some dinner. I live right over there." Denise motioned in the general direction of her building. When he nodded and stepped back from her car, she slid it into gear and headed for her parking space farther back in the lot. Pulling herself together, she walked to her apartment, knowing she would have nightmares again. It had been years since she experienced such a strong physical reaction to the memories.

With any luck this would be a short episode.

Denise ignored the waiting mailbox tonight, desperate to get inside before anyone else stopped her or noticed the tears now running wild down her face, despite her efforts to wipe them away. The halls were dark and musty like the string of hovels her birth mother had dragged her through, but all similarities ended when she entered her apartment.

The scented oils plugged into electrical outlets infused the air with the smell of strawberries. The walls were off white, the carpet light blue—a color she'd always considered daring for an apartment building, considering what tenets could do to carpets, but a color that always gave her comfort. The kitchen and bathroom floors gleamed. Bright pictures and flowered crafts, mostly supplied by her roommate, dotted the walls.

The apartment was quiet. Her roommate, Lily, was probably stocking shelves at the toy store. Lily hated the graveyard shift, but Denise was grateful to have the place to herself. Just this once. She inserted a thanks for small miracles into the silent prayer she offered for the little girls. A note was taped to her bedroom door.

Denise,

When you get a minute, could you send my cousin a list of companies who hire people with your skills? He's trying to find a job in the area.

Lily

An email address followed. Denise pulled the paper from her door and tossed it onto her laptop, which was sitting on the desk beside the door. She'd worry about it later. She hurried through a shower, collected her dirty clothes, and took them down to the laundry facilities on the first floor.

While the washers did their magic, Denise returned to her apartment, put on some grinding rock music, and emptied her dresser drawers. Her room was in perfect order already, but she managed to spend the next forty-five minutes scrubbing every nook and cranny. She rearranged the drawers and gave the space a white-glove cleaning.

The distraught look on the little girls' faces haunted her through it all, making her heart weep. Denise knew well the confusion and terror of being taken from home. The loss of control, the uncertainty—not knowing if the place she was going to would be better or worse. The emotions pouring through her pushed Denise to keep cleaning. The anxiety attacks hadn't been this bad in years.

After moving her laundry to the dryers, Denise turned to her tiny bathroom. She scrubbed corners of the floor with an old toothbrush and reorganized bathroom drawers. She stretched and rubbed her sore back muscles before bringing her hands around to look at them. Her fingers were long and thin just like the rest of her body, and just as suited to basketball as her well-trained muscles, but now the skin on them was red and irritated from all her scrubbing. She put away the laundry before deciding to give into the exhaustion bullying her. Though she still felt anxious, most of her desperation had drained away, and she figured she might as well try to sleep. She had to work in the morning.

Denise's fingers flew over the keyboard at work a month later as she created software. A system upgrade the previous night had left a tangle of bugs in its wake. She paused to consider the next line she should add and then typed it in. She spent the whole day, including her lunch break, fixing the issue so she could return to the Web page she'd been working on.

It was late afternoon when Joan walked into the room Denise shared with four other programmers. Joan was a dirty-dishwater blonde receptionist who knew the business better than almost anyone.

"What's going on?" Denise looked up from her computer and smiled. She grabbed the remains of her frozen yogurt and scooped out a final spoonful before tossing the Styrofoam bowl in the trash.

"Southwick said to bring these to you." Joan handed Denise a sheaf of papers. Denise opened them and saw they were specs for a new program she was going to write when she finished her current project.

"I told him I wouldn't be ready until Monday. That was before this mess came up." Denise rolled her eyes and flipped through the file a little more. "They're not complete either. Surprise, surprise," she said, glancing over at Jake Cornwall, the twenty-eight-year-old office jokester who sat next to her. He nodded.

"He's been too busy clearing his office to deal with silly details like paperwork," Joan said with a wave of her hand. "He's got interviews for his replacement today. I get the feeling there's one who looks pretty promising. They flew him in from Chicago."

"I hope he's not some newbie out to prove himself. A ladder-climber who's going to go ballistic over every flaw." Denise held back a grimace. Wally Southwick hadn't been a pleasure to work for; still, when he decided to take early retirement, everyone wondered if his replacement would be better or worse. The mention of Chicago nagged at the back of her mind, but she couldn't remember why.

Joan pointed at Jake's Room Defender, a movement-sensitive and remote-controllable machine that shot foam discs at anyone within range. "Don't turn that on today if you value your job," she told Jake. "Southwick will have your head if you make him look bad."

Jake nodded again. As soon as Joan left, though, he leaned over. "Better buckle up, DeWalt. Whoever they hire, he's bound to be twice as ambitious as Southwick. The young geniuses always are." His eyes skimmed over her. "Then again, maybe he'll have a soft spot for you as the only woman in the department."

Denise grabbed a pen off her desk and tossed it at him, hitting him in the shoulder. "Whatever." She couldn't hold back a smile though, coming up with another possibility. "You never know, maybe the person they choose won't be a guy. Could be a woman, maybe *you'll* end up in the soft spot."

Jake grinned. "There's something I could handle. Too bad the rules outlaw interoffice dating." He seemed to consider this and then winked at her. "You and me could even go out."

"Yeah, shorty, like that would happen. Get back to work, Cornball, I've got things to do." He shrugged, and she shook her head. Jake was only a friend, more a brother than anything. She glanced up and caught smirks from a couple of the other guys sitting near them, but she ignored them.

The afternoon was almost over when Denise caught her first look at the promising interviewee. Southwick ushered him into the room like an old friend. The younger man exuded authority and self-confidence from the tip of his well-polished shoes to the mass of brown hair on his head. His body was broad shouldered and powerful looking as well. But it wasn't until he turned to look around the room that Denise saw his confidence went all the way to the core.

His dark eyes saw right through her, jolting her and stealing her breath. There was something familiar about him. Denise wondered if the lightening bolt of recognition she felt was where his aura of power was coming from. Or was it the other way around? His eyes widened for a moment before he blinked and returned his gaze to Southwick.

Denise could feel her pulse beating a wild tattoo in her veins. She calmed her expression and fought to make her insides comply as well. Maybe he'd attended the University of Utah or had a sibling who did. Or maybe he reminded her of someone she once knew. She clung to those explanations, though none of them accounted for the something more than recognition bouncing around inside her.

When Southwick reached her and Richard Jensen extended his hand, she took it in her own. A strange tingle began at her palm and extended up her arm. She met his brown eyes—eyes that would have seemed too big on any other face. Somehow the strong chin and cheekbones seemed perfectly suited to them. "It's a pleasure to finally meet you, Denise." The words flowed like Southern honey from his lips—strange for a guy from Chicago.

"Finally?" Denise smoothly withdrew her hand from his grasp, desperate to break a connection that had her hair standing on end. She wondered why her hands weren't shaking when her insides were doing a tango.

"I'm Lily's cousin. You're the one who told me about this company," he murmured.

"And we're certainly glad you did. I'm sure Jensen here will do well, though he'll have quite a job to fill my shoes!" Southwick said, pounding Richard on the back and grinning.

"Oh." Denise felt stupid the moment the sound left her mouth. No wonder he had seemed vaguely familiar. Lily had shown her his picture after Denise had sent him a list of companies he might want to check into. "Well, welcome to our little family." Hoping to inject a note of levity, she jerked her thumb toward Jake. "Don't take the joker here too seriously. And don't let him anywhere near your soda if you don't want it tampered with." She forced a smile and hoped it looked sincere.

Richard glanced over at Jake and smiled, turning his slightly nicer-than-average face into something only a step below breathtaking.

Or maybe she was a bit short of breath after all. His gaze returned to her. "I'll keep that in mind."

They were gone before Denise could decide what she thought about Southwick's replacement. Richard Jensen couldn't have been more than a few years older than her twenty-six years. She remembered the jolt that had run through her when their eyes met, but then she pushed it away. She didn't have time for strange fantasies.

As Denise pulled into the apartment parking lot that evening, she told herself she had completely cut Richard Jensen from her thoughts. She ignored the fact she was reminding herself every few minutes that she wasn't thinking about him—that didn't count. She collected the mail from her box and waved at the redhead working in the apartment manager's office as she walked past. The sign out front said there were openings in the complex. With over 350 apartments squeezed together, there were always openings.

The apartment was silent. Lily was probably out with John. Denise made a face at the thought. She pulled out her laptop and checked her personal e-mail—answering a long note from her brother, Gerald—and then visited the online bulletin board for adoptees.

Denise had stumbled across the adult adoptee website several years earlier, coming across a link and deciding to see what it was all about. To her surprise, she had found a few people there who had been through experiences similar to her own. She soon found a support and camaraderie with this group that she had never felt before. None of them knew her real name or what state she lived in, but among these people she felt more herself than anywhere else.

For the past couple of years, she had been using her Internet search skills to help others find family members. What had started as a lark gave her great satisfaction.

It had been a slow day on the bulletin board, with no new requests for help finding family members, but it was almost a relief to have another day off. After twenty minutes, she was typing a note to her brother, Gerald, who attended Utah State University.

She heard the front door open. Lily's laughter and John's low tones trickled in from the living area. It occurred to Denise that she could use a workout, especially if John was going to be over for long.

John was a real estate agent from a well-known family who was already making a name for himself in Utah Valley. On the surface, he seemed like the perfect man for an elementary education major like Lily. He made a good income and seemed nice enough. But the subtle eyebrow raises and fleeting smirks she often caught told her there was far more going on below the surface.

If there was anything she had learned in her years living under her birth mother's thumb, it was how to read people.

By the time Denise changed into workout gear, Lily had dinner started. Lily's long, sable locks were pulled away from her bright, happy face with a large barrette. "Hey, I saw your car in the lot and wondered where you were." Lily put a pan on the stove.

"Hey, Lils, you've got a message." John smiled at Denise and greeted her. He handed Lily the phone, which was blinking to announce the in-line voice mail.

Denise never made an issue of her feelings about John, for Lily's sake. It wasn't Lily's fault John didn't seem to like Denise, or that his opinion of her seemed to drop after he heard she had been in foster care. He had been careful never to be less than polite to her, but he had still changed.

Lily dialed into the voice mail and soon let out a squeal. She scrambled for the pen and pencil on the countertop and dialed with a grin. In a moment she invited someone to eat with them. Lily loved to entertain, to cook for a crowd. It didn't surprise Denise that she would invite someone at the last moment, though she doubted John would appreciate it. He seemed to prefer having Lily to himself.

"What was that all about?" John asked, settling himself at one of the bar stools. He snitched some of the cheese Lily was shredding. When Lily slapped playfully at his shoulder, he merely grinned.

"My cousin's in town. He'll be up in a minute. I'm sure you'll love him."

The doorbell rang seconds after Lily finished the thought. Seeing that Lily's hands were full, Denise answered the door.

Standing on her doorstep was Richard Jensen.

CHAPTER TWO

"What are you doing here?" The words were out of Denise's mouth before she could stop them. The punch of surprise from seeing him was no weaker this time than it had been earlier in the day.

Richard didn't have a chance to react before Lily barreled toward him. Denise cleared out of the way, grateful for a moment to collect herself. "Richy, it's so good to see you. Come in, come in." Lily hugged him, grabbed his hand, and dragged him inside, shutting the door behind him. "Why didn't you let me know you were going to be here?"

The incredible smile Denise had seen earlier spread across his face. "I only found out a few days ago. I barely had time to get your number and address from your mom."

Lily introduced the two men and turned to Denise. "And this is my roommate, Denise."

"We've met," Denise said as she grabbed a cold water bottle from the refrigerator and took a swallow. She needed a moment to counteract the effects of his smile and the surprise of her racing heart. "I have to get to the gym. It was good to see you again." She wasn't very enthusiastic, but she figured no one would find it odd.

Discomfort filled her at having him see her in her slim sweats and old college T-shirt. She seldom dressed up for work, and that day she had only worn jeans and a simple red top, but now that she had her hair pulled back in two stubby dog ears and was kicking around in her ratty sneakers, she was uncomfortable. She felt homely and completely out of the league of someone as shined up as he was.

Not that she was interested anyway.

The fact that she was nearly six feet tall and as thin as barbed wire didn't help her self-image. She'd been told some men found her at least mildly attractive. When she looked in the mirror, however, she still saw that painfully thin, frightened nine-year-old with eyes that were too large for her face.

"You know each other? How?" Lily looked between the two of them. Denise hoped her expression was as bland as Richard's.

"You know my boss is moving on? Your cousin's taking over." Denise inched closer to the front door.

Lily turned back to her cousin, her excitement nearly palpable. "You're moving here? Do you need to find a place to live? Have you found an apartment? I can help you look if you like."

"I already found one." Richard lifted the sheaf of papers in his hand. "No one answered when I called earlier, but I was hoping you'd be home by the time I got here, so I decided to drop by. I stopped at the office on the way in and the manager showed me 208. The painting and repairs will be done by the time I get back to town."

"You mean 208 of this building?" The man would live four doors down from her. Denise wasn't sure what to make of that.

Richard turned, his eyes assessing her. "It fits my needs, and as you know, it's close to work. My flight leaves in the morning, so I don't have much time to look. Why waste time driving around when this one will do?"

"Very pragmatic of you." As a rule, Denise tried to keep her business and personal lives separate. She joked with the guys at work and some-times met them to play a game of hoops, but that's where it ended. With his relationship to Lily, and the way her heart seemed to flip into overdrive whenever he was around, she would have to be extra careful to keep her distance.

She refused to consider it might already be too late.

"I don't believe I've ever heard anyone use that word in real life before." He looked pleased, curious.

"Well, now you have." She didn't know what else to say. Denise turned to smile at Lily instead. "I gotta go. Cliff will be waiting for me," she lied before ducking out the door.

At the gym, Denise suckered some new guy into a game of basketball and beat the pants off him during the two hours of their play. Even after a hot shower, she was still anxious when she returned to her apartment, which was now empty. She decided to tackle the kitchen and started by cleaning out the fridge, then moving to the cupboard doors.

She was scrubbing the floor with a heavy brush when Lily returned, Richard in tow. Denise called out a hello in return to Lily's greeting, but otherwise ignored them. Her back ached, her hands were sore, and her head pounded when she did a final rinse on the floor. But she was finally starting to feel ready to settle down for the night. She rinsed the bucket out in the sink, before rinsing and sanitizing the sink. When she turned, she found Richard leaning against the counter on one hip, watching her.

"Looks like they're in full retreat," he said. His face was unreadable.

"What?"

"All those dirt particles that had considered settling in your apartment. They wouldn't dare come within fifty feet of here now." He glanced around and then looked back at her. "If you're as focused on your programming as you are on your cleaning, I'm going to like working with you."

Denise wasn't sure whether to take that as a compliment or not. She knew she'd been giving into her obsessive-compulsive tendencies. But they would pass in a day or two. She promised herself they would pass. The silence lengthened while sounds of Lily moving around her bedroom floated out to them.

"You don't like me," Richard said after a long moment.

You make me nervous. I never allow a guy to make me nervous, no matter how good-looking he is. "I don't know you, Mr. Jensen."

His eyebrows lifted. "That's what puzzles me. Most people like me until they get to know me, at least. And let's drop the Mr. Jensen nonsense. Call me Rich."

Lily came out with a photo album in her hands. "I knew I would find them here." Her eyes shifted between them, and her eyebrows lifted slightly. She continued, setting the book on the countertop. "Aren't you tired yet?" she asked Denise. "I thought you'd be sleeping when we got back, what with that marathon workout you must have had."

Denise forced a smile. "Just getting the weekend cleaning out of the way early. I'm bushed. Good night." She flicked her gaze in Richard's direction to include him, but didn't make eye contact. She hoped the night's family togetherness wasn't a hint of things to come.

Her night was dreamless, and she slept twelve hours, but Denise woke feeling as groggy as ever. A note on the kitchen counter said her mother had called, and with a sigh, Denise picked up the phone and called back.

"I was starting to wonder if you were avoiding me," her mother said when she realized who was calling.

"Sorry, it's been a crazy week, and I crashed early last night. What's going on?" Denise pulled out milk, cereal, dishes, and a banana while she talked.

"Busy, busy, you know me. The adoption fair is next weekend, and I wondered if you could help."

"Mom." The word came out as a whine. "You know how I feel about that."

"I hoped maybe you'd gotten past things enough to help out this year." The disappointment was evident in her mother's voice. Denise would rather be slugged than deal with that kind of disappointment. She considered the guilt it brought on as akin to emotional blackmail, and Jennette DeWalt could compete with a Jewish mother in that department.

"I'd love to help you. I stuffed envelopes for you last month, and I'll help set up, but I can't help at the fair. You know that." Unable to think about the adoption fair without her stomach twisting in knots, Denise only volunteered to help with the parts that didn't involve the children. When people started arriving, she'd duck out until they were gone—it made it easier to pretend the event wasn't connected to adoptions or foster care. Dealing one-on-one with these kids made it difficult for her to distance herself from her own memories of these activities.

The network of adoption organizations her mother had gotten involved with when Denise was in her teens held a bi-annual adoption fair, one in the spring and one in the fall, to help kids find families. Denise was all for kids getting out of the foster-care cycle and into solid homes like the DeWalts gave her. The first time she helped, however, it had taken only one glance at two children to send her into a spin of nightmares that lasted a full week—not that Jennette had ever known.

"You never have enough help setting up and tearing down. I'll be happy to help out then."

There was a short pause on the other end of the line, and when Jennette spoke again there was only a trace of disappointment in her voice. "I appreciate the help." Then she moved on to talk about her niece's upcoming wedding.

Fifteen minutes later, Denise stood in a hot shower until the tension in her shoulders and back loosened up. It seemed tension was a constant companion lately.

Despite several rain showers over the next week, the weather was perfect for the adoption fair Saturday—sunny and hot for late September. As she pulled down a beanbag toss booth in a downtown park, Denise couldn't help but envy the fun the kids must have had, focusing on happy faces instead of the purpose for the event.

Hearing a child ask about the clown board sitting next to her, Denise turned to look at a woman with two small children out for a walk in the park. "Hello. Do you like clowns?" Denise asked the little boy.

"Yes. And I like parties," the boy said. Denise figured he must be three or four.

She smiled and the woman asked, "What's this all about?"

Denise explained the purpose of the activity. Most people smiled and acted delighted when they heard about these events. This woman pursed her lips instead.

"My nephews were removed from my sister's house because of drugs when I was in high school. None of us know where they ended up. Do you think they were adopted, or would they still be bouncing around the system? I always wonder about them." The woman's blue eyes grew sad, and she shook her head, as if to clear it.

Denise clenched her hand around the bolts she had just removed from the game. "How old were they? Why didn't they go to family?" What she wanted to ask was why the woman was telling a complete stranger about all of this.

"The boys were real young. Two and four. My father was gone, my mother was really sick. I was only allowed to stay at home because I was about to graduate from high school."

Denise imagined the confusion the two boys must have gone through, being removed at that age. She had been nine, old enough to understand the concept of why she wasn't living with her mom anymore. She forced a smile. "At that age, I'm sure there was no problem placing them in an adoptive home. They're probably happy and well-cared for. It's too bad some of the kids who were here today weren't in a more settled home at those ages." Denise could feel the sting of tears behind her eyes, but she pushed them back as she tried to distance herself from the conversation. She did not cry in front of strangers.

She very seldom cried at all.

The woman shifted the baby from one hip to the other and looked more closely at Denise. "How are you connected to this group?"

"Default. I was one of these kids once. My adoptive mom asked me to help out, so here I am." Denise wished the woman would move along so she could finish up. She needed a pickup game of basketball right now. She could feel the tension growing in her back.

Setting the baby on the ground, the woman dug into the diaper bag she was carrying, and handed each of the children a cracker. Her eyes, however, barely left Denise. "How old were you?"

"Nine."

"Did you ever get back in contact with your family?"

Denise could feel the implied criticism in the words, but she wasn't going to cower to a stranger. "No. I don't know that I had any family besides my birth mother, and I'm not interested in seeing her again."

"I would love to see my nephews again. Don't you wonder about cousins, aunts, and uncles?"

With a tight smile Denise excused herself, saying she needed some other tools to finish her job. When she returned a few minutes later, she was thankful to find the woman gone.

When she got home that night, Denise defrosted the freezer and scrubbed the furthest corners of the refrigerator before starting on the oven.

CHAPTER THREE

Denise walked into the kitchen for breakfast on Sunday, dressed and otherwise ready, but faltered for a moment when she saw Richard leaning over a bowl of cereal at the kitchen counter. "What are you doing here?" She wished the words back as soon as they were spoken. It appeared she didn't know any other way to greet him. "I mean, welcome back. I hope your trip was smooth."

He turned and his eyes flitted over her, taking in the simple blue dress that showed off her calves. A smile of appreciation teased the corners of his mouth by the time his eyes returned to hers. "I moved into my apartment last night. Lily said I could eat here today since I didn't have time to go shopping." He had been wearing casual office clothes when she saw him the first time, but today he was dressed for church in a navy blue suit, a white shirt, and a subdued blue tie.

She thought he looked better in his suit, much better, and that hint of a smile teased heat into her cheeks. She dismissed the subject from her mind, not needing the distraction. Instead, she rounded the counter and pulled out dishes for her own breakfast. Several seconds passed in silence before she decided manners required her to carry on some conversation. And he was her boss, so it wouldn't hurt to be civil. Much. "How was your trip out here? Did you get everything settled in Chicago?"

"Yes, the movers beat me here by an hour and were all unloaded. The drive was long, but uneventful. Lily said you helped your mom with some fair thing yesterday. How did it go?" He scraped the end of the cereal from his bowl onto his spoon.

Realizing she hadn't thought about it since she entered the room, Denise wished he hadn't asked. "Fine, great. You ready to start work tomorrow?"

He shrugged. "I guess we'll have to wait and see."

Lily walked in and redirected the conversation, much to Denise's relief. She soon escaped back to her room with her breakfast.

Though Denise interacted with Richard as little as possible without coming across as rude, she was very aware of his presence in the room at church. Despite her resolve to focus on class, she found herself unable to keep from glancing in his direction several times, catching his eyes on her more than once. The memory of the jolt of recognition she felt when they first saw each other still lingered, regardless of her attempts to excuse it as her imagination.

Lily went to Richard's apartment after church, and Denise puttered around her apartment most of the afternoon. She had been invited to her parents' for dinner, and she knew she would see her sister Paige and maybe Paige's boyfriend, Cliff, as well. Needing something to do with herself until then, and something to keep her mind occupied, she pulled out a cookbook and made some snickerdoodles.

Denise was just pulling the first tray of cookies from the oven when Lily and Richard came back into the apartment, laughing. "We thought we were so tough, jumping from all of three feet up," Lily said.

"Kids always think they're so tough," Richard agreed. He sniffed the air. "Whatever's cooking smells great."

Denise slid the new tray of cookies into the oven and set the timer. "Give them a few minutes to cool, Richard, and you can have some."

"It's Rich," he corrected her. "Do you do a lot of baking?" Rich slid a cookie off the tray with a spatula and passed it from hand to hand to keep it from burning him.

Denise shook her head. "No, *Rich*, I'm usually too busy. You could have waited a minute for that, you know." She pulled a small plate from the cupboard and set on the counter in front of him.

His grin made her heart stutter. "I like 'em hot." But he set the cookie on the plate.

She turned back to the sink and swallowed to clear her throat. "You'll burn your mouth, but I guess that's your problem."

Lily laughed and pulled out three glasses for milk. "You always were the most impatient boy I ever met."

"I don't know what you're talking about. I'm a paragon of virtues." Rich acted offended, but his expression quickly melted into a smile.

Lily laughed again, and then scooted a couple cookies onto another plate. She and Rich retreated to the sofa to eat. "Come join us, Denise."

"I need to get to my parents' home for dinner, but thanks."

Lily took a phone call from John while Denise rolled the last batch of cookies in cinnamon.

"It must be hard to be the only female in the department," Rich said from behind Denise, causing her to jump a little.

Denise shrugged. It wasn't as though the guys made her life rough. She was more put off by Rich's sudden topic of conversation. "Not so bad. I can beat most of them at basketball as well as hold my own at work, so I earned their respect early on. I get along fine with everyone."

"That's good to hear." He leaned against the counter and pilfered another of her cookies. "Any office politics I ought to be aware of?"

Denise considered that, thinking about the various personalities in the office. "I don't know much of the gossip. Be careful with Murphy," she said, referring to the boss of the local office. "I'm not in the loop much, but you might want to watch out for a few weeks to figure that out. Joan is the office manager. She's the sweetest person who ever lived and knows the office better than anyone. If you get her in your corner, she'll make your life easier. If there's anything non-programming that you need to know in the office, she has the answers."

"Thanks, I appreciate the heads-up."

"Sure." Denise pulled out the second tray of cookies and put in the last one. "Your family lives in California, don't they?"

"Yeah, but they moved there when I was in college. I grew up in Louisiana, outside Baton Rouge."

Denise nodded. That explained the lazy Southern accent. "Lily never mentioned that." She set the kitchen timer. "Then again, we don't really talk much about her extended family."

"John's coming over soon. I wish you were staying for dinner," Lily said to Denise as she hung up the phone a moment later.

"Thanks, but I can't."

A few minutes later, Denise grabbed the plate of cookies and her wallet and hurried on her way. She soon found herself wandering around the temple grounds in Provo, killing time before dinner. She needed time to clear her mind if she was going to push away the questions of her past. She couldn't go there, not now, not ever again.

Early that morning, she had woken from another nightmare, sweating, breathing heavily, and practically having a panic attack. She had groaned when the clock told her it was nearly time to get up. Denise wanted to blame the nightmare on the nosy woman from the day before and firmly place the responsibility on all people who think it's okay to pry. She knew, though, that she hadn't finished her latest episode from seeing the kids taken away by the case worker weeks earlier.

Don't you wonder?

The words echoed again in her head as she rounded a corner of the temple grounds, and Denise worried they would never leave.

Pushing the question away again, she tried to find something else to think about. Something that didn't include Rich. Her mind landed on Paige, her sister. Denise smiled. She and Paige had shared a love-irritate relationship for many years. They cared about each other, but they didn't really understand each other.

Paige was the pretty one, the one with all the dates. The one who rarely kept a relationship going for more than a few weeks at most. Until Cliff. Denise pushed a strand of hair the wind had caught away from her face and turned the corner around the temple so she would be facing the wind.

It took no more than a glance at the temple to remind Denise she'd never been inside. She would have to enjoy the spirit of the place from the grounds instead. Feeling the peace she always garnered from the temple grounds seep into her, she checked her watch and saw she wouldn't arrive at her parent's home too early if she went now.

She didn't have to wonder why she left her apartment so early; she had made a conscious decision not to spend any more time than necessary with Rich. Her instincts said getting too close to Rich would be easy but dangerous. Part of her called out that there was something special about him; she should get to know him. Another part of her screamed out to stay away before he could hurt her. She chose the second option.

He was her boss after all.

She glanced at her watch, noticed the time, and then picked up speed, returning to her car.

Chapter Four

Ten minutes later, Denise pulled into the driveway at her parents' home, a brown brick house with tall trees and a sagging porch. Her parents had built it before Paige was born; they were almost the first family in the neighborhood. The large driveway was now riddled with long cracks from the roots of the neighbor's tree which had been planted too close.

The front windows sparkled, flaunting bright red and blue curtains. A cheesy fall wreath hung on the door, greeting visitors with a wooden "Welcome" sign tole painted and inserted in the middle. The wreath, or one like it, always seemed to hang there ever since the first day Denise arrived, fourteen autumns before. Nothing ever changed here.

In the driveway, a blue Honda sat next to her dad's beat up truck. It looked like Cliff was there with Paige.

Denise wandered up the walk and stepped inside. "Dad still hasn't fixed the door," she mumbled to herself as she leaned back hard on it to make it shut tightly. She found the fact strangely comforting. A yapping mongrel dog ran around the corner of the hallway into the living room to greet Denise. She smiled and leaned down to pick up the wiggly ball of fur and snuggle her, while balancing the plate of goodies in her other hand. "Cookie, it's good to see you too."

Cookie wriggled joyfully in her arms as Denise continued on to the dining room.

Jennette called out, "Denise, is that you?"

"Yes, Mom, it's me." Denise pulled faces at her favorite mutt. "Did you miss me, baby?" she asked the dog. Jennette was in her usual spot in the combined dining and kitchen area of the house.

The fact that these areas were open to each other had always made it convenient for her to keep an eye on her kids as she cooked or cleaned. The large room was pivotal during those years when children sat around the table and did their homework right after school. A seemingly endless parade of foster kids had wandered through when they needed a safe place to stay while their parents worked their lives out, and nearly all of them had spent time parked at the table doing homework.

Though she hadn't really minded the other kids coming and going, Denise had found that the worst part of living with other foster kids after she'd been adopted, was seeing them go home, knowing she never would. Denise always wondered why her birth mother couldn't have made the effort to pull her life together so she could have gone home, too. Why had Denise not been worth the effort? Not that she cared, she reminded herself. She was much better off away from Daphne, the junkie who gave birth to her.

Forcing the questions away, Denise smiled and put Cookie on the floor. She slid the plate onto the countertop and then walked around the island to give her mother a hug. "You look well today. Those kids in your nursery class must have behaved."

"Mostly. Nate Carling tried to flush all of the little animal figures down the toilet, but we caught him before he blocked the pipes. Meanwhile, his twin, Sally, managed to mix all of the kids' shoes into the bag of Legos during clean up. It took a while to figure out where they were. I had fun." Her eyes sparkled as she threaded the dish towel through the fridge handle.

"Sounds like a mad house—just up your alley." Denise turned to greet Paige. Her sister sat on the sofa with Cliff, who greeted Denise with a grin. She pushed back a wistful twinge in her chest as she saw the two of them sitting there—willowy, blonde Paige snuggled up against Cliff's tall, lanky frame. Paige had soft, classical features with just enough sass in her smile and eyes to make her face interesting, while Cliff's face was large with prominent cheek bones, a strong jaw, and the slightest cleft in his chin. They were both good looking enough to draw plenty of attention their way.

"What's up?" Cliff said, "I haven't seen you at the gym for a few days."

"Bad timing, I guess. You've spent too many evenings with my sister."

She smiled back at him and sat in a nearby chair.

"I don't know if that's possible, what with his school and practice schedule," Paige said with a teasing glint in her eyes.

Cliff tapped Paige's nose with a fingertip. "If you think things are busy now, just wait until the season starts." He glanced at the plate on the counter, then back at Denise. "You made cookies?"

"After dinner, sport." When Denise had introduced Paige and Cliff almost two months earlier, she hadn't expected the relationship to last more than a few dates. Cliff had returned from his mission in May then played on the BYU basketball team that fall. Paige had always had a thing for athletes, but this one in particular seemed to have caught hold and not let go. Denise was happy to see it. Cliff seemed a lot nicer than most of the guys her sister dated, and Denise felt an instant camaraderie with him on the basketball court—something she attributed to their mutual love of the game.

Whether he and Paige managed to make things work long-term or not, Denise wasn't complaining about him hanging around.

Monday morning, Rich pulled into the parking lot at work right behind Denise. She glanced over at him as he was getting out of his car and noticed he looked a bit nervous. She took pity on him and decided to try to lighten his mood. "Ready to move in and use your genius touch to remake the department?"

"Yeah." He smoothed his hair, which still looked wet from the shower, and turned toward the building. "Remind me not to puke, okay?"

Denise held back a laugh, mostly because he did look a little nauseated. "Relax, you'll be fine. I haven't heard of anyone biting yet, and I've been here two years."

She led him through the front doors and smiled at the receptionist. "Hey, Joan, guess who followed me in. Think you could let Mr. Murphy know Mr. Jensen has arrived?"

"Certainly. It's good to see you again, Mr. Jensen." Joan extended a hand in greeting.

He returned her smile, now looking as cool and calm as if he did this kind of thing every week. That was, until he looked back at Denise and their eyes met—that was all she needed to realize he was putting on a front.

Joan's laughter danced down the hallway as Denise turned away.

"Just oozes charm, that one," Denise muttered to herself before dropping her lunch off in the break room.

Denise saw little of Rich that day. At first, she figured he was settling into his office. Then she was too busy to give it another thought.

She stayed late at work, wrestling with computer code, knowing it needed to be up and running by the next morning. The trouble was, every fix she made seemed to cause a chain reaction in another part of the program, making it do something it wasn't supposed to.

After adding a few final keystrokes, she paused for a few moments to take another long pull from her can of juice before refreshing the page. As she sat back in her chair, thinking of how great a hot soak in the tub would feel on her aching back, she heard footsteps in the hallway. A glance at the clock told her it was nearly nine. *Who would still be in the building at this hour?* Wary, she sat up and looked out the door. In a moment, Rich stepped into the doorway.

Denise leaned back in her chair again. "Oh, it's you. I wasn't expecting anyone else to be here." Her heart beat quickly from nervousness, which hadn't escalated beyond control, thankfully.

"What are you still doing here?" His face was stern, and he tapped the edge of the papers he was carrying on his open palm.

She typed information into the site's search text box. "Finishing up this program. The Web page will be ready to go online tomorrow." She stood and stretched as she waited for the information to come back to her. "What are you doing here? Didn't you go home hours ago?"

"Lily and I were driving back from the grocery store when we noticed your car in the parking lot. When we saw the light on, I decided to come see if you were here. Do you often work this late?" he asked as he glanced at the clock.

Seeing the answers she sought flash onto the screen, Denise grinned. "Nope, just when I'm working to finish a project on time. I've been working on a few other emergencies this week and had to push to make my deadline. I'm done now. Finally." She set the sheets of paper on her desk and fiddled with the mouse as she saved and shut down all the programs.

Denise hunched over her desk, still standing, one hand on the desktop and one on the mouse. She glanced up and saw him watching her. "You can go, I'll be home soon."

"Are you kidding? You think I'm going to leave you here alone? It's dark out there." He gestured toward the window that showed the sun had been down for quite a while. "You never know who might be waiting in the parking lot."

"How gallant of you," Denise said with a roll of her eyes as she picked up her belongings and checked for her keys. "What would I ever have done without you?" She kept her voice dry to cover her amusement; he ignored it. Her stomach growled as she followed him out into the hallway.

He turned around and looked at her. "When did you eat last?"

"Well, *Dad*, I did have lunch about eight hours ago. But don't worry, I'll take good care of myself when I get home." She'd been taking care of herself since she was barely out of diapers and now Rich thought he needed to check up on her and make sure she ate dinner?

Rich ignored the barb and followed her out to her car. Lily was parked right next to it, and Denise waved a greeting to her roommate before she climbed into her own car.

As she followed them home, Denise wrapped away her irritation that Rich had treated her like some kid. She had moved out of the house the week after graduation and never gone home for longer than overnight again. She was perfectly capable of taking care of herself. Denise refused to acknowledge the warmth in her chest brought on by his concern.

Chapter Five

Tuesday night after grabbing some dinner, Denise holed up in her bedroom. Rich ate with Lily and John in the kitchen. The sound of their laughter trickled through the wall and door. Denise blocked it out and booted up the computer to check her email.

As she expected, her inbox was packed. She sorted through to weed out the junk mail and read notes from a few friends before tackling her emails from other adoptees. There were three search requests and a couple people responding after taking the next step on their journeys.

"Let's see what we can do for you, Mallory," she muttered as she pulled up another search. She filtered out possible answers for a woman she had been communicating with for months and emailed her the list of women's names to track down. "Good luck to you," she said as she pushed send. Denise wondered how much longer she would be able to put off her own search. Didn't she wonder about her extended family? Denise worried that the woman in the park had forced a crack in the dam. It had only been three days, but she couldn't get the question out of her head. The answer was yes, she wondered all the time. Was the life that she remembered the only possibility, or was there family out there that Daphne had never spent time with?

For years now, these questions had haunted Denise, though she tried to pretend they didn't matter. Did she dare find out? If she didn't search, would she be able to put the growing questions away again?

Still without answers, Denise shut down her laptop and grabbed her basketball shoes. She needed to work through this.

"Don't you have a place of your own?" Denise asked Rich with a forced smile when she sat down to dinner on Wednesday night. He was over visiting with Lily again. "Don't you have unpacking to do still?"

"Lily's been helping me. She organized my kitchen after her classes got out this afternoon, and I finished my room yesterday. I'm about done now."

"So soon?"

"Yeah, just like magic," Rich added, sidling up onto the stool next to her. "A la peanut butter sandwiches, or whatever that Sesame Street magician character says. It's good to be back around family again."

"He didn't have that much to put away." Lily set the pot of pasta on the counter in front of them. "Typical bachelor."

Lifting an eyebrow, Denise turned to look at him. "Do you watch Sesame Street regularly?"

"When you have friends with children, you tend to pick these things up," Richard explained. "Besides, he was using that line when we were kids. Don't you remember it?"

"I didn't watch much Sesame Street as a kid." Denise turned her attention back to the plate in front of her. The truth was, she'd seldom had a working television, but when she did, her mother was more worried about her own programs than she was about Denise's.

"I don't know why you bothered to put your kitchen things away. Lily seems bent on feeding you every meal anyway." She lifted a forkful of food to her mouth.

Rich laughed and looked over at Lily. "And I can't say how much I appreciate it. I've been cooking for myself for too long."

"Enjoy it while it lasts," Lily said with a smile of her own. "Midterms are coming up, and I'll be too busy to make anything for the rest of the semester."

"I'll have to take a turn cooking for you," Rich said.

"You cook?" Denise let doubt drip from each word. So far she hadn't seen him do anything more difficult than mix frozen lemonade.

"Sure." Rich grinned at her. "McDonald's, Arby's, Domino's, Wendy's—"

Denise couldn't quite hold back a smile as she poured her milk.

"That's not cooking. But I'm sure Lily will appreciate it anyway."

"Actually, I do know my way around a kitchen," Rich said. "I may not be a gourmet, but I've learned a trick or two over the years. We'll have to plan something."

Denise nodded but didn't take him seriously. Interacting at work had taken the edge of tension off from their first meeting, but she still didn't feel easy with him.

Shortly after eating, she hurried out the door, basketball in hand.

"Going to the gym?" Lily lifted an eyebrow, and Denise smiled back.

"Yeah, I figured I could use some exercise. There's bound to be some foolish guy willing to 'go easy on me.' There always is." She forced more bravado into her voice than she felt.

"She any good?" Rich asked after the door closed behind Denise. This made five visits to the gym for Denise during the seven days he had been in Utah. Like the way she was cleaning the kitchen that first weekend, it seemed a little obsessive to him. He told himself he shouldn't worry about her, she was a grown woman.

It didn't help.

"Oh yeah, she's excellent," Lily answered.

Rich allowed a smile on his face but kept his eyes focused on the countertop where he was playing with his keys. The week had been busy and crazy both at work and with unpacking. He made a concerted effort to ignore his feelings for Denise, but he watched her. It was impossible to miss the detail-conscious way she worked, the easy camaraderie she had with her coworkers, and the way she blocked herself off from them in all but the most casual ways. She was an enigma. "Excellent. Does she do anything badly?"

"Not much. Failure seems to be a foreign word to her." Lily covered the leftovers and stashed them in the fridge.

Rich's mind returned to Denise. She wasn't one who could trust easily. He wondered if he dared put in the effort to earn that trust. The jolt of recognition that came when he first saw her, the feeling that he had found what he was searching for, was overwhelming.

Rich wasn't one to believe in relationships cultivated on the other side of the veil continuing on in this life. Not that strongly, anyway. The need to get to know her churned inside him, but he wasn't about to risk his job over a little chemistry. And her response to him had been more than a little forbidding.

He stood, slid his keys into his pocket, and gave Lily a kiss on the forehead. She had homework to do before she went to the toy store tonight, and piles of paperwork teetered on his own kitchen table.

Lily and Denise lounged around the living room in their pajamas on Friday evening watching a chick flick and eating chocolate chip cookie dough. When the movie ended, they stayed there talking about hairstyles—or at least Lily was discussing hairstyles as she was considering a hair cut. Denise was nodding and agreeing with everything her roommate said. Lily lay on the couch, and Denise was spread out on the floor in front of her when Lily broached a subject that obviously bothered her.

"You haven't been sleeping well lately." Lily's comment was not a question.

Denise looked over in surprise. The nightmares had been very insistent lately. She tried to pass it off. "What makes you think that?"

"Last night I heard you scream something in your sleep. I was about to come wake you up when I heard you moving around; the water was running in the bathroom. It's not the first time I've heard it. You've been a little . . . off in the past few weeks too. What's going on?"

Denise wanted to laugh it off, push it away, and pretend it wasn't real. But she couldn't. She needed someone to talk to. She needed a friend who could be objective. Knowing she might regret it, but that at least Lily wouldn't spread it around, Denise decided to take a chance. "I've had a couple experiences that have reminded me of my past. It's been rough."

That was a gross understatement, Denise thought as she mentally cringed. Lily knew virtually nothing of the abuse and neglect Denise's mother, Daphne, had put her through, or of the rancid apartments and the men. Denise also never shared her experiences with the juvenile justice system.

Not sure how much to tell her innocent, naïve roommate, Denise decided to stick to basics. "I saw the cops arrest a guy a while ago, probably for drugs. Two little girls were taken by a social worker. At least it looked that way. I guess it could have been a family member, but I doubt it. Then I talked to a woman last weekend after the adoption fair. She asked me if I didn't wonder about my birth family."

Denise stood and walked over to the tiny living room window. Outside a couple walked hand in hand across the parking lot and into a neighboring building. "I keep telling myself I don't care, that it doesn't matter, especially if they're all like Daphne. But what if they aren't?" She whirled back around and faced Lily. "What if they're good people and they want to know me as badly as that woman wanted to know her nephews?"

Lily didn't answer, just looked at her expectantly, her long, dark hair pulled up with an elastic. She looked as sweet and innocent as Denise knew her to be. Lily had been very sheltered and was prone to look on the bright side.

"So what's the problem?" Lily finally asked.

"What's the problem? What if they aren't wonderful people? What if I check around and find out they're all in jail? What if I only had an uncle or something and he died when I turned eighteen and I lost my chance to meet him? Or what if they're perfectly respectable people, but they don't want me?" This was the possibility that hurt most. What if she made contact with her family and they didn't care?

"You're being melodramatic. It's entirely possible nothing bad will happen. What if they are decent people, they do want to know you, and you're shutting yourself off?" Lily's calm voice was almost maddening in its sensibility.

Denise gave herself a moment to calm down and think things through rationally. "Okay, say you're right and everything is dandy between me and my birth family. What about my adoptive parents? What do I tell them? When do I tell them? And if I don't tell them, how do I find out anything? I don't know what Daphne's maiden name was or her birth date. I don't know what state she was born in. I feel like I know nothing. My mom might be able to help me, but how could I hurt her that way?"

Denise returned to the sofa and sat heavily beside her roommate, burying her face in her hands as tears squeezed between her fingers. Crying in front of Lily was humiliating. "They're the only people who've ever been there for me. The only ones who stuck, and I was no fun at all to live with when I was a teenager. How can I hurt the only ones who care about me?"

"Would they feel hurt?"

The laugh that escaped Denise's lips was half sob. "I'm part of their family, legally. But I know my mom will feel somehow not good enough if I search. Intellectually, I think she would understand my need to search, but in her heart . . . it would hurt her. I'm not sure how my dad, Paige, or Gerald will react."

Lily draped an arm around Denise's shoulders and let her cry and reason out her worries to herself for a long time before Denise was feeling up to any answers.

"Feeling better?" Lily asked when Denise's breath calmed down again.

Denise sat now with her head leaning against the back of the sofa, so she could look up at the ceiling. Denise nodded without conviction.

"Good. No one can give you an answer, Denise. But I have a couple of questions for you to ask yourself. How long have you wanted to search? Is the desire getting weaker or stronger over time? If it's bothering you this badly, wouldn't your adoptive family want you to find your answers? Or would they rather you wake up screaming and wander the house in the middle of the night because you never resolved the problem?"

Lily's questions were almost as disturbing as the woman at the park's had been, but Denise knew she couldn't live like this for much longer.

CHAPTER SIX

Unfortunately, Lily was right. Denise spent a lot of time considering the possibilities over the next two days but could only come up with one option. She needed to talk to her adoptive parents about her desire to search.

Thursday evening, Denise waited until nearly nine before stopping by her parents' house. She pulled into the driveway and sat, her hands fidgeting on the steering wheel for a long moment. It was October now, the heat of summer had melted away, and the house was decorated for Halloween—the holiday where people faced boogey men. It seemed fitting.

With a deep sigh, she pulled herself from the front seat of the car and locked her door. She trudged to the front door of the house and pulled her key out to unlock it, but it opened when she tested the knob. Denise called out when she stepped into the house to let her parents know there was someone else there, but only Jennette met her in the kitchen.

"Where's Dad?" Denise fought the urge to bite her lip. The habit was a dead give away that she had something to say that they wouldn't want to hear. Jennette had told her that a couple of years before.

"One of his home teaching families had a problem, needed a blessing. I was just about to make hot cocoa. Care for some?"

"Yeah." Denise figured she could use something to play with while she talked. She said a quick prayer for strength, one of the many she had said that day already.

Jennette talked about things going on in the ward and neighborhood while she prepared the hot water. A couple minutes later, they were sitting across the table from each other, and Denise could see the look of expectation in her mother's eyes. Not much got past Jennette DeWalt.

"What's going on?" Jennette asked.

Denise smiled despite herself. "Work, the gym, church, the usual."

"Really? Normally you call if it's the usual on your mind. What's up? I can see something in your eyes."

Denise twisted the cup of cocoa on the tabletop and bit her lip. Her voice was low and hesitant when she began. "I don't want you to think I don't appreciate everything you guys have done for me, the family you gave me. I wouldn't hurt you for anything, not after everything I've put you through. But I've been wondering about my other family—my biological family." She glanced up and saw worry in Jennette's eyes.

There was a long pause while Jennette seemed to be fighting to stay calm. Denise wondered if she should have surprised her mom with the information like this. Was there a better way to approach the issue?

"I see. Are you ready to try and make contact?" Jennette's voice sounded almost normal. Almost.

Regretting that she had brought the subject up, for a fleeting moment Denise considered abandoning the whole project, but she knew she couldn't. "I'm not sure. Well, I know I need to; I haven't been able to get it out of my head. But I'm not sure if I *want* to. I'm happy with my life and being part of your family. I just can't seem to let it go. It's keeping me awake at night." She reached out and touched Jennette's arm, needing the woman to understand how important this was to her.

"You've been separated from them for a long time. I expected you to do this right out of high school, especially the way you were acting. I wondered for a while if you had made contact but never told any of us." Jennette's eyes were now focused on the cup in her hands, locked onto it as if desperate for something to hold.

"I couldn't do that." Denise shook her head. "Even when I was a snot-nosed teenaged brat I wouldn't have done that. I know it probably sounds like I'm ungrateful, but I don't have any other options. The need to know won't shake loose this time. But I don't want to hurt you."

Jennette laughed softly, but there was no mirth in it. "Everything I've read about reunion says it's a rocky road, lots of ups and downs. I have to tell you, a lot of the time it doesn't work out. Even if you make contact and manage to keep up something of a relationship, there's a good chance you'll never feel the connection you may be looking for.

"I'm not telling you this to discourage you. I've done a lot of study-ing over the years, and almost every story I heard said the person seek-ing was glad they did, even if it turned out badly." The words sounded almost bitter, as though she were speaking them against her will. She had received extensive training as a foster parent. By the time Denise had been placed in their house as a preteen, both parents had studied about nearly every conceivable problem a child might have, and their background on Denise's issues had been deep. It had been a blessing, though Denise hadn't seen it that way at the time.

Denise ran a finger around the rim of her cup, and then looked into her mother's eyes. "I've heard that, too. I already know there's a good chance this won't be a happy reunion. If Daphne is still around and hasn't killed herself with alcohol and drugs, the woman I knew may never for-give me for finding a life of my own."

Sighing, Denise ran a hand through her short hair. "Actually, I'd rather not meet her again, especially if there are other family members I can contact instead. I have to try something, though." Denise reached out and grabbed Jennette's hand, desperate for her to understand. "I don't know if I'll get any peace if I don't at least try. I feel driven. You and Dad have done everything for me. Please don't be mad."

"I'm not mad, but why now? Why not seven years ago when you were first old enough to make that decision on your own?" Jennette pulled her hand away and added a couple more miniature marshmallows to her drink.

"I couldn't have. I was still so angry with her and everything con-nected to her. I couldn't imagine taking the chance before." Denise took a long sip of her cold cocoa while the silence lengthened. "I'm going to need your help. I don't know where to start, what Daphne's maiden name was, or how many times she was married."

Jennette's eyes focused on Cookie for a long time before she answered. The mutt rested at their feet, her eyes begging for a treat. "Four marriages, by the time parental rights were terminated. That's what we've got on record anyway."

Denise looked up in surprise. "How did you know that? Why didn't you tell me before?"

"I figured you knew, and you never brought the subject up. The few times I tried to talk to you about Daphne, you got angry and refused to discuss it." She hesitated before continuing. "I have documents that might help you search, if you want them. There's your original birth certificate, at least. Not the one you get with my name on it if you requested one now, but one with your biological parents' names on them."

The look on Jennette's face, the desire to help warring against the desire to protect, made Denise's stomach tighten in a knot. "I don't know if I want to talk to her or just root around the edges. I just know I have to search." Worry overwhelmed her. "No matter what happens, it won't make a difference between us, will it?"

Jennette smiled wanly. "No, of course not."

Denise promised herself that she would make sure of it.

It was late when Denise returned home that night, and Lily was already at work. There was a message on her door saying Rich had stopped in to say hello, but she ignored it.

Denise felt more torn than ever about the search. She had hurt Jennette, and she knew that her father, Lynn, would be unhappy when he heard it all, if only because of the way his wife felt about it. They were like that, protecting each other, putting the other first all the time. Denise desperately wished she could have a relationship like that. She had once thought she would.

Brian had started out as a study buddy, a guy she occasionally played on the court—and beat more than half the time. That didn't seem to bother him much though, and when he had turned their friendship into something more, she had been cautious but interested. He took things slow. Despite her struggle with some issues from her abuse, after six months, their relationship was definitely headed toward marriage, and she had decided it was time he knew more.

Unfortunately, Brian hadn't asked enough questions about her past, and she had never volunteered the information. It wasn't until she started telling him the trouble she got herself into with the juvenile justice system that he hit his limit.

Funny, she hadn't even brought out the big guns.

He'd said they needed to step back a bit, take a break. Two weeks later he was engaged to someone else.

The jerk.

That had been the end of things for her dreams of future wedded bliss. She couldn't handle putting herself through that kind of hurt again. More specific memories of what had happened in her youth had surfaced since then, reinforcing her concerns about marriage, ensuring that she wouldn't take such a step lightly in the future.

The fact that Brian had found her too damaged to continue the relationship without hearing *everything* impressed on her that no one would take her if they heard the whole story. This thought brought her back around to Daphne.

In another week or so, she would have the information on her birth family. That would be the time to make decisions.

She hoped she was making the right ones.

The next week, Rich didn't see much of Denise outside the office. He was settled into his own place, and Lily often dropped in at his apartment for a few minutes. Despite all he and Lily could do to draw her out, Denise stayed firmly behind the brick wall she built.

Their time together in a professional capacity seemed to have eased the tension simmering between them. A little. But he was curious about the parts of Denise's personality that Lily hinted at. Parts the people at work never saw.

He was discouraged by the difference between her reaction to him and the rest of the crew. She and Jake teased each other a lot, but as soon as she realized Rich was around, she tightened up. He didn't seem capable of getting her to relax around him enough to have a normal conversation. But he didn't want to scare her off by pushing too hard, too fast. It was driving him crazy.

Thursday evening Rich drove over to the nearby gym. On her way out the door for a date with John, Lily had mentioned that she thought Denise might be there. He found he couldn't resist a little exercise. He walked to the front desk and paid for the night, glancing around. Stepping to the side, he could see someone consistently catching the net with a basketball in the next room.

"Do you need someone to show you around the weight room?" The perky girl at the front counter tipped her head and shot him a flirty smile.

Rich dipped his head a bit further to the side and saw Denise run into his view as she shot a three-pointer. She was poetry in motion, all long legs and easy grace. He grinned. "No, I think I'll just take a look around." He ambled in, taking a long moment to watch Denise's form and enjoy her catlike movements as she covered her half of the basketball court.

"Hey, DeWalt, you need a partner to play some one-on-one? I could go easy on you." Denise finished her shot and let the ball fall through the net before she turned around to see Rich standing with his hands on his hips.

She sized him up, wary, and then grinned, secure in her abilities. "You can't take it."

He raised his eyebrows at her comment. "Yeah? Care to wager some Hogi-Yogi on that?" He had noticed she had a fetish for frozen yogurt. If she was half as good as everyone said she was, he was toast, but he figured his ego could handle it.

"You're so on! I can taste it already," she said. "Going to fifteen?" He nodded. "You start, and I'll give you a three-point lead." She smirked as she tossed him the ball.

"Cocky, aren't you?"

"Confident."

She let him start with the ball, but stole it after only a few seconds. They bumped back and forth, then she twisted and shot for a three-pointer and missed. He collected the ball, teased her about her technique, but didn't get near the basket before she stole the ball again. This time she got across the court and sunk the ball in her hoop before he could catch up. The race was on.

Even with the lead, Rich lost the match. Twice. By a healthy margin. Denise was good. And by the time the game ended she was loose and friendly, bantering back and forth, letting confidence in her skills brush away the walls she usually wrapped around her.

"Do you ever lose?" he asked, breathing heavily as they walked off the court.

"Not often. A few times I've ended up playing against one of the college players, and they've taken me to the cleaners. I always lose to my sister's boyfriend." She grabbed her bag from the edge of the room and walked toward the door. She saw him grin as they headed for the parking lot. "I think I'm going to go home and hit the shower. You?"

"Yeah. I'll walk you to your car. It's dark out there."

"Thanks, Lancelot, but this isn't Chicago, and I'm not a wilting violet." She covered a laugh with a cough as Rich put a hand to the stitch in his side. "You gonna make it home without collapsing on the way?" she asked. Her eyes sparkled and her lips shifted with the effort to keep a smile from her face.

Still breathing hard, but getting better, Rich put on a desperate look. He had to milk the casual atmosphere while it lasted. She was so vibrant and alive right now, he could barely believe she was the same person who so often put up the obvious "do not touch" sign. "Maybe you'll have to carry me home. You wouldn't want me to get mugged because I collapsed in the parking lot."

"Tough luck, you're on your own, Lancelot," she said as she opened her car door. "I like chocolate, by the way. With crushed Oreos."

"What?"

"The yogurt. Payback. Chocolate."

"Right, you'll get it tomorrow." He watched her drive away before making his way back to his own car. If she was always so relaxed at the gym, he should consider getting a membership and actually using it. It had been too long since he had played a game like that one.

Chapter Seven

The next day, Denise sat at her desk, trying to find a good stopping point in her work so she could grab lunch. Rich walked in with a Hogi-Yogi bag and a drink holder with two sodas and two frozen yogurts.

"Payoff time," he told her. "I have your lunch. Do you want to eat at your desk, or are you going to step away and eat in a civilized manner?" It wasn't the first time he had chastised her about the way she ate at her desk when she should be taking a break.

"My lunch? The deal was for frozen yogurt." She looked up at him. There was a glint in his eyes that said he'd intentionally stretched their agreement.

"You skunked me twice, so I bought you lunch. I can't eat two so now you're going to have to help me out and eat it."

Aware of the guys listening in on their conversation, she picked up the pen on the desk and began rolling it through her fingers. "But I brought lunch."

"What did you bring, leftover pasta or something?" His comment made her wonder for a moment if he checked her lunch box, but leftovers were common for her. "It'll keep. Come on," he tipped his head toward the door.

"I'll be right there." She threw him an exasperated look. He smiled back and left the room.

"What's he paying back?" Jake asked with a grin.

Trying to make light of it, Denise smirked. "We ran into each other at the gym last night, and he challenged me to a game of one-on-one.

Sucker even bet me Hogi-Yogi. How could I back down from that?"

"You didn't warn him you could play?"

She laughed, deciding to keep the three-point advantage and final score to herself. He didn't need to be *humiliated*. "Yeah, but some guys have to try and prove something."

Rich waited in the break room for Denise to arrive. He knew he had thrown her a curve ball with the whole lunch thing. She could use a little unpredictability in her life, but he hoped she didn't get mad about it.

Denise came in and pulled out the chair across from him. Rich found his already-quick pulse pick up a little more speed. Just a friendly lunch, he reminded himself again. As if he wouldn't prefer a series of a-little-more-than-friendly dinners.

"Lily said you always order ham and cheese, but you're welcome to my turkey if you prefer." He held the two sandwiches up.

"You asked Lily? Why didn't you ask me instead?" she asked, taking the one marked ham.

The wall was up again and stronger than ever. He pretended not to notice. They both unwrapped their lunches. "You would have refused lunch, so I worked around it. I got you lemonade. I hope that's okay. Lily said you don't do caffeine or carbonation."

"Thanks." She took the plastic cup with a note of irritation. "They both dehydrate, and they cut your wind."

"I'll have to remember that." Rich sucked down a large swallow of his Coke and caught her fighting a smile.

"I was wondering about something."

Her mouth was full, but she looked at him encouragingly, so he continued, "When I looked at apartments, I noticed the two bedroom ones were $750 a month. Yet Lily indicated she was only paying $250."

Denise's gaze skated away from his. After she swallowed, she picked at the bread with her fingertips. "I do have the bigger bedroom. Hers is like a closet."

He wasn't going to let her dodge him, and he was more than a little curious. "Yes, but she seems to think rent is only $600."

Her lips curved up at the edges and she met his gaze. "I fudged the truth a bit. It was $675 when we moved in. I knew what her budget was and after several horrible roommates, it was well worth it to me to pay the extra. Since the contract is in my name, she didn't know when the rent went up." She pulled a slice of ham from her sandwich distractedly and then looked down and stuffed it back in. "I'd rather she didn't know. I can easily afford to pay the difference."

He found himself even more drawn to her easy generosity. She was such a study in contrasts. "I'll keep your secret."

She nodded and seemed to think that closed the subject.

They munched away in an awkward silence for a minute before Denise spoke again. "So how do you like your new job?"

He wondered if she really cared or was just trying to be polite. "A lot; it's going well, I think. I have a few of the details I'm trying to untangle, but I'll be able to step back soon and let most of you tackle things on your own again. How are things going on the Corbet project?"

Denise shrugged. "It's nothing serious. Basic code issues, none of it too difficult. They seem to be happy with the other work I've done for them, so we have a good dialogue in place, and I know they'll let me know if they aren't happy about any of it. We've worked through things before."

"That's important, good dialogue. That's something I want to have with everyone in my department." He watched her lift her gaze to his, and then look away, focusing on opening her bag of chips.

"I know we were a little worried about what might happen when you came in. Shake-ups are never a lot of fun, but you've gained everyone's respect." Her shrug was grudging but he figured she must have meant it. Denise didn't seem like the type to say so much if it wasn't true.

He read between the lines and shifted the conversation where he wanted it. "If not your trust, yet."

Denise looked at him in surprise. "What?"

"You don't give your trust easily. You pal around with the guys and put on a good show, but when it comes down to it, you're more of a lone wolf."

Denise lifted an eyebrow. "You don't beat around the bush."

"I find the direct approach is usually best. And I don't like to play games." He deliberately kept his voice light.

Her eyes never wavered, looking straight into his, but she matched his tone. "I don't play games, either. I like my life the way it is, and I don't need any help."

"You don't have room for any new friends?" He sent her a teasing smile, one that almost always worked on women. He saw the corner of her mouth twitch as though she were fighting a smile of her own, but her expression stayed bland.

She turned back to her chips. "I have plenty."

"You don't have any like me."

"There's no one else like you, Rich." He grinned, and she sighed. "There are reasons I keep work and my personal life separate. You're making that difficult. I'm not sure I like it." She hurried to qualify that. "It's nothing personal."

"Of course it is. It's personal to you. I understand you have your reasons." His fingers itched to push a lock of hair back from her face, but he knew she wouldn't like it. "Trust takes time. You might find you can even tolerate me, with a little practice."

She shook her head in resignation and took a big bite of sandwich. A couple women from advertising came in talking about some movie, ending their privacy.

Despite her reservations, Rich was hopeful; the basketball game had broken down a few of her barriers. All Rich wanted was a chance to see if first impressions meant anything this time.

Saturday afternoon, Denise was in the living room working on her laptop, searching out some names for people she met online. The living room window was open, letting in crisp autumn air and the sound of children laughing in the nearby playground. It would be Halloween in a couple weeks, a night for goblins and ghosties and far too much candy. The smile that thought brought vanished when she heard Lily and Rich come in the door. Forcing herself not to put things away too quickly, she finished up the job, sent the email with the information, and closed down her computer.

When she glanced up from her computer, Rich was looking over her shoulder. "What was all that?"

Denise hesitated for a moment. "I belong to an adoption website. One of the people on the site wanted information to search for his birth father. I looked up what I could find and sent it out." She turned toward him and set the computer on her lap. She knew she made it sound simple, but the search had been more exhaustive than some she'd done.

He dipped his hands in his pockets and his intense brown eyes grew curious. "You were adopted?"

"Yes," Denise said as Lily disappeared into her room with her book bag.

"Have you ever tracked down your own family?"

He always knew where to probe, it seemed. "Not yet. My memories of my birth mother aren't all that great."

"How old were you?"

Lily reentered the room and headed for the kitchen.

"I was eleven when I moved in with my parents. Now if you'll excuse me." Ruffled, Denise stood and pushed past, crossing to her room. "I have a lesson to finish preparing for church tomorrow."

Rich watched her shut the door behind her. He wondered if the reticence was more of the same wish for privacy or if she had really been more uncomfortable with the subject than most. "She doesn't like to talk about it," he said to Lily.

"No, not much. She wasn't some baby who was placed into a loving home at birth. She went through a lot of mess to get where she is. Give her time."

"Time I've got. I have to wonder if she'll ever get that far." The more Rich learned about Denise, the more she intrigued him. He glanced over at Lily and saw her knowing look. "I'm her boss, and the company is serious about no dating. They fired a couple of people a few years back."

Lily stopped and turned to him, her hand still on the open cupboard door. "Seriously? Who fires people over who they date?"

He shook his head. "There were rumors about problems. Problems between a worker and supervisor that ended up causing a real mess; I never got the details. The no-dating rule went into effect shortly after that. If we worked in different departments they'd probably ignore it, as long as we were discreet." Rich thought of the lunch a few days earlier. That hadn't been terribly discreet. He'd have to do better.

"We can be friends," he continued. "But one of us will have to switch companies if we make it more. I don't want to rush her, and I know she wouldn't let me if I tried. Instead, she'd run the other way so fast I'd probably never catch up." Lily laughed in agreement at that comment, but he continued, "I can't help but wonder if she's the one I've been waiting for."

He caught her lifted eyebrows but didn't give her a chance to speak. "It sounds crazy, but the feeling is so strong. We'll work through the rest when she's ready."

"If she ever is," Lily pointed out.

Rich pushed the possibility away. He needed a little hope.

Sunday evening Denise went to her parents' house for dinner again and brought back a manila folder. Jennette had unearthed all of the paperwork surrounding Denise's history and adoption that hadn't already been shredded. The woman who put up with so many teenage traumas without appearing to break a sweat had been obviously reluctant to part with the papers. It made Denise feel as though she were betraying the two people who never gave up on her, but she had to do it.

After dinner, Denise hurried home to an echoing apartment. She knew Lily would spend the evening with John. Grateful for some time alone, Denise dug through the paperwork in her room. She felt a jolt of surprise when she looked at her original birth certificate. Oklahoma? She had been born in Oklahoma?

The only birth certificate she'd seen before now was the one the State of Utah issued her when the adoption was finalized. Denise still had the original, though she knew Jennette had a copy in her files somewhere. When her eyes fell on her birth father's name and birth date, Denise felt torn. Did she want this to be true? Did she want this man to be her birth father? At the least, Denise was grateful it gave her an age and starting place for her search.

After setting that page aside, she ignored the phone and front door. It wasn't until Lily came knocking on her bedroom door after ten that she allowed herself to be distracted.

"Have you been shut in here all night? Did you eat?" Lily asked. "What is this stuff?"

Denise glanced at the clock and realized three hours had passed. "I ate with my parents. I'm going through paperwork."

Rich appeared behind Lily in the doorway, and Denise could hear John in the background. It sounded like he was on the phone with a real estate client. At 10 PM on Sunday. Lily explained once that John was little more than the hired hand and sometimes his clients were only available on Sunday. Denise pushed her irritation at his justification away; if it didn't bother Lily, Denise had no reason to fuss over it.

"What paperwork is that?" Rich asked.

A few seconds passed as Denise pursed her lips and tried to decide if she was ready to share. When she opened her mouth, intending to brush him off, her answer was a surprise. "My adoption papers, my foster care file—at least the parts my parents held onto. Paperwork about my birth family."

Rich joined her on the floor where she'd spread the papers around, set into neat piles. Her laptop sat nearby, with a word processing program open where she was taking notes. "Are you saying you're ready to look for your family? Do you need some help?"

Jennette had kept court summons and paperwork showing work hours Denise had completed as payment for some of her delinquent activities. Worried about what he would think if he read some of the papers around her, Denise hurried to place them out of reach. "No thanks, most of this only makes sense to me because I lived it. I don't want to miss something because you didn't know what to look for. Besides, I want to do this myself." *And I don't want you to know* that *much about my history.*

Lily sat on the bottom of the bed and looked down at them. She pushed her brown hair back from her face, the set of her chin and the glint in her eyes said she meant business. "But you'll ask for help when you need it, right?"

Not sure how to answer that, Denise looked back down at the paperwork. She didn't want to meet anyone's gaze. "This is something I have to do myself, a personal journey." Her hands fumbled the papers; she didn't really *want* to do it alone. The possible responses to her search terrified her, but she couldn't bear to have her secrets opened up to anyone else.

Rich took her trembling hand and squeezed it. "But that doesn't mean you won't need support. I can only imagine how scary it must be for you to go searching for your family. We can't do it for you, but we can help you, be there for you. If you'll let us."

Denise felt goose bumps rise where he touched her and held in a shiver. She closed her eyes for a half second imagining the strength he would give her, the comfort, but the image of Brian's cold eyes, as he'd said good-bye reared its ugly image, and she pulled her hand away. "I'll let you know."

CHAPTER EIGHT

Rich came around to the girls' apartment every evening the following week, pulling Denise into conversations. More often than not, John seemed to be around in the evenings, making the gathering feel almost datelike. That was disconcerting, but Denise managed to shrug it off since Rich kept everything super casual. When Lily decided to throw a surprise birthday party for John on Friday night, both Rich and Denise offered to help.

Denise's borderline OCD tendencies meant the apartment was always clean, but there were plenty of snacks to prepare. She got home from work to find Lily putting up streamers. A beautifully decorated homemade cake sat on the counter nearby. Lily's culinary skills amazed Denise as she wondered if a professional could have made the cake look any better. She sighed; slapping purchased frosting on a cake was the extent of her own skills in that area. And all too often she ended up with cake crumbs "decorating" the finished product.

Rich came in a few minutes after Denise. "What do you need?" he asked Lily.

"Help Denise with the vegetable tray she insists is required for these kinds of gatherings, would you?" Lily asked.

"Hey, we have to have a semi-healthy option available. Straight junk food makes you sick," Denise said. She caught Lily's teasing grin and let out a smile of her own. Lily's penchant for sweets and Denise's belief in a healthier lifestyle was an ongoing joke between them.

"I love junk food, and I don't get sick," Rich teased. Denise's elbow nudged his side. "Fine, I'll keep my mouth shut and help."

She held back a smirk. "Good thinking."

To her surprise, Denise relaxed with Rich as they stood side by side fixing munchies, though she sensed something was on his mind. Lily ran around the rest of the apartment putting up decorations and making sure they had enough paper plates and plastic cups and utensils. When Lily left a few minutes before seven to grab some ice cream from the store, Rich and Denise were still putting together the vegetable tray.

The party was turning out to be more of a production than Denise expected, and she wondered how Lily pulled it all together. Then again, John had been unhappy that Lily cut her hair. Denise figured Lily was trying to make it up to him by making a fuss, and she certainly went out of her way for this event. She wondered how Lily managed to get her homework done with the extra work for the party. Pushing the concern away, Denise focused on the food and her work partner.

When only carrots were left for the vegetable tray, Denise began putting together a seven-layer dip for the nachos sitting at the end of the counter. She glanced over and looked at what Rich was doing to the carrots. "They're supposed to be carrot sticks, not carrot logs."

"They're long and skinny," he said, looking back at the pile he had finished.

"They're bigger around than your thumb. Who's going to eat them like that?" She grinned to take off the edge of her criticism.

"I forgot you were a perfectionist." He cut the one in his hand lengthwise into a couple more pieces. "Is that better."

Seeing he didn't look the least offended, she pressed a bit more. "Fabulous. I thought you said you could cook. Even a six-year-old can cut carrot sticks."

"You would give a six-year-old a sharp knife? Are you crazy? You don't have kids cutting things like this until they are at least seven."

"Depends on the kid." Denise narrowed her eyes at the toothpick-thick sticks he was making now and set a hand over his. "Some people shouldn't handle a knife even when they reach adulthood. Maybe I should finish that, and you can spread refried beans with a spoon instead."

He brushed the finished sticks to the side and began cutting the next one into appropriate thicknesses. "Those are for the people wearing dentures. I didn't want their teeth to be damaged."

"You're nuts. How many people in our ward do you imagine wear dentures?"

"Well, there's the bishop. Of course, they might be all his own, they're doing amazing things to help people keep their real teeth these days."

Denise couldn't help laughing softly at the suggestion. "Our bishop can't be more than six or seven years older than you. You are twenty-eight, which is so old it's a wonder your dentist hasn't started discussing dentures with you yet."

He grinned at her, and they exchanged a glance before returning to their work.

Their talk had been lighthearted and casual for the past fifteen minutes, and Denise wondered how she could ever have felt uncomfortable around Rich. There were still plenty of things she had no intention of sharing with him, but he was a good guy. The fact that she was aware of every movement he made wasn't a reason to put up walls, she told herself. They could just be friends.

Denise told Rich about a project she got called in on at night a few weeks before he moved to Utah. "I ended up spending half the night working on code to get the site running again. They finally tracked the hacking down to a teenager in Montana. I'm telling you, if he would channel his energy in another direction, the kid could be a millionaire in five years. He was that good."

"I've seen your code. Your security is pretty tight, so he must have been good," Rich said. The vegetable tray was now complete, and he finished filling the center cup with dip, and then put the extra away in the fridge.

"Grab the salsa from the middle cupboard there, will you?" she asked, and moved closer to the countertop to let him slide past her. His compliment warmed her more than it should have, and she needed a minute to cope.

Denise heard the cupboard door open and the sound of canned food sliding around. "It's not here."

She set the spoon on the cupboard and turned toward him. "Oh, try the next one over. Lily never seems to put things in the same place twice."

"You allow that?" he teased.

"It's her cupboard." She shrugged, knowing he couldn't see it, or the way she tracked every move he made with her eyes. His arms were surprisingly muscular for a desk jockey, and his short-sleeved blue shirt emphasized his biceps and the width of his shoulders.

He opened the cupboard, picked the jar of salsa out, and then turned and placed it on the counter beside her. Denise looked up into his eyes when he placed his other hand on her shoulder. Her stomach quivered.

"You're a lot of fun when you let yourself be, Denise."

She couldn't respond to that as her mouth went dry. She swallowed, trying to get past the sudden lump in her throat. One of his fingers brushed her neck and she felt goose bumps run down her arm. The look in his eyes said more than she wanted to see. Why had she thought they could just be buddies, friends? The moment stretched out for several seconds as they stood, motionless, neither breaking eye contact as the moment wound around them. Hoping to bring some sanity back to the moment, she tried to protest, despite not wanting to step back from the situation. "Rich—"

"You make me want a relationship that a boss isn't supposed to want with his employee." His voice was low, barely more than a whisper.

Denise turned her head away, focusing on the sink, but Rich slid his hands up her neck and onto her cheeks, his gentle touch alone enough to have her turn and face him. One thumb brushed across her cheek, and the fingers of his other hand slid into her hair. "Rich, we can't." The protest sounded weak, even to herself. She wanted him to kiss her.

"For just a minute, I'm going to forget that you're strictly off limits."

When Denise looked up, his face was drawing closer, and she wondered if she would breathe again. His lips slid over hers, and she felt herself falling into the kiss. Her hands grasped the cotton at the side of his shirt, pulling him closer. His torso was solid beneath her hands, and the movement of his fingers on her face and in her hair sent shivers down her spine, into her scalp. Something inside her had wanted this since the first moment they met, fighting against the memories that warned her away. His soul called out to hers, and though she fought it, she couldn't beat it back. At that moment, she didn't even want to.

When he pulled away, they stared at each other for several long seconds. Denise wondered how she had ever reached this point. She'd already crossed a line she had sworn she would never cross again. Not only was one of them bound to be fired if they didn't pull back, but her feelings were entangled far more than she ever dared let them be before. It wasn't safe to go on.

But she really wished he would kiss her again.

Denise pushed him away and turned her back to him, concentrating on getting her breath back. "That can't happen again, Rich. You're my boss, and that's not going to change. We already took things too far."

"My feelings for you aren't going to go away," Rich said, putting his hands on her shoulders again.

Denise stiffened, wishing she didn't believe him. "You love your job; don't put it at risk over me."

"I love my job, yes. But I'm falling for you. Work is an obstacle, but it's not the main problem here. Something besides work has you running scared." He ran his fingers along a lock of hair by her ear. "Share it with me, Denise."

Denise hung her head, resting her chin on her chest. It took all of her will to keep tears back. She hadn't felt this way since . . . no, she'd never felt this way, not even with Brian. Somehow that made it even scarier. "You don't know what you're asking."

She gasped as she felt his fingers brush the hair away from her neck and his thumb rubbed across her exposed vertebrae. It sent a volley of shivers into her hair and made her uncomfortable as shadows of her memories crept into the corners of her consciousness.

"I know what I feel," he whispered into her hair. "And I know you feel something too, even if you aren't ready to admit it yet."

She fought the memories back. "You don't understand." She turned and pushed him away, putting some space between them. He gave way readily. "I'm not built for romance, and I'm not a good bet. It doesn't matter if I feel something or not." What mattered was the terror inching back into her chest as she worked to remind herself that her current situation was nothing like what had happened to her as a child. Rich was not one of Daphne's men, and she was no longer nine years old.

"You need time to get to know me. I can wait, try being friends first." He slipped his hands into his pockets, steeling himself for the change. "I wasn't going to push so far. I would apologize, but it wouldn't be sincere. I've wanted that kiss for weeks."

"I wouldn't believe it anyway." Denise had too many experiences with men saying things they didn't mean. She wouldn't be suckered now.

Rich's mouth lifted in what might have been mistaken as a smile, if someone hadn't heard the conversation. "There's that trust issue of yours again." He paused. "Tell Lily I'll be back in a few minutes; she left the drinks in my fridge." He walked out of the apartment without another word.

Denise fought the pain in her chest, the terror of knowing that he was already making progress, and that if he wasn't hallucinating about his feelings for her, this would end with both of their hearts broken.

John seemed surprised by the party, all right, but Denise didn't quite believe the perma grin he wore all evening. Lily left for work shortly after the party ended, leaving Denise with a mess in the house, but she didn't mind. She needed something to do with herself after her experience with Rich. She knew Lily would help with the cleanup in the morning but decided not to leave it for her roommate.

The next morning Lily thanked Denise for taking care of things, and then apologized profusely for leaving the mess in the first place. After taking care of her laundry, Denise did some weight training to work off some of her tension.

It was nearly dinnertime when Denise returned from the gym and a little grocery shopping to find Lily sitting on the sofa with a red nose and puffy eyes.

"What is it?" Denise asked, dumping her groceries on the counter. She hurried over to the sofa and set a hand on Lily's shoulder.

Lily shook her head and turned away.

"Is someone hurt? Are you sick?"

Lily shook her head after each question and then cleared her throat. "I didn't expect you back yet. I'm behind on my homework and everything. John's right, I just . . . I don't want to talk about it." She stood and walked to her room, shutting the door. The loud beat of eighties rock music came on a moment later.

Denise stood, uncertain of what to do. She didn't want to push, but there had been plenty of times growing up when Denise wished someone would come talk to her, care enough to push her.

Finally, Denise decided to give Lily a little time. If she didn't come out soon, Denise would go in and try to get more details. She put away her groceries and took a shower.

When she was dressed and came back out to the living room, the apartment was silent. Lily's door sat open, and her room was empty. Denise hoped it meant Lily felt better, or that Lily had decided to go speak with Rich.

Denise began to worry when Lily didn't return home before she went to work that night. But when she woke in the morning, she heard the sound of Lily's shower running and knew her roommate was alive, at least.

CHAPTER NINE

Since Rich's declaration a few days earlier, Denise had been treading with care around the office. She hardly saw Rich at work; he was spending a lot of time in meetings, but he still stopped by in the evenings—every evening—theoretically to talk and spend time with Lily, though half the time Lily was out, and Denise figured he knew it, but used Lily as an excuse anyway.

She was still going to the gym to work out four or five times a week, but Rich seemed to catch her at home nearly every night anyway.

Lily never spoke about her crying jag on Saturday afternoon, and Denise tried to respect her privacy, but the light had gone out of her roommate's eyes. After several days, Denise decided Lily shouldn't keep it to herself. Denise would make Lily talk about what was wrong.

Thursday night she came home from work and found Lily sitting on the floor between the sofa and coffee table, her books and papers spread across the table in front of her as she did her homework. Lily looked up, her smile a little brighter than the previous day, but not what it should have been. "How was work?"

"It was fine." Denise set the mail on the counter without sorting it and dropped her car keys on top, making her way across the room to the sofa.

Lily's gaze flitted back to the unsorted mail and her brow crinkled in surprise when she looked back at Denise. "What's going on?" Denise never left the mail on the counter like that, Lily had teased her about that fact more than once.

It was now or never, and though she didn't want to pry, desperately didn't want to pry, Denise couldn't let it go any longer. "You're the best friend I've ever had, and I hate to see you like this. Do you want to talk about what's bothering you?"

"You're going to make it hard for me to refuse, aren't you?" Lily turned back and looked at Denise, her face wistful, her eyes sad. "It shouldn't be that big of a deal, really. I . . . I shouldn't have tried to surprise John like that. He isn't really big on surprises. I knew that. He appreciated the thought, but . . ." she shrugged. "We'll get past this; things are already looking up."

Denise wondered if John really had appreciated the thought, or if Lily had forced herself to believe it so she could live with his disapproval. It made Denise want to go have it out with John. "He doesn't appreciate you enough. You deserve better."

Lily smiled, but her eyes became distant. "I love him, Denise. I've never felt this way about anyone, and he does appreciate me. I only need to adjust a little."

"You're great just the way you are. You don't need to change for him or anyone else." Denise modulated her voice to keep it sounding far calmer than she felt.

Lily's smile broadened at that comment, and she set her hand on Denise's arm. "You're such a good friend." She tipped her head, and her eyes twinkled. "Am I really the best friend you ever had?"

Despite frustration over the change of subject, Denise couldn't help smiling back. "Yeah. I've never had anyone close to my age that I could talk to before. Not really. If you need to talk sometime, I'm here for you."

"I appreciate that. John and I will work through things, so you don't need to worry about me. The course of true love never did run smooth. Speaking of which, how are things with you and Richy?" Lily wiggled her eyebrows.

If Lily was trying to find a topic that would drive Denise to leave the room, she couldn't have hit on a better choice. Feeling somewhat trapped, Denise scrambled to her feet and walked back to the counter where she quickly sorted the mail as she talked. "Rich and I are friends, and stuff." She wasn't sure what to say about her and Rich, the memory of his kiss warmed and confused her. It was definitely more than a friendly kiss.

"And stuff. Hmmmm."

Denise tossed the sales circulars in the trash and headed to her room to hide. "Yeah, I have some things to do before I head to the gym." She heard Lily's laughter behind her before she shut her bedroom door.

Denise had become much more of a regular at the gym. Two or three visits a week had blossomed to almost daily as she left the apartment as often as possible in an attempt to avoid Rich and the way he made her feel.

The flip side to all of this was that she started running into her sister's boyfriend, Cliff, more often. He always won, but she gave him a reasonable amount of competition, she thought. Cliff's willingness to keep their friendship based squarely on basketball made her easy and gave her a safe way to blow off steam. Besides, he talked a lot about Paige, helping her understand her sister better without increasing Denise's guilt for her part of their strained relationship.

After his winning basket Wednesday night, Cliff slid an arm around her shoulders and gave her a noogie.

"Hey, watch the hair. Don't you know girls hate that?" Denise ran her fingers through her hair, trying to put it back in place.

Cliff shrugged. "Guys hate it too." He didn't move his arm from her shoulders. "You know, Denise, I don't know why you and Paige don't get along better. She seems to think you're this recluse, but you're all right."

"Thanks, I think. I don't think she's dated anyone this long before. What's up?"

He removed his arm from her shoulders and picked up the basketball, which lay several yards away. He dribbled it back over to her, and aimed for a shot. "She's pretty great. I know you two don't talk too often, but we're not even starting to get sick of each other yet. Would you hate it if I stuck around a little longer?"

A smile formed on Denise's lips as she caught the twinkle in his eye. "How much longer are we talking about, a few months or a few millennia?"

The ball slid through the basket with a swish, and he grinned at her. "We'll see."

That surprised Denise. She expected him to nudge the issue away, like she would have done in his place, but the look on his face was an admission of long-term plans. Once again, she envied Paige. Not because it was Cliff she was getting serious with, just that she could get serious with anyone and take it all in stride. "That's great. I don't usually like the guys she dates, but I can't find anything annoying enough to hate about you."

"Brat."

"Creep." She walked up to him, smiling widely.

"Blockhead."

"Frog face."

He laughed and handed her the ball. "That's my brother's favorite. I can't quite seem to get away from it."

"That ought to tell you something. I'll have to make sure and use it often." Denise dribbled toward him, then turned around, her back to him to keep him from stealing the ball. He tried to block her as she made her way to the basket.

"So how about you? I haven't heard about you dating anyone. Do you keep that to yourself?"

"Guys around here are intimidated by my athletic prowess." Denise glanced over her shoulder and turned, feinting. She jumped a shot when he fell for the feint. It went through the basket. "The only guys I ever talk to outside of these four walls are at the office, and not only are most of them married, they're coworkers, so that's not an option." She played it as cool as she could while he went after the ball.

Cliff returned to the top of the key. "It's too bad Paige didn't get some of your athleticism. I'm afraid it didn't run thick in the DeWalt bloodlines." His grin was friendly and understanding; Paige must have told him most of the story, if not everything she knew. Denise wasn't sure how she felt about that, but since it didn't seem to make any difference to him, and she couldn't exactly change things, she let it go for now.

"Lucky for me, I guess. I'm still not sure where mine came from, not my birth mother. I never knew my dad." She ran after the ball and pivoted to return to the top of the key for her shot. She glanced up and found Rich standing nearby, his face inscrutable but hard. She wondered how much he'd heard.

She took the shot, but it hit nothing but air. Silence hung thick between them as she took the few steps back to Cliff's side, but she never removed her eyes from Rich's.

"Cliff, meet my boss, Rich. He's also my roommate's cousin. Rich, this is Cliff, he's dating my sister. He plays basketball for BYU."

The two men eyed each other with curiosity and shook hands. "I've been wondering about Denise's family. She talks about Paige, but I've never met her," Rich said. "She's mentioned playing ball with you a couple times."

"Yeah, she's a good partner." Cliff glanced back at Denise, then seemed to decide he was in the way. "I better be going, thanks for the workout. Coach should hire you to push us at training." He grinned as he grabbed his towel from the stands and beat a hasty retreat.

Denise felt her mouth go dry as she turned away and tossed another basket. This one went wild, unfocused, and didn't even hit the backboard.

Rich retrieved the ball, but didn't hand it back or take a shot of his own. He held it to his side and walked up in front of her, standing to give her a long appraisal. When he spoke, his words were low, his voice flat. "I can't get you to talk about your birth parents at all, but you'll talk to him?"

She clamped her lips shut to prevent them from quivering and took a moment to form a calm reply. "He knows the story; Paige told him. Enough of it in any case. I'm not trying to shut you out. I've just known him longer than you." He lifted his eyebrows, and she closed her eyes. "Or maybe I am. Look, none of that changes what's happening or not happening between us."

There was a long silence. "I started looking for a new job today. I can't start applying yet; I haven't been at Donaldson long enough to justify a move, but I'm keeping my eye out all the same."

Denise turned away. "Rich, don't do that. Please don't. I can't promise you anything, not ever. Work isn't the whole problem."

"What is?"

She felt his hand on her shoulder and moved away. "You don't know what you're asking. This is not the place to discuss this. I gotta go."

"Whether switching companies gets me a chance to be with you, or just some space so I don't have to walk by you every day and never be able to admit my feelings, I'll take it. It kills me to have to treat you like an employee when I want so much more."

Denise ground her teeth together. "I have to go. Bring my ball back with you, will you?" She didn't turn and face him, didn't dare for fear she would burst into tears before she reached the comparative privacy of her car. She strode over to where her gym bag sat and scooped it up, slinging it over her shoulder.

"Denise."

She felt a tug in her chest, a twisting pain, and she squeezed her eyes against it before turning to look at him. When their eyes met, the pain intensified. There was a chasm between them wider than the literal space on the basketball floor. They both wanted to cross it, but she couldn't take the chance. She knew when she did, he would hurt her. Or she would hurt him. Or both.

"Good night, Rich." She hurried out the door and into the crisp evening air. The weather man expected snow by morning, and for once she wished they would get two feet so she could work from the privacy of her bedroom.

The doorbell rang at six o'clock the next night. Denise had just begun looking through her cupboards, trying to think of something to make for dinner. A glance through the peep hole in the door showed it was Rich on the other side. She considered pretending she wasn't home but decided she might as well face him now.

She opened the door and let him in. "Lily isn't here; there's a note that she's at the library and that she'll head straight to work from there. You can leave a note for her if you like."

"You know I didn't come to see my cousin." He moved into the room, a couple of plastic grocery sacks dangling from one hand, and closed the door behind him. Rich circled partway around her before stopping to face her.

The directness in his eyes made her palms itch. "What did you have in mind, exactly?"

He set the sacks on the counter, and began unloading pasta, tomato sauce, onions, garlic, mushrooms, and half a loaf of French bread. "Unless you have serious objections, I was hoping we could make dinner together and talk. We both have to eat, and friends have to start somewhere."

"And if I do have objections? What if I have a date coming over?"

An eyebrow went up on his forehead. "I would have a serious objection to that, though I couldn't do anything about it. But I suppose we could reschedule if that were the case." He paused as if uncertain. "That was hypothetical, wasn't it?"

Denise enjoyed the worry in his eyes for a moment, and then decided to let him off. "Yes. This time. I suppose if you promise to keep your hands to yourself, we can try talking."

"If you insist. Now, come help me cook." His voice was as warm and smooth as chocolate fondue.

Deciding she was probably safe, and that his word was worth more than most, Denise walked over and picked up the package of mushrooms. She circled the counter and picked out a knife, and then grabbed a plate to begin cutting. When she saw him drawing closer out of the corner of her eye, she looked up and took an involuntary step back.

"I don't bite." He stepped a little closer before pulling another plate from the cupboard.

He removed a saucepan from a cupboard, put a little oil in the bottom, and turned on the heat below it. "Do you want to talk about last night?"

She finished slicing the mushroom in her fingers and picked up another. "Not especially. But I guess we should. You want the whole story?" A glance in his direction told her he did. His expression was so calm and unworried, it made her want to punish him. To punish him with the truth. And though she knew that would be the end of their relationship, it would be best if he understood the situation now, before things got even more serious between them.

CHAPTER TEN

"My birth mother was a drunk and a druggie," Denise began. She didn't lift her head to look at Rich, choosing to focus on her slicing instead. "She flitted from man to man, looking for someone to make her happy. She married several times, but more often just moved her boyfriends in or moved us in with them. When Daphne—I can't even call her 'mom'—got soused or high, she got mean and stupid. Sometimes she hurt me, then shut me in the other room so she could have her party. Usually, I only came away with bruises."

She slid the plateful of mushroom slices into the saucepan, and grabbed the onion on the counter beside her. Memories swirled around her, making her throat constrict, her heart race. She could almost smell the moldy apartment from her past. "The night they took her to jail and put me in foster care, she broke my arm, but she was too high to understand what she had done. I lay in the next room, listening to her partying with her friends, knowing in the morning she would realize and take me to the doctor, and that if I left the bedroom before that, disturbed her party, I would pay. She would be sorry about that too—later—but it wouldn't stop the immediate pain. Luckily, that night the neighbors decided enough was enough and called the cops to break up the party."

Rich placed a hand on her arm, Denise wondered if he already regretted asking to hear the story. His face had taken on an almost permanent wince in the past ten seconds. She shook off his touch and continued, "I went into a shelter home. I was scared and worried. Daphne went through treatment, saw me at supervised visits once a week, but never quite managed to stay clean. The Robisons told me from the start they would keep me if I didn't go home, but their daughter was about my age and she hated me on sight. It took a couple months, but eventually we fought enough that they sent me on.

"The Carters were nice too. Erica was the best mom I'd ever seen, though she's only on par with the one I ended up with. I stayed there over a year while Daphne continued treatment. She took the required random drug tests and failed at least once a month, but I know she got high a lot more often than that." Tears threatened, and Denise paused for a moment to reign in her emotions. The oil popped in the pan, and she checked the heat level before returning to her onion.

When Rich reached out a hand toward her shoulder, she moved away. If he touched her or showed any pity, it would be that much harder to get through it.

"Without the drugs, she never hurt me, never tried, but I could never understand that while she always said she would get clean, that she wanted me home again, she never really did it. Nothing I did was good enough." Her voice quavered, and she cleared her throat. "I always wondered if there was something wrong with me that my own mother couldn't make me a priority in her life. Other people's mothers managed it."

Rich tried to speak, but Denise shook her head. He'd asked for it, now he would get it. She wrapped up inside herself. "Better heat the water."

When he got out the pot and started filling it with water, she continued. "Things were starting to come together. I was adjusting to my new home fine and the termination of parental rights began. Then Erica and her husband began fighting and the fights escalated until he left. They had a baby of their own and a toddler, and Erica didn't think she could handle one more child alone, especially if she had to go back to work. I understand now, as I couldn't have at the time, that she felt unable to take care of me, to meet my considerable needs by herself. But I figured I was almost eleven, I could take care of myself, if she kept me. I was mad at her for a long time."

The onions joined the mushrooms, and she pulled out the garlic. "Instead, I went to the DeWalt's. They had fostered for several years before I came along but never adopted. I don't think they intended to adopt me, but after a few weeks they decided to keep me. I remember my mom coming in to talk to me, telling me they would push through an adoption as soon as I was ready. I told them I was ready when I was twelve, but that was mostly to spite Daphne. I made their lives a nightmare clear through my teen years. I got into trouble in school, was caught shoplifting a couple times, spent time in a detention center, caused trouble at home. I deliberately tested the limits, pushing to see how far I could go before they stopped loving me."

"They didn't stop though, did they?"

Denise shook her head, giving herself a minute to work the lump in her throat out of the way to continue talking. "No, they never gave up. By the time I hit college, I quit pushing so hard. I even gave religion a real chance and was baptized when I was twenty."

She looked up from the garlic she was mincing, meeting his eye. Denise expected her admission to confuse and disgust Rich. That her mother was a druggie and had beat her, that she had been in trouble as a teen—most people would be horrified at the thought. Brian was especially disgusted by her juvenile record; it was the last straw for him. It still caused a twinge of pain, but she realized now it wouldn't have worked with Brian anyway. Her other baggage would have gotten in the way very quickly.

Instead of freaking out, though, Rich reached over and smoothed back the hair from her face, tucking it behind her ear. "I can understand questions. I can understand lack of trust. You were too young to go through that kind of trauma."

His gentle acceptance broke her angry resolve, and she felt the prick of tears at her eyes. Denise turned away and scooped the garlic into the pan with the mushrooms. She gave it a stir with the spoon Rich had placed nearby. She wouldn't turn back until she was in control. Crying in front of him was not an option.

"Are you okay?" He sounded worried, and she felt her control start to slip again. When he set a hand on her shoulder, she shrugged it off.

"Don't get all mushy on me. I don't want it." She pulled out the green pepper and began slicing pieces to add to the pan.

"I'm sorry." Rich backed away. "Have you heard from any of your family lately?"

"No, not since before I came to the DeWalts. Daphne either stopped trying to clean up to get me back, or the state decided she'd had enough chances. I never met my father. Daphne always said he knew about me and didn't care. I never saw any of my aunts or uncles. I don't know anything about Daphne's family."

She turned to open the cans of tomatoes. "I recall a long line of Daphne's boyfriends and a couple short-term husbands, but I don't remember any other family hanging around. The only people I ever called aunt or uncle weren't really related, I don't think." She dumped the tomatoes into the saucepan. "How about you? You have a perfect family: mom, dad, brother, sister."

"Yeah, I was lucky. But you have that now with your adoptive family, don't you?" Rich played with the French bread a little.

"I know my parents love me and would do anything for me, but sometimes I feel too . . ." *Damaged.* But she couldn't say that. Denise was surprised she'd even started the sentence.

"I don't really belong," she continued. "I know better, but in my heart, I still believe that." She set the knife on the counter, then turned and looked him in the eye. "Do you know what it's like to be eleven and have no one in the world who wants you? To have no one care about you enough to stick?" She shook her head. "You couldn't imagine it."

Rich's hand covered hers as she reached for the knife. "I care enough to stick now."

Denise paused. "You don't even know me. I don't know if I have anything to offer you, Rich. Don't take chances for someone who may have nothing to give back."

"It's too late." He removed the knife from her hand and set it aside, and then took her hands in his. "I admired you for your work ethic, your stubborn pride, your integrity. Still do, actually. But now I love you for all that and more." She tried to pull away at his words, but he held fast, his voice becoming more urgent. "I love you. Don't tell me it's too soon, that I couldn't know. What I feel for you isn't going to go away. It isn't my imagination. It's real. I've prayed about it. You may think now that you have nothing to give me, but I'm not ready to give up on you yet. You said yourself this search is a journey."

He loves me? How can he say that? "Don't go there Rich. You don't know what I came from. I don't know what I came from—other than Daphne, and she wasn't anything great. You don't know what I'm capable of." Denise felt shame as a tear squeezed from her eye and slid down her face, but he was faster to wipe it away than she was.

"Didn't you say she was only abusive when she was intoxicated? You don't drink, don't do drugs. I don't see a problem. I don't think you realize what you're capable of, the goodness inside you. Don't you think the Lord wants you to be happy?" His fingers lingered along her jaw, lifting it to face him again. "You need a little more time, that's fine. I need some time to get another job, anyway. We can do the friend thing in the meantime and get to know each other better. I want to be there to support you as you go through all of this."

Denise turned back to the sauce, picking up the spoon again, desperate for something to busy herself with. "Rich, I still think it's a mistake for you to get a new job. You're doing great, and everyone loves you at the office."

"Are you saying you want to switch jobs instead? I have a hard time believing that." He found a serrated knife and started preparing the French bread.

"I don't think there's a good answer for now. Don't be too hasty."

As she added herbs to the sauce, Denise realized with a sinking sensation that he was telling the truth. It warmed her that Rich could take so much of her history in stride. Unfortunately, there was more she wasn't going to share, not unless she had to, and she was sure it would be the end of everything good in their relationship.

Saturday Denise took her first step on her own search. A detailed search online brought up a long list of Loren Miners, the name of the father on her birth certificate. According to the foster care paperwork her mother had held onto, Daphne said Loren wasn't actually her father, regardless of what the birth certificate said, but Denise hoped he might have some information for her anyway. She reduced the list to men whose ages made them possible choices, then further cut the list to men who lived within two-hundred miles of the town she was born in.

She set a hand on the telephone receiver, wondering what she would say if Loren answered, what she would do if none of the men were the right one. Or what if he were dead? She considered pretending to be a disinterested third party, a go-between.

She had done this kind of work for another adoptee when he wanted to contact family back in July. Denise contacted the family member and asked if she would be willing to exchange letters or talk to the adoptee on the phone.

The birth mother had ended up denying any interest in knowing her son. Denise had left the woman with an email address to contact her if she changed her mind. Weeks later, she had. Last Denise had heard, the relationship had stalled. What Jennette said about reunions being rocky wasn't an exaggeration. From what Denise had heard, she wasn't sure if she was ready for it. But the aching in her heart and the unanswered questions had finally won out, and she decided to make the call. Taking a deep breath, and dialing the code to keep her number confidential, she began.

Though she had originally planned to write, Denise had made the decision to call based on the concern that Loren wouldn't respond at all if left to think about it. She was pretty sure Daphne had been telling the truth this time, that he wasn't her father, so he shouldn't feel threatened.

The first number she had was disconnected, the second brought an answering machine. On the third, a man answered. He denied knowing anyone by the name of Daphne Callister. A fourth call produced a grieving widow, her Loren had died only three weeks earlier. Denise didn't have the heart to quiz the poor woman but made a note to call her back in a few weeks if nothing else proved fruitful.

She stood and walked into the other room, stretching her legs and getting a glass of water from the sink. The thought of continuing with the calls was daunting, but she promised herself when she reached ten names she could quit for the night and try again the next night. A couple minutes later, she was back on the phone. Two more disconnects, a wrong number, and then she reached another woman.

"Hello, is Loren Miner there?"

"Just a moment."

A few seconds passed before a deep voice answered on the other side. "I'm Loren."

Denise felt as though her stomach was turning over. Her mouth grew dry, but she wet her lips and forced herself to speak. "Hello. My name is Denise. I'm looking for the Loren Miner who was married to Daphne Callister twenty-five years ago. Is that you?"

There was a long silence on the other end of the line, and Denise started to wonder if he was going to answer her or if he had already hung up.

"Yeah, that was me."

CHAPTER ELEVEN

Denise let out a breath of air she hadn't realized she was holding, and her heart began to pound.

"Denise you said? You must be her baby girl." He continued, "I have to tell you, I didn't know your mom when she got pregnant with you. I don't know what you want, but I'm not really your father."

Despite having been pretty sure of that fact before, Denise still felt a bit let down. If he had been her birth father, most of this would have been over. "I didn't know, but I thought as much. Look, I just need a little information, whatever you can remember. When I was nine I was put into foster care and eventually adopted. I'm trying to get in touch with my biological family, but I'm not sure how to reach Daphne, or preferably, her other family."

"I can't help you there. We lost touch while you were a baby. Sorry."

"Wait, wait, please. Don't hang up." Her heart pounded with worry that she wouldn't get anything from him. "Please, I just have a couple of questions."

"What are they?" His voice was cautious, bordering on belligerent. She couldn't blame him for not wanting to be caught in the mess again.

"First, do you remember, or did you know the names of any of her siblings? I was told her parents are dead, but I wondered if there was anyone else I could contact: a brother, a sister. Anyone." She began stalking back and forth across the room. "I have nowhere to start."

"Yeah, there were a couple brothers. Ned and . . . Dennis, Darryl, I don't remember, something like that. They were in school or something, so we never met. Didn't you ever meet them?"

"If I did, I don't remember it. Ned, though, you're sure about that one?" She scratched a note and circled it several times in black ink.

"Yes, I'm sure. Daphne was the oldest, she said. I think he was in college or something. One of the brothers was." His answer was firm.

"Do you remember the name of my father? Do you know if she even knew who it was?"

"I don't know. She was never a terribly . . . faithful woman. She claimed your father was her previous husband. I can't remember his name, some guy she grew up with in Southern Utah." He paused for a moment before coming up with a name. "Pete something. She claimed he was the father, but I don't know if she knew for sure. Ned would probably know who he was, if you can find him. They grew up in a small town, that's all I remember."

"Every town south of Provo was small then," she muttered under her breath, making another note. If they grew up in Southern Utah, there was a decent chance Ned was still in the state. "Thank you for your time, Loren. It means a lot to me to be able to track someone down. It couldn't have been easy to live with Daphne." She glanced in the mirror at her face and wondered how much she looked like her mother.

"No, but I was a grown man making my own mistakes. I straightened up a few years after the divorce. I always wondered about you. I'm glad to hear you're doing well. Good luck with your search."

"Thanks." Denise said good-bye and hung up the phone, tears sliding down her face. Her feelings were all jumbled up between disappointment that Loren hadn't been her father, excitement to have a direction to search next, and fear of being rejected when she did find Ned. After a moment, she pushed the emotions away. She had a name. One more step. One more piece of the puzzle. She walked over to her computer and entered the new information.

A quick search on the Internet found a stack of Ned Callisters in the intermountain region, many within ten years of Daphne's age. She considered calling him too, but she wasn't sure she was ready for that. Denise had been pretty sure from the beginning that Loren wasn't related, but Ned was another story. She wrote out a letter and addressed a couple dozen envelopes with her return address blank and only a first name. She would get a postbox the next day on her lunch break. That would be the most anonymous, safest thing to do. She glanced over the letter again, wanting to be certain it said enough, but not too much since so many people would be getting it.

Dear Sir,

I am seeking information about a family member with your name. If you are related to Daphne Callister, who lived in the State of Utah fifteen years ago, I would appreciate a response. If not, sorry to waste your time.

Sincerely,

Denise

She hoped that would be enough and sealed the letters. What happened next would be anyone's guess.

She started checking her mailbox on Thursday.

It was empty.

On Friday it held a free shampoo sample she'd ordered online.

On Saturday and Monday, it remained empty. Tuesday there was a letter.

Denise, I'm not the Ned Callister you're looking for. Good luck . . . .

The man continued on to tell her in excruciating detail about his military service fifteen years ago. Denise scanned over it and tossed it in the garbage before leaving the post office.

She returned to the office feeling disappointed and almost ready to give up. Her concentration at work was beginning to suffer, and she found the office banter more distracting than ever.

When Rich joined her at her desk after lunch to discuss a program she was working on, he asked, "Anything?"

"Not unless you want to count a lonely old man requesting a picture of me in a bikini." She pulled out the specs she was working from and set them on the desk, then met his gaze. The look on his face said he wouldn't mind seeing her in a bikini. She elbowed him, and he wiped the look from his face.

"No luck, then. Don't worry, it'll be fine. Now, where are you?" He picked up the papers and began flipping through them.

Partway through the discussion, a woman from advertising stopped by Denise's desk to drop off some papers that were faxed to her department by mistake. She eyed Rich appreciatively when they were introduced and stayed several minutes longer than necessary to flirt with him. Denise was all too aware of the wide smile Rich gave the woman as they spoke; she saw the way he charmed the younger woman without even trying.

It galled Denise to realize she hadn't even considered his previous social life, the number of women who must be interested in him. Several of the women in their singles ward flirted outrageously with him. What did he see in her?

When Jake teased Rich about the woman after she left, Rich shook his head and returned to the assignment he and Denise had been discussing. When Jake pressed the issue, Rich said he was "kind of seeing someone" and the subject was dropped.

That night, she was looking up a family member for another adoptee when she heard a knock on the front door of the apartment. Lily was at the library doing homework, so Denise answered it. Rich stood in the hallway, his hands resting in his pockets, an easy casualness exuding from him. "Hey, Denise, I thought maybe you could use some company." He walked into the room without invitation and brushed some hair from her eyes as he slid past her. He glanced at the kitchen. "Not in the middle of dinner? You care to grab a bite?"

"No, I had a sandwich earlier. I'm busy now." Denise watched him wander further into the apartment, before turning to her, wearing an easy smile.

"I can sit quietly like a good boy. The truth is, there's nothing on television, and I wanted a little company."

"I'm sure you can find that almost anywhere. I'm surprised you hang around so much, with all the desperate single women out there. You must have a dozen or more admirers in our ward alone." She turned and walked back toward the front door, feeling like a fool for bringing it up. The thought had been on her mind for hours, though, and it was wearing on her.

Before she could open the door for him, he grabbed her elbow and stopped her. "What's going on?"

"I'm busy tonight. I'm sure you can find other company." She lifted her eyes to his and saw amusement, irritation, and curiosity all warring with each other in their brown depths.

A huge grin swept over his face. "Are you jealous?"

She could feel the anger and humiliation bubbling up inside her. "That ego of yours is really out of control."

"You *are* jealous." He moved closer and set his other hand on her shoulder.

She pulled away. "I'm busy."

"Are you asking if I've dated much in the past? What is this?"

She folded her arms over her chest and decided to stop behaving like a child. At the very least she could have an adult conversation about it, even if it made her feel defensive and about three inches tall. "Maybe I am."

He nodded, though he looked incredulous. "Fine. I dated plenty. I was looking for a relationship, eventually a wife, so yeah. I dated."

"Fine." She turned and tried again to get the door for him, but he didn't let go of her arm.

"You know how I feel about you, Denise. You have no reason to worry."

His words rankled, causing her back to stiffen. "I don't know why I should be worrying. After all, you're just *kind* of seeing me. Nothing serious. But that's okay, I'm used to being nothing serious. I actually prefer the status. Now, I have a lot to do, if you don't mind."

"Now you're offended. I *am* only kind of seeing you, compared to what I want. I'd like to see a whole lot more of you on our own time, and the way I feel about you is serious." He ran his hands from her shoulders, down her arms to her elbows and back up again. "I've told you how I feel about you. You're one in a million, or ten million. No number of dates with other women in my past can change that. They just make me more certain that I want to be with you."

"Pretty words confuse the issue." Denise fought her desire to cry. Now was not the time. She wouldn't cry over him: not because he dated others, and not because he claimed he didn't want to date others. There was something achingly sweet about his declaration.

"They're not just words." He leaned in and planted a kiss on her forehead. When she closed her eyes, he followed up with a soft brush of his lips across each of her eyelids as well, melting her reserve. "Come with me while I get some dinner. I promise to get you back before too long so you can get back to work. I'll get you a chocolate shake or something."

Without knowing how it happened, she found herself bundled in a coat and walking out to the car with him. He held her hand in his and stopped to open her door. She wondered as she slid into the car what kind of dream she was living in. When would reality intrude and destroy the moment?

CHAPTER TWELVE

Though Rich and Lily made efforts to distract her, the empty mailbox teased Denise again for the following week. The thrice-weekly nightmares were robbing her of sleep, and her apartment was cleaner than most hospitals. By Thursday morning she was making far more mistakes at work than usual. When Rich called her into his office, her blood pressure spiked even higher. She knew she hadn't been working well.

"Shut the door," he told her. His face was unreadable, his eyes focusing on a paper on his desk.

Denise took a seat across the desk from Rich and clasped her hands in front of her. "Is something wrong?" she asked.

He looked up from the paper and pushed it to the side. "The Cramer project is supposed to be done tonight, right?"

"Yes."

"I understand you don't have any vacation days planned in the near future."

Denise grew wary. "No."

"And that you haven't taken more than two days in the past twelve months, even though you have almost two weeks saved up."

"That's right. I haven't gone anywhere."

He leaned forward, setting his elbows on the desk and clasping his fingers together in front of him. "I think you need to take tomorrow off."

It took her a moment to process his words. Her temper spiked. "What? I know I haven't been up to my usual performance, but that doesn't mean you have to put me on detention." Denise leaned forward, placing her palms on the edge of his desk. "My errors haven't been that much worse than the ones the guys do regularly."

"No, they haven't, but they've been much more than I've come to expect of you. You're stressed out, worked up about that letter. I'm not telling you to take a week, but obviously you need a break." His words were calm and measured, and it was clear he was trying not to upset her.

Denise couldn't have been much more upset if she tried. "Don't play Lancelot and don't play games with me, Rich. If I'm not good enough, say it. I'm the woman, I have to be better than the men to measure up to them; I understand. It's either that, or you have feelings for me, and in an attempt to keep from showing me favoritism, you have to be twice as hard. That's fine. Maybe *I* should be looking for another job."

Rich sighed and rolled his head on his shoulders, cracking his neck. "Denise, I'm not playing favorites, and I'm not trying to be extra hard on you. All I want is for you to take a break, to calm down. You're going to break down if you don't take some time off. It's only been three weeks since you sent the letter. If I didn't have feelings for you, I might not require you take a day off, but we'd still have a discussion."

"And what, exactly, am I supposed to do with a whole extra day? Sit in my apartment and twiddle my thumbs, stare at the television, and pretend I'm watching while I go quietly insane?"

"You've already scrubbed the life out of your apartment again. I don't know, read a book, watch a movie. What do you do for fun?"

"I program. I play basketball. Apparently you won't let me do the first, and I can't do the second all day long."

Rich ran his hands over his face in frustration. "Look, I don't know what you'll do. We can sit down tonight, and you can tell me every reason why I'm a big, stupid, idiot, or we can plan something for you if you like. I'll be happy to get you a picture of me so you can play darts with it if that's what you want. If you come in tomorrow, you're fired. Understand?"

Denise stood and leaned across the desk to tower over him. "You'd love that, wouldn't you?"

His eyes flashed. "If it wouldn't be a sure way of alienating you, I'd be tempted to do it now. Get back to work."

Without another word, Denise turned and all but stomped out. She glanced in his direction as she turned the corner of the hallway and saw him rubbing his forehead. *Sure, now you're starting to regret it. When suave doesn't work, you just bully your way through like any other man. Maybe it would be worth showing up tomorrow to call his bluff.*

Instead of heading straight back to her desk though, she detoured to the restroom. Being one of only a dozen women in the building had its advantages, and the likelihood of having five private minutes in the restroom to calm down was one of them.

When she came out of the restroom, Joan was leaning against the wall in the hallway. She handed over a can of vegetable juice and sent her a sympathetic smile. "You looked about ready to spit nails when you came out of there. I've been told you're taking a vacation day tomorrow."

Denise cracked the lid and was grateful she didn't drink alcohol. The way she felt now, she would have kept drinking until she passed out. She thought she could use a little oblivion about now. "Against my better judgment, I am."

"He's worried about you. So am I. You've been walking around in a haze for weeks. I don't know what's bothering you, sweetie, but I have a good listening ear."

Somewhat mollified, Denise forced a smile. "Thanks, I just needed a few minutes to calm down and a little pick-me-up. A bunch of personal stuff is going on right now. I'll see what I can do to be less . . . distracted next week. Meanwhile, I still have work to finish up today."

Joan patted her on the shoulder, and Denise returned to her desk, sending scowls at anyone who looked ready to ask her what was going on.

When lunchtime arrived, Denise grabbed her box from the refrigerator. She swiveled back around to find Rich leaning against the doorway, his hands deep in his pockets. "You going to check your mail?"

She looked away from him and nodded. Though her anger had cooled some, it hadn't gone away yet. Her trips to check her mailbox now made her physically ill. Denise knew she wouldn't be able to eat until it was out of the way. After weeks of waiting, she wasn't sure if she wanted an answer or not. Not knowing was driving her crazy. On the other hand, finding out could have negative repercussions. She wasn't sure what to think.

"You gonna forgive me?" His words were barely more than a whisper.

She looked back at him and allowed her face to soften. "Not for a couple of hours."

He nodded but looked relieved that she didn't plan on holding the grudge too long. When she walked toward him, he let her pass into the hall. Denise gripped the handle of the box tighter and dug the keys from her pocket as she passed Joan's desk on her way to the parking lot.

When she pulled up in front of the post office, Denise sat in the car and watched the door open, letting out a man in his early twenties. She had checked the box every day but Sunday for the past two weeks and found only disappointment. *Am I wasting my time? Is finding my family worth allowing myself to get so out of control?* Rich had been right, she'd scrubbed every inch of her apartment again that week, and the nightmares were coming more often again. *But I've already waited long enough to search. Now is the time, if only for my own peace of mind. Knowing the worst couldn't be more difficult than wondering day in and day out.*

But, she asked herself as she got out of the car and walked toward the building, what would she do if the search proved fruitless? What if no one answered, or if the right Ned Callister refused to make contact with her? She shook her head to clear the thought; it wasn't productive. She needed to focus on the positive, not on what could go wrong.

Her hands shook as she slid her key in the box and twisted the lock. The door swung open, and she pushed away a tingling excitement at the sight of an envelope in the box. She reached in and pulled it out. *N. Callister* was written in the top left-hand corner.

She stopped short and took the envelope between her hands; she flipped it over to look at the blank back, and then turned it back to the front. Ogden, Utah, the return address said. If this was him, he lived only an hour away.

She heard the scrape of boxes and looked up to see a woman smiling over at her, a smattering of freckles covering her cheeks and nose. Denise smiled tightly, stuck the letter in her pocket, and hurried back out to her car.

She drove down the street to a park, though it was cold and windy, and she had no intention of getting out of the car. Her lunch was forgotten as she came to a stop and pulled her key from the ignition. The letter shook in her hands as she stared at the return address again, and she could feel her heart pound. This was it. This was what she waited for all week. The moment of truth. What if it ended up not being him after all? She didn't think she could handle that again.

She flipped the letter over and ripped it open, leaving a large jagged opening across the flap. Her fingers shook so much she could barely get the letter out and open it. It was two pages of ruled paper, torn from a spiral-bound notebook and covered in large blue-ink letters.

Denise,

I am Ned, the brother of Daphne Callister. You didn't say that you were her daughter, but I know she had one with your name who would be around twenty-six now. If so, welcome to the family. I'm sorry I didn't write right away. We were out of town last week and didn't get your letter until our return. Then I didn't know what to say. Nothing seemed quite right.

My wife, Sharon, and I are glad to finally hear from you. We've been hoping you would decide to search someday. We have four children and my brother, Derrick, and his wife, Sue, have two. There is more to tell, but I want to be sure you are who I think you are. If so, please call us.

You are probably wondering why we never contacted you or tried to help. The truth was, we never knew where you were or that you were in state's custody until after rights had been completely terminated and the adoption was final. When we heard, the state wouldn't give us any information about you. It's a miracle to hear from you after all this time.

A phone number followed, along with an email address. Tears poured down her cheeks. Someone wanted her; someone cared about her. Her other uncle's name was Derrick. She had six cousins. The fact that Ned filled her in that much reassured her that this was no hoax. No one else would have known enough details about her past.

It took her a moment to consider what to do as she eyed a phone booth not far away, one with four walls to cut out the wind. Denise dug her calling card out of her pocket and took a deep breath before stepping out into the wind, afraid that if she waited, she would talk herself out of calling.

Her fingers shook as she dialed the long string of numbers, waited for the prompt, and then dialed some more. She fidgeted with the phone book and shook more from nerves than the cold as the line began to ring.

CHAPTER THIRTEEN

"Callister Air Conditioning, this is Ned." His voice was high for a man's, though mature, as Denise expected. Warm and friendly. She found it reassuring.

Her heart soared to her throat, making it difficult to speak. "Hi, Ned, this is Denise, your niece."

The two seconds of silence that followed was agonizing and seemed to drag on forever.

"Denise, I'm glad you called. I've been wondering how soon I might hear from you. I didn't expect it to be yet." He hesitated, and she wondered if it was because he felt as wrong-footed as she did or if she sounded too eager and he was second-guessing his decision to write her back. "We've been wondering about you for years. We would have contacted you sooner. We put feelers out on databases and everything, but we didn't know your new name." He sounded glad as he rattled on, and she felt relieved. "How have you been? What are you doing?"

"I'm a computer programmer, I work in Utah Valley, as I'm sure you guessed by the address."

"That's great. We're dying to meet you. Can we come down this Saturday, or would you like to come up? We have a lot of extra space at our place. We'd love to have you."

It was all moving a little too fast for Denise; her heart pounded, nerves fired in her fingertips, and she wondered for a moment if she was going to pass out from hyperventilating. "Wow, I hadn't thought past this phone call, really. I didn't dare. You're not that far away. I . . . You know, I have the day off tomorrow. Maybe I'll come up for a couple of days. I have to teach a lesson in church Sunday, but I can be there by noon tomorrow. Maybe we can meet for lunch."

"That sounds great. We'll have the spare room ready for you."

That thought scared her. He may be family, but he was still a stranger. "No. That's maybe a little too quick for me. I'll get a hotel room for the night, this time."

"You're sure? We'd love to have you, and there's plenty of room."

"Yeah. It's no problem." Denise bit her lip for a moment while she debated her next question. She needed to be prepared for the possibilities. "I'm not sure I'm ready to see her again yet, but do you know where Daphne is?"

There was a long pause, and she wondered for a moment if he was going to tell her she was dead. "Yes. She's in prison, at the Point of the Mountain."

Denise wasn't sure what to think about her mother being at the state prison at the summit bordering between Salt Lake and Utah counties. It wasn't like the woman hadn't done anything to deserve it in Denise's memory. But she hadn't quite expected that. Daphne always seemed to worm her way out of everything. Denise would think about that later. "Where do you want to meet for lunch?"

She wrote down the address to the restaurant he mentioned and hung up the phone. As soon as the phone hit the cradle though, her stomach started to clench, and she wondered if she'd made a huge mistake. She muttered under her breath as she reviewed her situation. "Can I face them alone? I could take Rich along—no, that's ridiculous," she shook her head and tapped her fingers on the telephone. "He has to work."

"Besides, it would be too much, too soon for us." What she had told Rich was true—she didn't know if she had anything to give him. Maybe if she was able to face her past, she would be ready to face a future.

She knew three weeks wasn't so long to wait to hear once she had mailed out the letters, but it had seemed like forever. Now that she had spoken with Ned, she worried that she was taking things too quickly. Denise took a deep breath and let it out slowly, trying to calm the adrenalin racing through her system.

She returned to her car and rested her head on the steering wheel, willing herself to calm. Surely she could pull everything back together before her lunch hour ended. She checked her watch and noticed there were only twenty minutes left for her lunch. She put her key in the ignition and flipped it to accessory, switched stations, and turned up the radio as AC/DC screamed out the lyrics to "Thunderstruck." After a few minutes of the pounding beat, her hands had stopped shaking, her breathing was normal again, and she was ready to return to work even if she wasn't completely calm. She switched the station and pulled out of the parking lot as John Denver crooned about sunshine making him cry.

A glance at her watch as she walked back in the front doors of the office told her she would be working her way through the peanut butter sandwich and apple she had brought at her desk instead of in the break room. That was fine, she had done it plenty of times before. She smiled at Joan, projecting calm.

"You look better."

"I feel better. Thanks." She continued to her office and settled into her chair. It was an hour later when she looked up to see Rich enter the room. He greeted everyone and headed to Mick's desk, but glanced back at Denise, a question in his eyes.

Denise nodded and wished she had two private minutes to talk to him.

He smiled and turned his attention back to Mick, though she could tell he was dying to talk to her. Eager to put the anxiety that had plagued her for the past week behind her, she focused on her screen and blocked out the noises around her.

It was nearly four when Denise returned to Rich's office with the paperwork for her now-finished project. "Here it is, ready to go," she said as she handed it over.

"No bugs?" Rich asked. He studied her face, as if searching for the animosity he found there earlier.

"In one of *my* projects, are you kidding me? I thought you expected a higher level of professionalism from me." Denise stopped herself from fidgeting under his searching gaze and forced a half smile. She knew she owed him an apology.

Her smile seemed to reassure him, and he flipped through the pages. He pulled the web page up to look at it. "It looks great. You've done a good job with it. I'm sure Cramer will be happy." He looked back up into her eyes. "You look better."

She was ashamed of the way she'd overreacted earlier, of the way everything had gotten out of control. "No apology could be sufficient after the way I behaved this morning, but I'm very sorry." She smiled faintly. "My lunch break was fruitful, and I'm no longer ready to strangle you." *Only myself.*

"Strangling your boss is against the rules," Joan said as she breezed into the office, handing Rich a stack of faxes. "Although I could give you a pass if you had a good enough reason."

Denise laughed, though it felt a little forced. "I have a visit to make to family tomorrow, my uncle." She sent Rich a significant look. "So I'll go finish things up and try and get some housekeeping done before five."

"Denise, didn't you stay until eight the other night working on this project?"

She turned back to look at him. "Yes."

"Go home, you've put in your time. Have a good weekend." He waved her away and turned back to his work.

"Thanks. I think I will." She turned and followed Joan out of the office.

"Feeling better?" Joan asked when they reached the door to Denise's office.

"Yeah. I know I've been a pain this last week, but I'm going to do better; and now I have a day off tomorrow, I have more time to spend with my family."

"Good." Joan winked at her and then turned toward her own desk.

Denise went in and shut down her computer. She changed her voice mail to say that she would be out of the office on Friday.

"What? Are you leaving already?" Jake asked.

"No point in my starting a new project an hour before close. You boys have a great weekend." Denise grabbed her water bottle and strolled out of the office.

After reserving a hotel room for the following night, Denise managed to reach Jennette and let her in on the latest developments with Ned.

Jennette acted positive and upbeat about the possibilities over the next couple of days and asked Denise to come home for dinner Sunday to tell them about it. When she hung up the phone, however, Denise was left to wonder how much of her mom's chirpy happiness was real and how much was a cover. She still felt like she was being disloyal to her parents and did not want to hurt them, however unintentionally.

The thought had crossed Denise's mind to keep the reunion details to herself, but she couldn't. Jennette and Lynn would be much more upset to learn about everything later, than if she kept them apprised.

Denise was dialing Gerald's number to talk to him about it when the doorbell rang. Promising herself she would call later, she hung up. She swung the front door open to find Rich standing outside. It shouldn't have been a surprise; he'd told her he would come over this evening, even if they had been in a fight at the time. But seeing him at the door shot a jolt through her system. The sunny bunch of yellow daisies in his hand were only part of the reason her throat closed up and her mouth went dry. "Hi." It was the best she could manage.

Rich stood to the side of the door and shifted his feet. "So you got your letter and things went well? I've been thinking about it all afternoon."

She beckoned him in, took the offered flowers, and walked into the kitchen to put them in one of Lily's vases. She turned to face him before speaking. "I don't deserve these. I'm sorry I was so out of control this morning. No amount of stress is justification for acting like that." Denise sniffed the flowers, absurdly touched by the gesture. She set them on the counter and turned back to him.

He reached out and took her hand, linking the ends of their fingers together and waited until she met his gaze. "Consider it forgotten."

Too mixed up by the feelings he generated in her, she pulled her hand away. "Care for a drink? Looks like juice or water," she said, scanning the contents of the fridge.

"Water, but I can get it myself." He pulled out a glass from the cupboard and filled it at the sink. She could sense him carefully feeling his way around the situation. "You're going to see your uncle?"

"Yeah, he offered for me to stay with him and his wife in Ogden." His eyes looked wary, and she smiled. "I told him I wasn't quite ready to make that step, but I am meeting them for lunch. I got a hotel room instead."

He brushed the hair back from her face, letting his fingers hover near her cheek without touching it for a brief moment before he retracted his hand. "You sound excited."

Denise told herself not to squirm: he hadn't touched her or anything, hadn't pushed, though she could see the desire to in his eyes. "I am, and terrified. I was worried. Really worried. And when I opened the letter I did kind of explode. All of the worry and anger built until I was strung so tight."

"I know." He walked around the counter, pulled out a bar stool, and sat.

"Then I called. He was so excited to hear from me, and . . . it felt good to know someone from my family cares." She took the stool next to him, and he picked up her hand again.

"I was worried what might happen when you got the letter, especially with the way you've been acting the past day or two."

"I'm sorry I've been so hard to deal with the past little while. I've been distracted and sulky all week." She tried, casually, to disengage her hand from his. His expression didn't waver with the attempt, and he didn't let go.

"Distracted and worried, more like. Though there was some sulky thrown in this morning. Promise you'll try and handle the next step a little better? It's hard on all of us when you wig out like that." He ran his thumb along her knuckles, causing her to shiver.

"Promise. I appreciate you being so supportive. I had no idea what to expect. Still don't, not really. But at least I know they're open to meeting me." Giving up on getting her hand back, Denise accepted the comfort he offered and relaxed. It felt strange, but perfectly normal to have this kind of conversation with him.

"I wish I could be there with you tomorrow. But maybe it's easier that way. How do you explain what I am? I'm your boss, but we don't just have a working relationship. I'm not exactly your boyfriend, though don't let anyone con you into a date on that score or I'll have to pop all of their tires."

Denise laughed, allowing a bit more of the tension to leave her body. Rich would no more pop someone's tires than he would make a six-course French meal. He didn't have it in him. "So, what are you?"

Rich lifted her fingers to his lips and kissed the pads along the tips. "The man you're going to marry someday."

CHAPTER FOURTEEN

This time Denise did pull her hand from his and stood, moving away. "Rich, you're moving too fast."

"It's not a proposal, just a statement of intentions. Someday."

She pressed a hand to her stomach and turned away. "How many women have you used that line on?" It took a great deal of effort to squash the glimmer of hope his words provided. She'd let herself hope once before and had been destroyed.

"One so far. I don't intend to need it with anyone else."

He had all the right words, exactly the right tone of voice. It unnerved her. She turned to see him standing, both hands planted on the counter behind him. His expression was calm and serious, his eyes a little grim, as if she were trying his patience. "What about all those women you dated in Chicago? None of them turned your fancy that direction?"

With two steps he crossed the distance between them, sliding his hands into his pockets in a deliberate move, but she felt almost as penned in as if he put one on each side of her. "No. I admit, Denise, I dated quite often in Chicago. Seldom seeing anyone more than a couple times. Even those I dated longer can't hold a candle to you. You're the one who matters to me."

"It's hard for me to believe someone like you would want a messed up person like me when you could have your pick." She smiled as she spoke, acting as though it were a backhanded comment, but she worried he would wake up one day and realize what a rotten deal he got with her.

"Someone like me? You mean a charming, intelligent, irresistibly good looking . . . ." She sent him a scathing look. He grinned back.

She didn't realize how good he was at reading her, sensing her insecurities until he picked up her hand, and clasped it in his. "Trust takes time, but I'm good for it. You have nothing to worry about from me. I'm going to be there for you."

"That doesn't mean you have nothing to worry about from me. If you're determined to be in love with me, if you're sure it's me you want, heartbreak is almost guaranteed." She kept her voice light.

When he leaned a little closer, she wanted to back away but knew he would only follow, so she held her ground. "That's a chance I'll have to take. Love is trust and letting yourself be vulnerable." His free hand slid into her hair along the side of her face, cradling her cheek. "I think you're worth the risk." His lips lingered over her forehead and cheeks. He pulled her close and laid his cheek on her own.

The gentle acceptance nearly shattered her self-control, testing her ability to keep her heart from completely falling. She couldn't decide whether to pull him closer or push him away. Finally, he moved back. "I found a great listing for a programmer using Flash today," he said. "It pays better than the one you have now. Your boss wouldn't be such a paragon of virtues, I'm sure. But you could survive."

She pulled away, needing the space, needing to get out of the confined kitchen where there was nowhere to go. "Being a bit presumptuous, aren't you? Can't wait to get rid of me?" This time her voice was soft and teasing; she was desperate for a change in mood.

"On the contrary, I'd hate to lose you at the office. But I'd hate even more to continue this half-relationship we're in for much longer."

She stepped into the living room, gulped in a deep lungful of oxygen, but found his cologne hovering in the air, his presence pulsing through the room. If it had been an uncomfortable or threatening presence, she wouldn't have worried so much. The trouble she got into in high school, the physical conditioning she kept up, had taught her to hold her own. But the threat he presented went far beyond the physical. "You could always walk away from me." She looked him in the eye and hoped he wouldn't walk away. No matter how much she pushed, she hoped he wouldn't budge. She needed him. Denise fought down the shock of terror that realization caused.

"Not a chance." His kissed her on the tip of the nose. "Your parents didn't walk away, did they?"

She shook her head. It was hardly the same thing. "I still don't know why they didn't. You know, they read my file before they took me in. My whole file, beginning to end. They knew everything there was to know about me, but they still took me."

"They let foster parents read the kids' files?" Rich lifted an eyebrow.

"I don't think they actually get that in-depth often, I never heard them mention that they read anyone else's, but the law says they have the right to know everything the case worker knows, so they knew everything. Everything."

"How did that make you feel?" He took her hand in his, stroking his thumb across her knuckles again.

"It depended on the day. Sometimes it made me feel violated. They knew everything, I didn't have any secrets, not any important ones. Other times it made me feel safe. They knew the worst about me and still wanted me. They had lots of extra classes over the years to learn to help me and the other kids who lived with them. I doubt there's any emotional disorder or behavioral problem out there they haven't studied. They were my rocks."

"Everyone needs a rock." Rich brushed his lips across her knuckles. He turned in surprise when Lily walked in.

"Sorry, I can leave if I'm interrupting something." Lily's eyes danced in amusement as she watched Denise put a little more distance between them, pulling her hand free, but Lily was already moving to her room.

"I was about to ask her to see a movie. You want to come?" he asked.

"That sounds great. John and I were planning to catch one anyway," Lily said. "We'd love to join you."

"All right."

Denise sent Rich a surprised look, and he picked up her hand again, running a thumb over her palm. "I thought maybe I could use a chaperone. I promised myself I wouldn't kiss you again until you were no longer my employee."

She looked pointedly down at their joined hands and back up at him.

He shrugged and put on a self-deprecating smile. "I never said I was perfect."

The sun hid behind a veil of clouds and snow threatened as Denise made her way through the Salt Lake Valley traffic the next morning and continued on to Ogden. Thanks to good directions, Denise was easily able to locate the restaurant and find a decent parking spot.

Denise bit her lip subconsciously as she looked around the lobby of the restaurant a little before noon. A couple in their eighties sat at a bench, and a young pair of college students stood nearby. It was the forty-something couple that caught her attention. The man was tall and blond, with twinkling brown eyes and a nose much like her own. The woman was shorter, with dark hair and looked nervous. The clincher was the polo shirt the man wore with a Callister Air Conditioning insignia.

Taking a deep breath for courage, she walked over. "Are you Ned?"

He smiled, showing straight, even teeth. "Yes. You must be Denise." His hand opened and closed for a moment, then extended to be shaken.

Denise shook his hand and Sharon's.

"How was the drive?" Ned asked when it was obvious no one knew where to start the conversation.

"A little crazy, but not too bad." Denise wanted to wring her hands but forced herself to keep them at her sides instead. Then she caught herself biting her bottom lip. She was relieved when a waitress walked over and directed them to their table.

"Ned said you're a computer programmer. What do you do, exactly?" Sharon asked when they were seated with the menus in front of them.

Denise explained her job and talked about what she had done since high school. She gave a general description of her adoptive family.

Ned and Sharon showed pictures of Denise when she was still a toddler, talked about their kids, and asked more questions about her adoptive family. The food was great, and they lingered for over an hour before Sharon reminded Ned they both needed to get back to work and they were forced to part.

"Come to dinner tonight," Sharon said. "Derrick and Sue are coming with their daughter." Her eyes shifted away for a moment, but she didn't elaborate and returned her gaze to Denise. "We set it up last night, unless you don't want to. They're staying the night at our place and hanging out tomorrow."

"That would be great. Thanks." Denise got the address and was about to leave when Sharon placed a hand on her arm.

Sharon let out a huff of frustration and nodded her head, as though she had come to a decision. "Derrick's daughter, his Kaylee. . . . She's your sister. She's scared but anxious to meet you, and," Sharon seemed uncertain of what else to say, " . . . fragile. If you don't want to meet her, I need to know now so we can make other arrangements for dinner. She doesn't know about the visit tonight, only that we talked with you, so if you decide you aren't ready, I need to know now. I considered springing it on you tonight, but I just can't."

Denise's heart leaped in her chest. "Sister? I have a sister?" How could that be a problem? It seemed something to be excited about.

She had never been close to Paige, never felt a connection; there were too many bad memories from their early years. But she and Kaylee could start out fresh, if Kaylee wanted things to be good. "That's great," she finally managed. "I can't wait to meet her."

That left the rest of the afternoon to drive around, do some Christmas shopping, and replay the lunch conversation. They hadn't talked about why she was removed from her mother, what foster care was like, or any of their responses to it yet. Denise was just as glad to put it off until she knew them a little better, but she was sure some of it would come up before she returned to Orem.

Denise wasn't sure how much her aunt and uncle knew about her life with Daphne or how much they would ask. Even though they were family, she didn't know them yet and she wasn't ready to get into the gory details.

After checking into the hotel, Denise followed the directions to Ned and Sharon's house. Her stomach didn't tremble as it had before, which she attributed to their easy acceptance. But there were new people to meet, new experiences, and she still felt nervous about it.

She pulled up in front of the sprawling brick house. A circular driveway provided plenty of parking and led the way to their three-car garage. The yard was filled with flowerbeds, trees, and bushes, though they had lost all of their foliage weeks earlier. Now it was dotted with Halloween decorations, including a big bag of leaves decorated like a jack-o-lantern. Denise double-checked the address on the paper Ned had given her. This was it.

There were no other cars parked out front, so Denise figured she had beat Derrick's family here, but she tried to prepare herself to meet them. They may have parked in the garage or something. "Ned and Sharon are perfectly nice people, and they said the others were anxious to meet you. Everything will be fine," she reminded herself as she walked to the door. Before she knew it she was pushing the doorbell.

Sharon greeted her with a smile. "Come on in. You beat the others, but Sue is notorious for running late, so they'll be along eventually." She led Denise through the comfortable entryway into the sparkling kitchen, which was ringed with a butterfly border. Rich smells of beef stew floated from the crock pot and mingled with the smell of bread baking in the oven. Sharon had even whipped together a pan of brownies for dessert. "So what did you do this afternoon?"

Ned came in and greeted them, and Denise answered, "Window shopped mostly. It isn't very often I take the time to just bum around."

"A spot of retail therapy, even if I don't spend much, always makes me feel better when life gets a bit out of control." Sharon shared a female grin with her niece.

"I don't usually enjoy shopping. I guess I'm more like a guy that way. I'd rather be playing basketball than hassling with lines of people in stores. Thankfully the lines are still pretty short at this time of year."

"So you play ball?" Ned asked, and Denise realized she had left that out of her life's story.

Denise felt her pulse begin to even out as she sat on a bar stool placed at the island where she was talking with Ned and Sharon. "Yeah, it was a great outlet in high school, kept me out of trouble—mostly." The doorbell rang, sending her pulse rate spiking up again.

"Hold that thought." Ned disappeared down the hall to answer the door.

When Ned returned to the kitchen a moment later, he brought along a man who looked a bit like him, only with darker hair, a tiny woman with big blue eyes and a brilliant smile. And trailing a little behind, stood a teenage girl of fourteen or fifteen with honey-colored hair, blue eyes that were a mirror of Denise's own, and the same pixielike chin she had. Despite those similarities, Denise thought her younger sister beautiful.

Chapter Fifteen

A smile quavered on Kaylee's lips as Sharon made introductions, and Denise stuck her hands in her pockets in self-defense. They were family, so shaking hands seemed a little strange, though she'd done so earlier that day with Ned, but she couldn't quite bring herself to hug a stranger. Instead they stood around staring at each other while Sharon and Sue carried on an awkward conversation about their children.

Though she tried not to stare, Denise kept finding her eyes sliding back to her sister, studying the similarities and differences between them.

The ears, the shape of the nose. Kaylee's jaw line was softer, and the girl was at least six inches shorter. Denise had reached her full growth of five foot eleven by the time she was fourteen, something she'd considered a major inconvenience, until Jennette and Lynn convinced her to try out for her high school basketball team. Though Kaylee's arms were moderately muscled, she lacked the build of an athlete.

"You baked bread too?" Sue asked as Sharon pulled the loaf out of the oven and slid in the pan of brownies.

"It's one of those pre-frozen deals, so don't get all worked up about it. A good stew practically begs for fresh bread. Now sit, everyone." Sharon waved toward the dining area before tipping the loaf of bread onto a clean towel to cool.

Though she managed to get in plenty of questions about her aunts and uncles during dinner, Denise found the same questions she answered at lunch coming up again. "So, how did you manage to get adopted by family?" she asked Kaylee.

Derrick answered, "Shortly after your adoption finalized, Daphne went into rehab. She contacted us, and we found out she was pregnant." He took his wife's hand and glanced at her before returning his attention to Denise. "Sue's first pregnancy was very difficult. She almost died, so after Luke was born, we considered adoption. The timing was perfect. We spent the entire pregnancy unsure whether she would go through with it in the end, but she did, and we couldn't be happier." He ran a hand over his daughter's hair, affection glowing in his eyes.

It hurt Denise's heart to see how loved her sister was, while it gladdened her at the same time. Kaylee seemed shy but interested in the answers Denise gave about her own life, asking an occasional tentative question when the other four adults in the room gave her a chance.

"You said something earlier about basketball," Ned reminded her a moment later.

"Oh yeah, I started it at my parents' insistence when I entered high school and found I had a bit of natural talent. Four years and several thousand hours of private practice later, I ended up on my college women's team."

"You played basketball in college?" Kaylee's eyes went wide when she heard that news.

"Yeah, I loved it. I still play a pick-up game pretty regularly," Denise said as she pushed around the last couple pieces of carrot in her soup bowl.

"Wow, did you ever think of playing pro?" Kaylee seemed mesmerized.

Denise laughed. "No, I was never that good, but I had an injury my senior year that made it impossible to go pro, even if I had been that good. That was fine, I love basketball, but computers are really my first love. And the tiny bit of spotlight I received when we played for the national title my junior year was more than enough. What about you? What do you do?"

Kaylee pushed away her empty bowl and shrugged her shoulders, as though she didn't have anything to say. Sue spoke up when it became obvious Kaylee wouldn't. "She plays the cello, she's very good. She's played a little with the city orchestra and is first chair in her school orchestra too. The conductor thinks she'll be first cello next year, and if she keeps applying herself she could be really great someday. Even play professionally."

"Really? That's great. I love music, but I can't play anything. I'm a total loss."

Kaylee gave her a disbelieving look. "Have you ever tried?"

Remembering the way she argued against the piano lessons Jennette made her take, then seldom practiced, Denise shook her head. "Not really. I took a few lessons when I was a teen, but I didn't want to be there. Piano was for wimps. If I was going to play an instrument, I wanted it to be something cool, like a guitar or drums. And I think I may have rebelled out of spite since all the good little Mormon girls seemed to play piano, and I was determined never to be one at that point." She stopped herself, realizing what she'd just said, and hurried to cover it. "I wasn't always a gem to live with, but I got better with age."

A first real smile spread across Kaylee's face, and Denise smiled back as Sharon brought in the dishes of brownies and ice cream. After dinner was over, Sharon hustled Denise and Kaylee into the family room to talk while she and Sue cleaned up dishes and the men went out to look at Ned's new ATV. Denise wondered if it had been an intentional ploy to let the two sisters get to know each other without all the distractions. When an hour passed and they were still alone, she knew she was right.

Kaylee's reserve slowly fell away as they talked. She shared memories from her childhood, stories of things she did with friends, their parties, the concerts she played at, and her hopes for the future. Denise found herself feeling jealous that her little sister lived what seemed like a simple, easy life. In many ways, Kaylee's life seemed more idealistic than Paige's. She hadn't shared her home with other people's kids, after all, and her older brother protected her as often as he tormented her.

Warring with the tiny pangs of jealousy was a deep sense of gladness that Kaylee had been spared the nightmare Denise lived through. She was grateful Kaylee lived such a great life and wanted to ensure Kaylee's life continued to be so carefree. She'd never had a younger sister, not really. Not like this. Paige was several years younger, but their relationship had always been awkward, colored by her own jealousy of Paige and whatever resentment Paige felt toward her. With Kaylee, Denise could start fresh.

Eventually everyone else wandered in to join them. Ned's kids were hanging out with friends that night and would be there the next day, so it was only the six of them, a fact Denise appreciated when the conversation turned to the less pleasant facts of her past.

"I don't remember much about growing up, where we lived, what we did. We were always moving, always in a new apartment, new neighbor-hood, new schools, new state. What can you tell me? About me, about

Daphne growing up, our moves, anything really," Denise finally asked Ned, her curiosity burning.

It took Ned a moment to speak, as if he wasn't sure where to begin, or how much to tell. "Your mother started drinking in high school. She dropped out of school, moved out of the house, and moved in with her boyfriend. They were married soon after; both of them were druggies holding down low-paying jobs. That didn't last long.

"She moved out again and found another husband. I don't know how many she went through, but it was during her second marriage that she became pregnant with you. Pete Sumner was my favorite of all the men she went with. At least the ones I met. She wasn't around much; she kind of skated in and out of our lives, and half the time we didn't know how to find her. Most of the time, actually." Ned played with the glass of ice water he brought back with him, rolling it sideways in his hands as the memories poured out.

Derrick put in his two cents. "I have no idea how she ended up with Pete. He'd been a big athlete in our high school and played some on his college team. He quit college to work when his mother got sick. That was when he met Daphne again. She was at the driest point I'd seen in years. She'd been out of the area running around and returned home because she was out of money, I think. We saw her more when they were married, partly because Pete thought family mattered."

Derrick took a sip of his soda, and Ned picked up the conversation again. "They were married fast, within weeks, completely obsessed. When she started back down the spiral of drug and alcohol abuse he slid with her, a little, though I got the feeling he was uncomfortable with the amount she used. They both grew up in LDS homes in a small town and both rebelled at the first opportunity. If you've never lived in a small town, you don't realize how easy it can be to feel suffocated by people's expectations. Especially if you're someone trying to find yourself but have little guidance at home. Not that our parents didn't try."

"But I don't think they really understood Daphne. None of us did," Derrick said. "She was never close to our parents—Mom was often sick and Dad traveled a lot. After Mom died, the family kind of fell apart. I was on my mission when we heard about the car accident that took Dad."

The mood grew solemn for a long moment. Though years had passed, it was clear to Denise the loss of their parents had been difficult, and still was. Ned broke the silence. "When Pete's mother died and his marriage with Daphne was getting rocky, he wanted to move to Virginia to work for an uncle with a car lot and clean up their acts. He could return to school again, do something with his future. Daphne didn't want to move anywhere and so because of that, and a long list of other reasons, they finally split. I know your mother blamed it all on Pete, but I doubt he had more than his share of the blame. Daphne never was easy to live with."

Denise nodded. She had never done drugs, tried alcohol, or gotten too intimate with guys—primarily, she supposed, because of Daphne's example—but she still gave her parents plenty of trouble when she was a teen. "Do you know what happened to Pete? Does he know about me?" She had to ask. Pete sounded okay compared to Daphne, and she was desperate to find something worth holding onto.

She realized these people shared her blood, and they seemed well-adjusted and happy, but she longed for more. It was comforting to see the love and respect in her aunt and uncle's home. Something good came from the Callister line.

Despite all she accomplished, she still yearned to know that at least one of her parents had redeeming values, made something of life. Obviously, that person wouldn't be Daphne. Denise would be happy to settle for Pete. If he was her father. She needed to consider the possibility that he might not be. Denise wouldn't put it past Daphne to tell everyone she was one man's child, when in reality, she came from someone else.

"I know he went to Virginia, but I haven't heard much of anything since. I don't have any other specific information. When he left, we didn't see Daphne around for a long time. Didn't know you were coming along until you were several months old, and she had remarried. Pete didn't learn about you until a couple years later, from what I could gather." Denise furrowed her brow, and Derrick seemed to sense her confusion. "After Daphne split with husband number three, she tried to get Pete to pay child support. He decided he wanted some visitation, maybe even sole custody, and she disappeared."

Denise stood and walked across the room, running a finger along the rim of a small stone bowl that decorated the fireplace mantel. "Loren Miner, was he number three?"

"Yes, Loren. He's the one on your birth certificate, but he wasn't your dad."

"That's what he said when I talked to him."

"You talked to him? When?"

She turned back to face them and explained the steps she had taken to find them.

Ned nodded in understanding. "Daphne told me a few years ago that she never came back to see us because she was afraid Pete had filed something with the state, that you would be taken from her and given to him to raise if we could find you. I guess Daphne traveled all over the place for a few years, Colorado, California, Wyoming, Nevada. She stopped in to see us for a couple hours one afternoon when you were three. She found jobs wherever she could, married another deadbeat for a year or so when you were four.

"She didn't marry again after that, preferring the ability to walk away when she had enough. You'll have to fill in most of the gaps during this time. By the time she got back in touch with us again, your adoption was finalized, and we couldn't contact you. I think it killed Daphne to lose you, but she was too proud to ask for help. Too certain she could do it on her own."

"She was too high to care most of the time," was Denise's bitter reply. Knowing Daphne had kept her apart from her family so she could ignore and abuse Denise herself made her angry. She fought back the emotion, but it wasn't easy.

"If it helps to know, she did go through three treatment centers trying to clean up," Sharon said.

"Was that before or after the state terminated parental rights?" Denise asked.

"After." Ned's voice was low, and he looked uncomfortable at admitting she hadn't tried until it was too late.

"She told me she was pregnant when the state took you away. The baby was stillborn. That was her third pregnancy. Do you remember the second one, when you were about three?"

Denise was floored. "She had a baby? I . . . don't remember that. Another stillbirth?"

Sharon shook her head. "Like Ned said, we saw you when you were three, and your mother was very pregnant. She wouldn't talk about it, and we didn't hear anything else from you for years. When we asked about the baby later, she said she'd chosen a private adoption. I got the feeling there was a little something extra for her under the table as an incentive to give her baby away. Maybe I was wrong, but Daphne seldom did anything for free, and I can't see her giving her kid up without something for herself. At least not back then. She still won't talk about it much." Denise nodded that she understood. She remembered that part of Daphne's personality only too well.

Ned picked the story up again, "The adopted baby would be twenty-one now, turning twenty-two this month, maybe last. All we know is the adoption happened in Utah; she never even mentioned if the baby was a girl or boy, and she won't discuss it with us. Your mother never had any others—that I'm aware of."

He seemed to hesitate, but seeing the encouraging look from Denise, continued. "She has done all kinds of illegal things to finance her drug habit. She was jailed a few years back for running a meth lab. When she got out, she seemed to do well for a few months, then slid again. This time she's in jail for burglary. She and a friend were high. It only took a few hours for the police to track them to the friend's house where they found thousands of dollars worth of electronic equipment."

He closed his eyes and turned his face away, as if wishing he could avoid telling her the rest. "She also got trigger happy in her hopped up haze and shot a security guard. He recovered but that added to the sentence. Daphne never was a happy person. She spoke of you sometimes, wondering how you were, regretting that she hadn't been there for you. I'm sure you don't have many happy memories of her, but she did love you, as much as she was capable."

"Yeah, I just bet." Fighting the anger that seemed to rise like a volcano inside her, Denise noticed the silence fall as everyone watched her. Her hand fluttered to her mouth and she settled back into a chair, her knees weak. "I'm sorry. That was uncalled for." *But my mother shot someone. For drugs. I came from that.*

"No, you've been through a nightmare. You have a right to be angry," Sharon said.

"No, I need to forgive, or I'll never move past everything." The response was automatic. She believed it, deep down, knew it was true, but wasn't sure it was in her to forgive Daphne. She wasn't even sure she wanted to. Believing a principle and following it weren't the same thing.

She evened her breath and forced herself to look them in the eyes, trying to stay calm. "You didn't know anything about me being put in state's custody until the adoption was finalized? That was over three years." She knew the question bordered on accusation, but she needed to know why no one had done anything.

"Since Mom and Dad were gone, we had both moved on," Derrick said. "I don't know if anyone in Annabella knew where we were."

"There was no Internet to make tracking people easy like it is now," Denise agreed, but couldn't quite excise the bitterness in her throat.

"What happened to you?" Ned asked after a long moment.

After glancing at Kaylee, trying to decide if the younger girl should hear everything, Denise began. She told him everything she remembered, or a shortened version of it, at least. Cleaned up and sanitized. Of growing up in hovels and sitting quietly, or pretending to sleep while her mother partied. The men who filed through the dingy apartments. Getting used to one new man before having him or Daphne decide to leave. Eventually she stopped trying to make a relationship with the new man, and many times she worked to avoid them.

She didn't tell them about what sometimes happened when her mother passed out or left her alone with these men. They didn't need the extra guilt. And Denise could tell Ned felt guilty. Besides, the memories still nauseated her.

Denise explained her life in foster care, giving the highlights, laughing about foster sisters and brothers, and finally landing with the DeWalts. It felt almost false giving them only the highlights, but she couldn't share the whole truth with these near strangers. Sharing what she had was difficult enough.

"I think they saved me in ways I hadn't thought I could be saved. They've really been there for me over the past fifteen years." She forced a smile.

Silence hung in the air while everyone digested Denise's words. Sharon's face showed tear tracks, but she wiped them away and put on a wavering smile. "And now, are you dating anyone? You told us about your job and roommate, but you never mentioned a man. A cute girl like you has got to have one. If not, I know some eligible bachelors." She wiggled her eyebrows and wiped at a damp spot on her face.

Coloring a little, Denise focused on the hands clasped in her lap. "We're . . . I don't know exactly. There is someone, sort of. We're taking things slowly, I guess." *At least I'm trying to.* "We'll see what happens." She shrugged, trying to pretend it didn't matter.

"We would like to meet this young man sometime. Maybe when we're in Provo next. We should be down before Christmas," Sharon suggested.

"That would be nice. I'm sure Rich would like it."

After returning to her motel for the night, Denise found herself too wound up from the things she'd learned and talked about that night to settle down. She walked laps around the courtyard in the cold and dark until her nose felt numb and her toes turned to ice cubes.

Denise loved her own family in Orem, but she couldn't help but feel cheated at not having had contact with her extended family for all of these years. How did Daphne justify keeping her from her family, not allowing her to have relationships with people who loved her?

Tears threatened to fall, stinging her eyes, but she refused to give in to them. If she did, she just might cry all night. More than anything she wanted to call Rich and talk about what she learned, to share her excitement, her worry, and her anger. But she knew she couldn't call; it was late, and she knew if she gave in and shared it all with him tonight it would prove he was important to her, too important to give up easily. She couldn't rely on him because he might not be there for her in a few more weeks.

It was late when she returned to her room for bed, but sleep didn't come easily.

CHAPTER SIXTEEN

After sleeping in and eating a quick breakfast at the hotel, Denise returned to Sharon's house midmorning to visit with the family again. Kaylee was sitting at the table with the adults looking a little lost when Denise was shown into the kitchen. When Denise heard Kaylee asking her mother to take her shopping and Sue's obvious reluctance to deal with the traffic and mall, Denise offered to take her. "I'm usually not much of a shopper myself, but it could be fun hanging out at the mall with my little sister."

Kaylee smiled shyly at her, and Sue agreed to let them go. She sent Kaylee with some money, and Denise soon found herself on the road. An hour passed as they sucked down sodas and wandered from shop to shop. Denise picked up a few more Christmas presents, though it was barely after Halloween, and Kaylee bought a cute T-shirt.

Though she hadn't had much practice with girl talk, Denise enjoyed listening to her little sister talk about hanging out with her friends and the crazy things they did on orchestra trips. She noticed, though, that it sounded as if Kaylee spent untold hours practicing her cello, in addition to piano lessons. Denise figured she would have felt stifled at that age. The younger girl's life sounded tame and innocent to Denise, who had been into much more trouble at Kaylee's age. Of course, Kaylee's life was too disciplined to leave room for getting into trouble.

"You don't talk much about what you did when you were a teenager," Kaylee pointed out as she poked through an earring display and looked intrigued at a nose ornament.

"You don't want to hear about my teen years. I was a brat who thought she knew everything and could take care of herself. I made a huge mess of things, and it took me years to straighten things out. It's amazing how the little decisions we make can have a big impact." She tried to keep her voice light and casual, but her feelings on the subject were anything but casual.

"What kind of decisions?" Kaylee asked; with a fascinated expression she fingered an eyebrow stud with a purple jewel on the end.

After taking a moment to consider the effects of telling the truth, whether it might encourage or discourage her little sister, Denise moved closer and lowered her voice, not wanting to share the story with random strangers. Since she was so far from home, at least they were strangers. "I was a mess by the time I moved into my adoptive home. I didn't have anyone in my life I trusted, not like you do with your parents. I got into fights at school and was caught shoplifting a few times. The juvenile detention center is not a fun place to visit—it didn't take me long to decide I didn't want to go back."

Kaylee's eyes widened, and then she shivered. "I don't blame you."

"I focused on school before I graduated though, got good grades, a basketball scholarship. Focus on where you want to be and set a goal. Don't get distracted. You won't regret it."

As they walked past a beauty supply store a few minutes later, Kaylee looked longingly at a poster in the window. A twenty-ish looking girl with white blond hair sporting black and hot pink streaks looked out over the hallway from the oversized picture. She looked confident, amused. "So, what do you think of hair dye?"

Denise studied the poster, then her sister. "If you're talking about that," she pointed to the poster, "I say Sue would freak."

"You think I might talk her into strawberry blond?"

Understanding Kaylee's need to make a statement, do something, have some control, Denise considered again. "Maybe if we gang up on her you'll have more leverage. Nothing brassy or outrageous, just a boost of color." She leaned in conspiratorially and dropped her voice a little. "But, if you ask first for something brassy and outlandish, maybe she'll be relieved when you settle for something more tame."

A smile spread on Kaylee's face as she considered the possibilities. "I hadn't thought of that. I'll give it a try."

They grinned at each other for a moment and continued down the hall.

After a nice family dinner and an afternoon of idle chitchat with everyone, Denise headed home with Kaylee's promise to keep her updated on Operation: Color Change.

And a sheet of paper was tucked into Denise's wallet with the date and time of Kaylee's next orchestra performance.

"Denise did say she would be home tonight, right?" Rich asked Lily, checking his watch for the fourth time in twenty minutes. It would be seven soon, and he wished Denise owned a cell phone, a suggestion she'd scoffed at just last week, saying that she didn't want to be at everyone's beck and call all day.

"Yes, definitely tonight. She left a message on the machine last night after I left for work saying she had a family thing this afternoon and would be back tonight. She has a lesson to teach tomorrow, remember?"

"Right, Relief Society." Rich turned his eyes back to the game they were watching, but his mind stayed on Denise. She was a grown woman, after all. She could take care of herself. Surely if she decided to stay another night, she would call and let them know. She and Lily always watched out for each other that way. He wondered how things were going with her family reunion since the previous day. Was she happy or would she be angry and disappointed when she came home? Another week like the past one could drive her over the edge. And he wouldn't be far behind if that happened.

John rolled his eyes and picked up his glass of soda: Coke from a can, three cubes of ice—it was always the same. Rich learned Lily kept the cans of soda in the fridge specifically for John; she was a root beer girl herself, and Denise eschewed anything carbonated. "I'm sure she'll be here soon enough. Sit down, Lily, and quit fluttering. You're distracting me from the game." The Clippers-Bulls game was on and John's attention had been riveted all evening.

The sound of the door opening broke into Rich's thoughts, and he was relieved to see Denise was well, if a bit worn looking. Her arms were full of grocery sacks and mall bags, and her gym tote hung from her shoulder. "Hey all, I'm home."

As soon as she emptied her hands, Rich slid a lock of Denise's hair behind her ear, wishing he dared pull her into his arms. He could see from the way she barely met his gaze that she would balk if he tried and wondered why she held back from him. "How was the trip?"

"Exhausting, but nice. I have a sister and another sibling." She smiled, but it looked forced to Rich. "Daphne doesn't talk about the third one, apparently. We're not sure how to find him or her, but my uncles promised to try and get more information from her. My sister is also my cousin, since our uncle adopted her." Denise began unloading the groceries, putting them into the cupboards and fridge as she told him about her little sister in tones low enough not to disturb John's game.

"Whoa, slow down. You had fun?" Rich asked, running his eyes over the shining glow of her cheeks. He would have thought her happy if her eyes hadn't said there was more she wasn't telling. Since it didn't appear she was ready to discuss that though, he decided to bide his time.

"I did, it was great. Thoroughly overwhelming. I'm not sure I can keep everyone's names straight. Oh, and Ned knows who my dad is. I'm not sure how I feel about everything. It makes me feel a little off balance, but I'll figure it out."

The haunted look in her eyes grew when she mentioned anything having to do with her mother. This worried Rich, and he realized there was a long road before she would be free of the pain she carried around with her.

He listened to her chatter while she put away the groceries, seldom meeting his gaze. Though she put on a brave front and acted excited about the meeting, something wasn't right, and Rich knew he had to find out what.

Sunday dinner with her family went well, Denise thought, as Jennette returned to the kitchen for dessert. Paige had brought Cliff again. Denise liked Cliff more every time she talked with him. She marveled that he put up with Paige's shallowness, then realized that Paige seemed steadier with him than with any other guy she'd dated. It made Denise wonder if it was Cliff's influence, or if she had been like this all the time, and the other guys she dated were the problem.

The subject of Denise's visit with her family came up as they were cleaning after dinner. Paige was horrified when she found out that Denise contacted her biological uncle and had plans to try and reach her father and possibly Daphne in the future.

"Don't you remember what that . . . woman put you through growing up? The drugs, the beatings, the empty promises? How could you want to see her again, to go through all of that again? Are you crazy?"

Denise ground her teeth together but turned to face her sister. "A little bit, yeah. I think maybe I am. On the flip side, I never had a chance to make my peace with her." She closed her eyes at the thoughts of how her life could have been and fought back the wave of anger. "Though right now, I'm so angry at her, peace is the furthest thing from my mind. I'm not saying we'll have a long and loving relationship. My birth dad may not be interested in meeting me at all, but I have to find out." *If you knew where Daphne is right now, you'd really flip.*

"Don't you have any consideration for *my* parents' feelings? How can you bring up that woman in this house? How can you treat everything they've done for you like nothing?" Paige thrust the carton of milk she was holding into the fridge and slammed the door shut.

"Paige, you're out of line," her mother said, the lines around the eyes showing how strained she was.

"Mom," Paige protested.

"No, this is her journey, and she has to make it." The obvious pain on Jennette's face cut Denise to the bone. It was clear Jennette wasn't entirely happy about the developments but was trying very hard to be supportive.

"Mom, give me a minute." Denise took a calming breath. She turned back to Paige. "Before I started this, I thought about it for a long time. I know Daphne far better than you ever could, or at least what she was. You've learned bits and pieces; I lived it every day for nine years. I talked with Mom before I tried reaching my other relatives, and she gave me information that led me to Ned. Trust me when I say that nothing my biological family could offer me will ever take the place of what I was given here.

"Contacting Daphne is still way down the road. I don't know when I'll be ready, or if it'll be more than writing her a letter." Denise glanced in Cliff's direction and saw how uncomfortable he looked, standing at the end of the counter, his hands full of dirty dishes. She sent him an apologetic glance and looked back at her mom. Jennette's face was a little worried, but less so than before. Denise returned her attention to Paige. "This is something I have to do, even if no one understands it."

"Do you have to rub it in their faces though? 'Oh, my aunts and uncles are so great!' "

Paige's attacks exasperated Denise. "I'm talking about it with Mom and Dad because I think they deserve to know what's going on. I'm not rubbing it in their faces. Would you rather I went behind their backs with all of this?"

Paige sulked for several seconds. She shook her head. "I guess not. But I still think you're crazy."

"That makes two of us." Denise threw the rag she had been using to wipe down the counters into the sink of soapy water and turned to look out the back window.

"I think Denise is pretty brave," Jennette said in a strangled tone. "This is a hard road to take. She found some answers now, and more questions. I'm glad she's keeping us in the loop, and I hope you won't be so hard on her." Her voice was calm but firm, and Paige burst into tears and ran from the room. Apparently Paige was too caught up in her worries to notice the way her mother's hands fisted until her knuckles were white or the tight line of her jaw, but Denise noticed.

Denise turned to see Cliff look around at the rest of the family apologetically, set the dishes on the counter and hurry after Paige.

Refusing to give in to her own tears, Denise turned back to the window and stared into the yard, seeing nothing. Jennette was the only real mother Denise ever had—she wasn't about to forget it. Nor was she going to turn away from the support Jennette offered while it was available, even if her mom did have misgivings. If Denise only knew what they were. "Thanks, Mom."

Silence stretched for several heartbeats before Jennette answered. "Just be careful."

Chapter Seventeen

Things went better at work the next week. Denise wasn't as tense, managing to push her worries about family to the side as she focused on her computer.

Denise did an online search on Pete, and found a couple dozen names that looked like they might be him. She knew there was nothing she could do to track down her other sibling until they knew a gender and exact birth date, at the very least, and she didn't know if Daphne would ever part with that information.

Her fingers tapped on the keyboard as she prepared another letter, backing up, rewriting, deleting it, and starting over again. It had to be perfect: concise, specific enough so he would be sure he was the one she was searching for, but vague enough no one else could use it against her.

Though she was more nervous about getting in touch with Pete than she had been with Ned, because his rejection would be that much more personal, she also felt a sense of comfort knowing that whether he wanted her or not, she had at least made other strong connections. Besides, she had reason to hope that Pete would be open to *some* kind of contact

As she hit the print button and her laser printer began spewing out pages, she told herself it didn't matter that Paige didn't understand. The printer stopped, and she added paper to tray two, then clicked on resume.

Her mind drifted to Rich as she reached for her stack of envelopes. He was offering her a life with him. Someday—eternity. It wasn't that she didn't believe in the concept. Through a long struggle in high school and college, she'd gained a testimony of her own and knew that the concept of eternal marriage was true. But she never thought of it being applied to her.

A year after Denise had been baptized, Jennette had begun talking about being sealed as a family in the temple. Denise had deflected these comments by saying she wasn't ready to go yet.

The paper formed crisp edges under her fingers as she folded and stuffed each sheet into an envelope. She had never been ready to go to the temple. There was far too much baggage to deal with. Denise glanced at a picture of the Manti Temple Lily had hung on the living room wall. Feeling a hollowness in her chest, she looked away.

Now she was putting her hope in the hands of the man who might be her father. After all these years, would he still care? Had he cared in the first place, or had his apparent desire to get custody been a form of punishment for Daphne for something she did to him? She addressed the letters and stamped them, ready to mail. Feeling antsy, she changed into sweats and grabbed her basketball.

The gym was not as busy as usual, but she hardly ever made it in on a Monday night. Five guys were running some drills at one end of the court; Cliff was one of them.

"Hey, Denise." He waved her over. "We wanted to play a game, but we're short tonight. Care to join?"

Denise looked at the other guys and saw the disbelief on their faces. She hadn't seen any of them before, but as they were all tall as trees and quite adept with the ball, she figured they must be on Cliff's team. "Somehow I don't think any of these guys wants to play with me," she said, looking back at Cliff.

"Well, you are pretty lousy, but a game's a game, right? Even if you do shoot like a girl." Cliff sent her a calculating look and sighed as if to say he supposed he could do worse. "I guess I'll take you on my team, if I have to. Rooke, wanna join us? These other losers will have to fend for themselves. Under the circumstances, my team ought to be shirts."

The other three guys shook their heads and removed their T-shirts, and then got into position. One dark-haired guy took a look at Denise and cocked his head. "I get her, I always did like to guard the easy ones."

Denise sent him a disparaging look as she took the ball out of bounds and tossed it in to Cliff.

The game was intense, and the guys' surprise that she wasn't a pushover on the court, even if she wasn't as good as they were, was golden. It had been a long time since she played against a group of guys more intent than she was. The guy guarding her found his task wasn't as easy as he expected.

When the game ended, Cliff's team lost by one point. "Good workout guys. Are you all on the BYU team?" Denise asked as she stretched out her muscles. She had worked harder than usual, and her college injury was starting to feel sore. She ran a hand over it and decided a little babying was in order when she reached home.

"Yeah. Games started a few weeks ago," Rooke, a gangly eighteen-year-old redhead said with a grin. "You're something else, girl. You can play on my team any day."

"But you lost," one of the other guys said.

"Yeah, if she had been on that team and you were on ours, they would have won by more than one point," Cliff said.

Denise laughed; the idea was absurd—she didn't have anything on these guys.

"So Werner, how'd you meet this spitfire?" Rooke asked. "I thought you already had a girl."

"Denise is Paige's sister, so behave yourself."

"Oh, I can behave." Rooke slung an arm around Denise's shoulder, a move which emphasized the fact that he was several inches taller than Cliff's six-foot, seven-inches. "You wanna grab a bite, baby?"

Again, Denise had to laugh, the whole thing was so exaggerated she knew he wasn't serious. "Sorry, Stretch, not only are you too young, you're not my type."

"Oh, what type's that?"

"I hear she goes for computer geeks."

Denise turned around when she heard the voice and looked into a pair of dark brown eyes. She smiled despite the mixed feelings racing through her. "Rich, are you following me?" Rooke's arm slid from her shoulders.

"Naw, I've been swimming. I needed to blow some steam after that marathon meeting today. You too apparently." He walked over and settled his forearm arm on her left shoulder, a territorial gesture that amused her rather than irritated.

"I met you once before, didn't I? The roommate's cousin?" Cliff asked as he came over and held out a hand for Rich to shake.

"Yeah, you're dating her sister. Cliff, right?" Rich looked Cliff over and nodded.

"I better book it. I've got homework before curfew. Catch you later boys." Rooke shot Denise a look. "You can play with us anytime."

"Thanks," Denise said with a laugh.

"Oh and girly, that guy ever gets boring, give me a call." Rooke winked before heading through the double doors.

Denise's laughter followed him down the hall.

The other three guys found similar excuses to head home, leaving Denise with Cliff and Rich.

"How long have you two been dating?" Cliff asked.

"Oh, we're not really . . . I mean we're—"

"Almost two months," Rich interrupted Denise. She sent him an irritated look.

"I got ya." Cliff looked back at Denise. "You're embarrassed to be seen with him in public. That makes sense to me. He probably can't even hold his own on the court."

Giving up, and with no idea how to explain since she didn't understand it herself, Denise decided to play along. "That's true about the court. It's sad, really. I'm not sure where the genes come from, but he doesn't have it. That's okay, he knows everything about putting together a mean website." The conversation was almost conspiratorial, but open enough that a glance was enough for her to see Rich fighting back a smile.

"I'm telling you, Cliff, it's the way to any girl's heart," Rich joked.

"Basketball always worked for me. Of course, Paige wasn't very impressed with that."

"Paige?" Denise sent him a disbelieving look. "Are you sure you read her right? That doesn't sound like my sister."

"There's more to me than my muscles." He seemed almost defensive.

"That was never in dispute," Denise assured him, realizing she spoke before her brain engaged. "Of all the guys she's dated, you're far and wide the best. Solid major, RM, and a nice guy. Don't get me wrong, but Paige has a penchant for dating jocks. She usually gets sick of them way before now though, so you must be doing something right."

"I guess that's a lucky thing for me." He shrugged off what she realized must have come across as only half complimentary.

Denise shifted gears. "Look, I wanted to apologize for your getting sucked into the mess Sunday. Paige's pretty protective of our parents. I think she never let herself think of them as 'our parents,' which is mostly my fault. So . . . you get scenes like Sunday."

Cliff's shoe scuffed across the parquet floor. "I was sorry she freaked out on you. I can see you wanting to figure out your past. My family is kind of a Heinz 57 mix too; most of us were adopted, so I understand the drive to look for answers. I'm sure she'll see it's not the end of the world. Give her a little time. I'll work on her for you."

"I will. Thanks." Denise realized Cliff was what Lily would call a kindred spirit.

"It's getting late," Rich reminded Denise.

"You're right. I'll catch you later. Coach has us on a curfew." The roll of Cliff's eyes said exactly how he felt about that.

Before the parking lot scene a couple months earlier, it had been nearly a year since the last time Denise woke shaking and dripping with sweat from one of her nightmares. But though it had calmed some since they started again, she still woke in a panic a couple times a week.

Still shaking and sweaty, Denise threw back her bedcovers and climbed out of bed. She learned long ago that it took a great deal to fall back to sleep after one of these nightmares, and it was already five in the morning. She showered and dressed, worked through her morning routine without a thought, but she couldn't settle down.

When Lily returned from work a few minutes before seven, Denise was eating breakfast. It was a little early, but not so much that Lily commented on it. Exhaustion rang in Denise's brain and the unforgettable images of a man entering her room, a room she hadn't lived in for seventeen years, wouldn't shake loose.

Desperate for something to distract her, Denise left for work early, letting herself in with a key and sliding in at her desk.

Everyone else arrived an hour and a half later, and the day progressed like normal. The same chatter about the previous night's game, the same questions about code, the same lame jokes that bounced from one guy to another. It was infuriating that life would seem so normal on the outside while her brain screamed at her that nothing was right.

Denise found her thoughts trailing off to some of the worst memories she had, making concentration impossible.

She had blocked out the noise and activity of the guys around her, so she jumped when Rich walked in, setting off Jake's Room Defender. Rich sucked in a quick breath of surprise and shook his finger at Jake, but continued on to Mick's desk with a hint of a smile on his face. Jake put on a chagrined look but smirked as soon as Rich turned away. The Room Defender was everyone's favorite toy.

While working through a couple problems with some of the other guys, Rich threw Denise a worried look, and she returned her gaze to the computer screen. She brushed the hair back from her face and wondered how awful she must look that a glance told him something was wrong with her. He didn't need to know about the nightmares, the real horrors she lived through. What she had already shared with him was enough.

Knowing she'd lost sight of this issue in the past few weeks, not given it the full weight it deserved, made her mad. She was mad at herself for risking his heart, mad at him for pressuring her when she said she couldn't be what he needed, and most of all, mad at Daphne for letting it all happen in the first place. How could a mother have kept her daughter from people who loved her, allowed her to be hurt so much—been the one to hurt her so many times.

Pushing away from her desk, Denise made her way to the soda machine and purchased a can of vegetable juice. Rich's face swam before her eyes. *I love him, and I never thought I would love another man.* She took a sip of her drink, not leaving the privacy of the hall's dead end.

Though how I can compare this to what I felt for Brian . . . that was far more desperation than love. I wasn't really risking as much then, and the risk now is more than I can handle. She took a deep, cleansing breath and then headed back to the office. *Tonight it ends. Tonight I let him go before I get entangled any further in this mess. If I let it go any further, I'll have to tell him everything, and then I'll have to deal with him pushing me away instead.*

She couldn't eat when lunchtime came. The sandwich and apple she brought sat in the break room fridge in her lunch box as she wrestled with her focus and the code she needed to do her job. The others all left for the day. Still she stayed. She hadn't finished half a day's worth of work yet. Hadn't made more than a minimum of headway on the page she was building. It was the first time in memory that she couldn't work through the stress, to wrap it away, and move on.

As the twelfth hour of her workday approached, she shifted her attention to the computer screen. She could make this work, she knew she could. She was smarter than the code. Surely.

"Denise? What are you still doing here?"

When she looked up, Rich stood in the doorway, his face full of concern. Already on edge, the emotion that rose inside her just seeing his face was almost more than she could handle, and she looked away while she shoved it back inside. "I'm wrestling with this problem. I'm sure I'll get it soon."

Rich walked around her desk and slid Jake's chair over by her own. He peered over her shoulder. He asked a few questions about what she was trying to accomplish, then added a line of code. It was simple, not more than a few commands, yet when he hit execute it did everything it was supposed to. "You must be tired, you're good enough to have seen that right away."

After all her work, it was more than Denise could take and she fell back on anger as she saved the changes and stood to leave. "Fine, you're the young genius. You do my job."

She took three steps before he grabbed her elbow, turning her around. "What's the problem? You've been moody and distracted all day."

"Obviously my work isn't good enough for your high standards." She wondered if Rich could feel the chill in her gaze as she glared at him. She forced in a little more frost, her best defense from the tears she was on the verge of letting loose.

"Forget about work. What's wrong?" He held her by both elbows now, his eyes searching her face.

"I'm not upset."

"Obviously you are. What is it?"

"Let me go. I don't want to talk to you." Denise pulled on her elbows, but his grip tightened. "I have nothing for you." She wasn't talking about work anymore.

He seemed to sense the change in topic, and an edge of fear entered his voice. "No way. I'm not going to give up on you like that. You may as well talk to me."

He pulled her a little nearer, and her nightmare returned. It was no longer Rich's face in front of hers but another. A man pulling her closer, smiling lecherously. Panic bubbled up inside her as she felt herself being sucked back into her childhood. She cowered and pulled away from him, sobbing. "I said let go of me!"

Rich's hands unclamped when he saw her panic. He stood in shock as she stumbled the few steps to the wall by the doorway and crumpled onto the floor.

Joan appeared at the door. "What is going on here?" Her jaw dropped as she glanced at each of them.

Denise sat huddled in the corner, pain and terror ripping through her in huge sobs. She pulled herself to her feet and stumbled out of the office.

CHAPTER EIGHTEEN

Denise's reaction terrified Rich, made him desperate to go after her. Then he looked at Joan and saw the fire burning in the woman's eyes. It hit him that this looked bad. Really bad.

Rich sought something to say that wouldn't sound ten times worse than it was. Something that would release him to go help Denise. "I could tell she was upset, it was even affecting her work, and I asked her to talk about it. She . . . I don't know what happened exactly." He took two steps toward the door, but Joan held out a hand to stop him.

"Rich, I don't know what happened here, but I intend to get to the bottom of it. If you've been harassing her, your career is over."

Rich tried to find the right words. But nothing sounded right. He wanted Denise to share what was bothering her. He loved her. Taken out of context, the whole thing would have sounded horrible. Again, he felt caught between showing Denise that she was important to him, showing her he would be there for her, and not pushing her too hard. "But I—"

"Go. Now." Joan's voice was hard, her gaze flinty.

Feeling helpless, he left.

Denise stumbled out to her car and drove it into an adjoining parking lot that couldn't be seen from the main building. She didn't hear the sounds of cars rushing past her on the nearby road, didn't notice how much time passed as she felt the adrenalin pumping through her, heard echoes from her past, and struggled to push the emotions back. The cloak of calm was more difficult to wrap around her than usual, and when she felt ready to start the car again, she realized it had been more than forty-five minutes.

She almost detoured to her parents' house, knowing Rich would be at her place, wearing a path in the carpet. *I have to face him and let him go, it's the only fair thing to do. Then I can finish with these tears and put it behind me.* She didn't find the thought comforting; instead, she hurt worse than ever. *What other option is there?*

She found Rich pacing in the hallway outside her apartment. She stopped when she saw him, noticed the haunted look in his eyes, and felt swamped by guilt. Her gut tightened even further. "I figured you would be inside," she said as she walked past him and pulled out her apartment key.

"Lily's not here to let me in. I have to talk to you, Denise. I promise I won't touch you if you don't want me to. I'll sit clear across the room if I have to, but I have to . . ." He trailed off as she held the door open for him.

He walked in, and she pointed to the sofa. "Sit."

There was a moment's hesitation before he complied. He turned back to her with more questions in his eyes than she knew what to do with. Denise rubbed the back of her neck and took over on the pacing. Shame and embarrassment warred with the knowledge that she had put him in an uncomfortable situation at work. Joan was bound to have questions about what she saw.

"There are things I haven't talked to you about. Things from my past that I don't want to talk about. Ever. I had a dream last night that shook me up all day. I'm sorry it distracted me from my work and made me so emotional. I'll talk to Joan tomorrow, straighten everything out with her. I won't let you lose your job over my panic attack."

"Forget the job. I don't care about that. What happened in there?" He clasped his hands in front of him, his knuckles turning white.

She buried her face in her hands and ran over the possible responses. He was not getting a play-by-play. She wasn't going to burden him with even the general idea of what was bothering her. Denise turned and looked him in the eye, her hands forming balls at her sides. "I remembered some unpleasant memories, and I was already upset and short on sleep, so I over-reacted. I know it's not your fault. I haven't explained things. I just . . .

lost control. I hate losing control, and that only made it all worse. When Joan came in, one thing piled on top of another. It's been ages since my last panic attack. It doesn't happen regularly anymore." *At least not until recently.*

"You've been pushing me away ever since you came back from meeting your family. Something changed between us. I was so worried about you, about the way you were acting; I'm sorry if I scared you. I know things in your past were horrible, and I don't want to add to that, but I need you to talk to me." He paused for a moment, considering. "It wasn't just the dream, was it?"

Denise waved his concern away as if it didn't matter, though she knew it mattered to him. Now came the hard part. "Rich, you're a great guy, you've meant a lot to me, but I don't think we should see each other outside of work anymore. I'm going to apply for that job you showed me as a joke last week, or was it the week before that? It's time I made a change."

Rich stood and strode across the room to her, stopping several feet away, hope fighting with worry in his eyes. "But once you've switched companies—"

"No." Denise shook her head. "I don't see how. I can't go there with you or anyone else. I know what you want, but I can't give it to you, and I doubt I ever will. I've never wanted marriage." *Not as much as I do now.*

Disbelief seeped into his face. "Denise, you're killing me here."

"I'm sorry, Rich. I told you I would break your heart. I didn't want to." She closed her eyes to shut out the hurt on his face. "I don't—I *can't* give you what you want. Not now. I'm so sorry." Tears came to her eyes again. She didn't think she'd been through anything harder in her life than letting him go.

Pain radiated from him when she looked him in the face. "I can wait."

"Don't, Rich. Don't wait, find someone else, have a family, make something of yourself. I've never worked for anyone like you before. You're the best boss I've ever had, one of the best people I've ever known. Don't let that go." She rubbed her forehead where she could feel a migraine growing as tears threatened to pour out of her. She turned away. "Please go. I need to lie down now. Fits of hysterics do that to me."

After several seconds, he turned and took two steps, then pivoted back. He held her gaze for a long moment before whispering to her. "I love you, Denise."

Denise turned away, unable to meet his eye any longer. She barely contained her sobs until he shut the door behind him, and she was able to hurry to her own room to empty the pain in her heart.

The next morning, Denise showed up to work early and was waiting by Joan's desk when the woman came in to open up. "I need to talk to you." A night of little sleep and long hours scrubbing walls in her apartment left Denise tired, but with a clear idea of what she had to accomplish that morning. At least where Joan was concerned.

Joan nodded and led Denise into a conference room nearby. They sat at the table, Joan on the end, Denise just around the corner. Joan took Denise's hands and looked her in the eye. "Tell me what happened yesterday. What did he do to you?"

A lingering headache had Denise almost as keyed up as the day before. The headache could be melted away with time and medication, but reality still had to be faced. She had filled her heart with prayer since rising that morning, desperate for help to explain what happened with Rich the previous night to keep Joan from freaking out over his concern.

She sighed. "I had a difficult experience yesterday morning and didn't get enough sleep. It hung with me all day making me distracted and . . . Rich was worried about me. He could see I was pushing what was bothering me away and . . . Let's say I had an unhappy flashback to my troubled childhood. I panicked, even though I know Rich would never hurt me."

"What did he do to you? You can tell me." Joan seemed convinced that there was more to it than that, and Denise wished she had tracked the woman's number down the previous evening and talked it over before Joan's imagination had blown everything out of control. Of course, she wouldn't have been ready to discuss it then.

"Nothing." Denise shook her head. "He really didn't do anything. He didn't hurt me or threaten me or do anything inappropriate. I just freaked out. I have panic attacks sometimes, and with everything going on in my personal life lately, it doesn't take much to set me off. I'm thoroughly embarrassed, and I don't know how to explain it." If Joan had been less of a friend to her over the years, Denise doubted she could have told the woman so much. Even this was extremely difficult for her.

"Give me the word, and I'll see to it that he's suspended from work until further investigations can be made. I like Rich, but he can't do this. I won't let him." Joan's eyes were shiny, but her voice was deadly serious.

Denise grasped Joan's arms and looked her in the eye. "Don't. I promise there's nothing to worry about. Rich didn't do anything wrong. I swear it. We're friends—good friends—and I've been going through a rough patch. I know he's been worried about me, but he hasn't hurt me or harassed me. I promise. He held my arms and asked me to tell him what was bothering me. I freaked out. That's all."

Joan gave her a long look. "Sometimes victims don't even realize when they're being victimized."

Denise's response was a bitter laugh. "Trust me. I know all about victimization. I grew up in a home filled with abuse, neglect, and chemical dependency. Rich has never been anything but kind and understanding with me." Denise put a hand on Joan's shoulder and looked at her earnestly. "He's a very good man and innocent of any wrong yesterday."

A surprised understanding entered Joan's eyes. "You're in love with him."

She hadn't planned on giving so much away, but Denise could sense that was part of the reason Joan accepted her word. "I don't know what I am anymore. Believe me when I say this is a personal problem, not something the boss needs to worry about. We're not dating, but we're close, and appropriate behavior doesn't ensure appropriate feelings." She brushed away the tears that slid from her eyes and stood, looking Joan in the face. "You haven't said anything to anyone else about last night, have you?"

Joan shook her head. "I was saving that until after I spoke with you."

"Good. Drop it. I swear, if you'd seen it all, it wouldn't seem as horrible as it must. I need to get to work, and you need to get this place opened up."

Before work and on her breaks, Denise applied for every programming job she could find. There weren't that many, but after contacting some old college friends, she managed to track down one or two that weren't listed on any database. She hated to leave Donaldson because she loved it there, but seeing Rich every day would kill them both. She didn't want to think about switching apartments too but hadn't ruled that out yet. Her friendship with Lily was too important to damage unless absolutely necessary.

Rich came into the room before lunch with a stack of papers. Denise glanced over to see who it was but didn't look at him after that, avoiding his gaze.

"Mick, you at a stopping point?" Rich asked as he walked over.

"Just a minute." Mick typed in a couple more lines and then saved his work. "Okay, shoot."

Rich pulled over a chair and sat down so they could get to work. Denise tuned them out until she heard Rich's voice again. Jake was pushing back from his desk when Rich asked, "You heading to lunch?"

"Yeah, do you need something first?" Jake asked.

"If you could hold on a bit, I've got appointments all afternoon, and I'll be in Pittsburg for the rest of the week."

"Sure." Jake sat again with a shrug.

Denise took that as her signal to leave. It was awkward working with Rich so near. Besides, her head was fuzzy, and she knew the break would help. She slipped away for a picnic in her car. The wind howled outside her car windows and late-season rain pelted the roof, beating off tempo with her music on the radio, but the half-hour's respite from the office helped ground her. Denise wondered if she would have been better off taking a break yesterday even if she didn't eat. Maybe she wouldn't have freaked out so badly if she had. That realization made her feel worse.

The doorbell rang soon after Denise dropped her keys on the hook inside her apartment door. A look through the keyhole showed a strange man with a vase of white roses. With a sigh, she opened the door.

"Hello?" Denise had been crying in the car on the way home and knew her eyes were rimmed with red.

"I have a delivery for Denise DeWalt."

"That's me."

The man produced his clipboard and had her sign while he mentioned what a maze her building was. Denise shut the door behind her and walked slowly to the kitchen counter. The card for the flowers sat tucked among the ferns and baby's breath, mocking her. She didn't even need to open it to know who sent the bouquet.

Still, after setting them down and looking at them for a long moment, she pulled it out to read anyway.

I HOPE THINGS START LOOKING UP FOR YOU SOON. REMEMBER, I'M HERE FOR YOU IF YOU NEED ME.

RICH

The tears started to fall again, but instead of pushing them away, she let them fall and opened a cupboard in search of dinner. The quote that the Lord wouldn't send more troubles her way than she could handle flashed through her mind. She laughed. *Surely, whoever said that was never in my place.*

The heady scent of roses filled the room as Denise put together a sandwich. The flowers were a reminder, all right. She wondered if she should make a trip home to her parents' and give them to her mom. The thought to simply toss them crossed her mind, but she couldn't. They represented the hope of something she had never allowed herself to believe in.

Aside from the issue of whether she deserved it was the question of whether any man deserved to be saddled with her. Intimacy had always scared her, and though she knew Rich would be good to her, she feared her past experiences would taint anything good she could have with him. Other people could have that kind of loving relationship, but it wasn't for her.

That thought staggered her. *Do I really feel that way? Is that what the gospel says? Of course not.* But it was the way she felt. She sat at the counter, her dinner forgotten. *Did that thought come from me?*

The front door opened, breaking her from her musings, and Lily breezed in, grinning madly. Denise turned away, sticking her head into the fridge as if looking for something. "Oh Denise, I was at John's and I wondered if you wanted to join us for a movie. I know Rich is gone. These are gorgeous. Did my sweet, handsome cousin send them?"

"Yes, it was nice of him." Tears still threatened, and Denise wondered if her voice sounded as strange to Lily as it did herself.

"Sweet, very sweet. But Rich always was the sweet type. You care to come with us?" Lily told her about the show at the dollar theater starting in forty-five minutes.

"No, thanks. I think I'm going to go to bed early tonight. It's been a rough week." Denise heard footsteps behind her.

"Rich said you had a bad day yesterday. He hated leaving you alone for the next few days." Lily placed a hand on Denise's shoulder, but Denise turned her face away. "Have you been crying?"

"It's been a rough couple days, and I'm exhausted." Mustering her courage, Denise turned to face her roommate, her best friend. "I need some time to think through everything going on. The stress of searching for my family is starting to get to me, and things with Rich have reached the point of no return." She paused, considering whether to go on and then did. "I broke whatever our relationship was off with him last night. It was getting too complicated. But I don't want to talk about it now. I'll take something to help me sleep and conk out for the night."

Worry covered Lily's face. "You broke up with Rich? Why? I thought the two of you were getting on really well. I thought—"

"I don't want to go into it right now. Ask me tomorrow or the next day, and maybe I'll be ready to go there." Denise averted her eyes again, certain Lily would read the truth in them—that Denise was almost as traumatized by the end of the relationship as she would have been if Rich learned everything and rejected her.

"But, Denise, are you sure you don't want to talk? I mean, I know sometimes you just want to hold back, even when it's better to talk."

Denise put a hand on Lily's arm. "I really need some time alone to deal with things. Please give me some time to work through it alone."

Lily pursed her lips but nodded after a moment. "Okay, if that's what you want. I've got to go."

Once she had the apartment to herself, Denise ate the sandwich, though she couldn't taste it, and headed to her room.

Sleep wouldn't come, and she was soon up and scrubbing out her kitchen cupboards. Again.

CHAPTER NINETEEN

As a general rule, Rich would have welcomed the opportunity to see a new city, to meet others in the company's sister office, and to network. This trip, however, was longer and more painful than he expected. He would have liked to spend the flight mulling over his personal problems, but Sam from advertising was going too and kept up an active conversation about his department, the latest football scores, his hope for the BYU basketball team, and his family. Rich seldom did more than nod and make sounds of agreement, but the chatter was enough to keep him from finding a solution to the mess in his life.

True to her word, Denise seemed to have managed to talk to Joan and smooth things over. He almost wished she hadn't. She was more important to him than his job was. Of course he realized he was being ridiculous; losing his job wouldn't solve whatever was hanging between them right now, and he didn't think she'd backed off of things with him to protect his job.

They didn't reach the hotel room until after two in the morning, and the next day was filled with meetings and appointments.

After a long run of meetings Friday morning, Rich welcomed a break and went in search of a free computer. "I need a laptop," he muttered to himself when he popped into his work email. He could have accomplished a lot at the hotel the previous night while lying in bed, unable to sleep, if he'd had a computer. The inbox was overflowing, and it took several minutes to separate the junk mail from the legitimate items.

He froze when he opened a request for a job referral for Denise from

Frandsen Computing—a competing firm in Utah Valley. His mouth went dry and his stomach dropped. "She's really doing it." It wasn't that he hadn't been hoping one of them would find something, and of course, he hoped she would find something first, because while he would gladly leave the company to be with her, he had an unspoken obligation to the company after they paid to relocate him to Utah only a couple months before.

Her reasons for finding a new job didn't make him happy though. She wanted to get away from him, and knowing that hurt. He sent back a note to the company saying what a great worker she was and then fired off a note to Denise.

> I HEARD FROM FRANDSEN COMPUTING TODAY. DON'T WORRY, YOU GOT A POSITIVE RECOMMENDATION. I WILL HATE TO SEE YOU GO. I HOPE THINGS ARE GOING WELL AT THE OFFICE.
>
> RICH

He didn't dare say more for fear someone else might read it over her shoulder. Soon that wouldn't be an issue anymore, if the referral email was any indication. Standing from the computer and heading back to his meeting, Rich thought back on everything that had happened, trying to figure out what went wrong. *Was there something I could have done differently? Is there anything I can do to repair the relationship?* He doubted it. Denise didn't act as though she wanted to fix things, and it had to come from her now.

The struggle was accepting what she felt, seeing if there was a way to alleviate it. If not, he wasn't sure where to go from there.

Three weeks had passed since she sent out the letters to her prospective fathers. Three weeks.

The mailbox remained empty.

Denise reminded herself that people get to the point of being ready to deal with reunion issues at different speeds. Hadn't she said as much to more than a dozen other adoptees? She had taken fifteen years to be ready to begin her search. Why should she expect Pete to respond the minute he got her letter? Maybe Pete was out of town like Ned had been. Maybe he had been too busy with the holiday to respond. Maybe he wasn't around any more. Maybe he wasn't even among the group of men to whom she had sent letters.

Ned and Sharon had been looking for her. Pete hadn't. Not that she knew of, anyway. Still, she had to curb her frustration as she shut the mailbox and turned the key to lock it. True, the letter would come to her postbox downtown, not at home, but checking the mail at home reminded her that she hadn't gotten anything that day.

It had begun to snow that morning; clouds hung low in the early December sky, and Denise wondered how much more snow would fall before morning. She was grateful she didn't work far away. The roads would be dangerous the next day.

She stomped off the snow from her boots and hurried down the hall-way, averting her gaze from Rich's apartment. She had spent as much time as possible with her family since he'd returned Saturday afternoon.

At work that day she hadn't met his eyes when they spoke. When she was contacted for an interview, she hadn't gone to ask for the time off, but rather wimped out and sent an email instead.

As her door clicked shut behind her, Denise wondered whether she should be happy that he'd given in so easily or irritated that he was in such a hurry to get rid of her. Still, she couldn't help but admit to some relief that things had progressed to the interview stage with Frandsen so quickly. It meant she was that much closer to putting some space between Rich and herself. "I should be happy about that, shouldn't I?" she asked aloud.

The apartment was cool. Lily had not worked the previous night and had probably been out of the apartment for hours, preparing for next week's finals. Denise turned the thermostat up ten degrees, took her lunchbox into the kitchen, and washed it out for the next day.

While she waited for the apartment to warm up, she walked to her closet and began to rummage. She didn't own very many outfits that would be appropriate for an interview, so it didn't take long to settle on a navy blue pantsuit and matching flats. She hung them in the bathroom to steam out the wrinkles during her morning shower. She returned to the kitchen to reheat some pasta for dinner.

The microwave was beginning to drone when the doorbell rang. When she opened it, Rich stood on the other side.

"Hey, Rich, sorry, Lily doesn't seem to be here right now." Denise stood in the doorway, not opening it enough for him to slip in.

"I didn't come to see Lily." His gaze was searing, and she had to avert her eyes. Being apart from him this past week had been hard, even harder than she expected.

"That's fortunate for you, I guess. Did you need to borrow some eggs?"

"Is your appointment tomorrow morning for an interview?"

Denise let a couple seconds pass in silence. "Yes. I don't know how long it will take them to make a decision, but if things go well, you may be looking for a replacement soon. You did say once that you would be glad to have one of us gone, even if we didn't work out. You won't have to pass me in the halls anymore." She tried to smile, but her heart wasn't in it.

"Under any other set of circumstances, I would offer you a raise, almost anything I needed to do to keep you on. You're one of the top programmers in the city. That's not a lovesick man telling you that either. As it is, the boss is going to wonder why I didn't fight harder to keep you. So am I."

Denise flicked her eyes back in his direction. He hadn't taken a step closer, hadn't leaned toward her, but the fire burning in his eyes made him seem uncomfortably close. It was almost suffocating, but she couldn't draw away. "Rich, I told you. I can't."

"You keep saying that, but I never get a real reason why. You won't tell me what's bothering you. You love me, I've seen it in your eyes, but you deny it. This is killing me Denise. I know you feel the same; why are you pushing me away?"

The sound of voices came down the hallway, and Denise turned her face away for a moment as a young couple renting a few doors down walked by. She knew her eyes were shining with tears and didn't want to face them. She didn't want to face Rich either.

She squeezed her eyes shut, then jumped when she felt his hand on her arm. "Denise, please let me in so we can talk."

"I don't have time to talk now. I have things to take care of. I never heard back from Pete, and I need to do some more investigating. Maybe later."

"I can help."

"I only have one computer. I . . . please go. Please." She met his eyes and swallowed hard to get around the lump that formed in her throat. She wanted nothing more than to fall into his arms and say that everything would be better. But she couldn't.

"You have me in a strange position." His voice was soft, but serious. "Too many people in your life didn't fight for you, didn't make the effort to show you they cared, that you mattered. You matter to me, Denise, and I don't want to make the same mistake. But I don't want to push you somewhere you aren't ready to go either. You mean too much to me."

Denise heard the sound of her pounding heart as he let that sink in. She wanted him to fight for her, but she worried if he did fight, it would still end up the same. In the end, she would tell her story, and he would decide he'd made a mistake.

His hand slid down her arm and gripped her fingers. "Think about it. We'll talk about it later." He turned and walked away, and she shut the door, leaning back against it as she fought the tears that threatened to fall.

Denise was scrubbing the nooks and crannies of the kitchen cupboard doors when Lily came home a couple hours later. The younger girl beamed and practically skipped into the kitchen, pulling to a stop when she saw the way everything sparkled, and the toothbrush Denise was wielding on the doors.

Forcing a smile and feeling a little better after cleaning like a mad woman since Rich left, Denise turned to Lily. "You don't look like you've been studying for finals. You must have had a date instead."

"Best date ever. I believe if I were still at Snow College, I would owe you dinner."

It took a moment before Denise was able to process that comment. She remembered the time her roommate had told her about the payments roommates made to each other for each new milestone in a relationship. Holding hands was M&Ms, kissing was ice cream, and dinner was . . . "You're engaged?"

Lily let out a high-pitched squeal and held out her hand, showing off a huge marquis-cut diamond. "We're thinking late May, right after I finish my student teaching. John doesn't see the point of my finishing up my student teaching now, but I couldn't imagine not finishing when I'm so close already. Can you believe it? I'm getting married!" She grabbed Denise and wrapped her in a hug.

Denise hugged her roommate back, thrilled that Lily was so happy, that at least things were going well for one of them. But it only made her own pain seem stronger, more powerful. And her future, all that much more empty.

The job interview went well, and when Denise returned to the office at ten-thirty, she was feeling confident about being hired.

Jake whistled long and low as she came in the door. It wasn't often she wore anything fancier than a T-shirt and jeans. "Where have you been, girl? You look pretty nice."

Denise smiled at him. "What, a girl can't wear anything nice without having a reason?"

"Not you. You're the original blue jean poster girl. Come on. What's up?" Jake asked.

"I had an appointment. Don't worry your pretty little head about it." Denise turned on her computer and pulled out her notes from the previous day. "Anything interesting happen this morning?"

"You didn't show up at the crack of dawn. That's interesting," Jake said. "Completely out of character for you. And you left a pen on your desk instead of in that pen and pencil cup you always use. You're getting sloppy in your old age."

"I'll take that to be a no." It didn't take her long to slip into work mode again, and because she was feeling good, the work clicked into place. She ate a tuna sandwich for lunch while sitting at her desk, to make up for lost time, and finished her project a few minutes after five. She ran a diagnostic on the program and smiled as she picked up her ringing telephone. "This is Denise."

"Denise, Frank Frandsen. We would like to offer you the position. How soon can you start?"

It wasn't until that moment that Denise realized how badly she didn't want to quit her job. Yet she knew she must. The new job would be interesting, a change of pace as she worked to keep a series of company websites updated. The pay was better, the vacation package an improvement, and . . . she would have a little more space from Rich, which was her main concern.

"That's great. I'll need to give my two weeks, and that puts us at Christmas week."

"I'll be out of town that week, so how about if you start the following week, December 29?"

"That'll be perfect. 9 AM?" She asked, her throat closing up from emotion.

"Yes. I'll be in touch by email if there's anything else."

"Thanks. Bye." Denise hung up the phone with reluctance. She swung her eyes back to the computer screen where the first test of the website she had just finished showed that her work was good.

"What was that? You're not quitting, are you?" Jake asked.

Denise avoided looking at him, focusing on the screen as she closed down her computer. "Yes, actually. I start just before the new year. Maybe Rich will hire another guy and you can be a fully-testosteroned team."

"I thought you loved it here." Jake touched her arm, encouraging her to turn and face him. "Why would you leave?"

It took some effort to force the smile she knew he would expect if he would believe her. "Frandsen Computing has offered me a raise, a better title, and . . . I think it's time to move on."

"Does this have anything to do with Rich?"

Denise had to fight the instinct to look around her, even though she knew the other guys had left earlier. Instead she gave Jake a steady look. "I don't know why you would say that. He's a great boss."

Jake rolled his eyes. "Come on, the air almost crackles around the two of you. You may think you're smooth, but I notice things sometimes, you know. I'm not stupid."

"This is about my career, Jake. Don't go laying blame where it doesn't belong. Besides, I have nearly two weeks of paid vacation left for this year and three more that have accrued for next year that I'll be able to cash out. Merry Christmas to me, you know. I'll have that down payment for a new car now, and I get a little time off during the holidays."

"This isn't about your car."

"Come on. How many times have you told me to get a new one?" *Dozens, at least.*

"You love it and will never replace it until it doesn't run anymore and costs too much to fix. Quit making excuses."

He was right, of course. "My reasons for leaving are my own. Don't worry, I'm sure my replacement will be as easy to tease as I am." Denise grabbed her lunchbox from the floor and stood. "I guess I better go let the boss know."

Denise didn't feel steady as she walked down the hall toward Rich's office. Her stomach turned into a tight knot of nerves and her legs felt weak. She didn't want to make any more changes in her life right now. But she had prayed about it. The time was right.

She knocked on the door casing when she found him talking on the phone. He looked up and waved her in. Rich finished his conversation but never took his eyes from hers.

"What's going on? You look nice. I haven't seen you in that before."

Denise broke eye contact and took the seat across from him. "I heard from Frank Frandsen a few minutes ago. They offered me the job, and I took it." She looked back up into his eyes. "I'll start right after Christmas."

Several emotions passed over his face, but Rich didn't say anything until it settled back into an impassive expression. He glanced at a calendar and then back at her. "We'll miss you here. Would you like the nineteenth to be your last day?"

"Yes. I did want to tell you that you are a great boss and it has been an enlightening experience working with you the past couple months."

Rich nodded, and Denise stood to leave. Before she reached the doorway, she heard his voice call softly to her, "I'll talk to you later."

She paused, gripping her hand tighter on the handle of her lunchbox, but didn't turn around. "I'm sure you will."

Chapter Twenty

After two days of not being able to find Denise at home, Rich saw her at church, but she had a guy with her. Jealousy raged through him as he saw how friendly they seemed, and then Lily mentioned it was Denise's brother. When Rich went over to talk to them, Denise left him and Gerald alone, disappearing down the hallway. She returned as class started. After Relief Society and Priesthood, she and Gerald disappeared again. Rich reached the outside door in time to see her car pulling out of the parking lot and wanted to swear.

Surely there must be a reason for all of this. He wouldn't have been given these feelings, this confirmation, if they weren't supposed to be together, would he? Discouraged, Rich waited for Lily to join him at the car to return to the apartment building.

Denise pulled in front of her parent's home, not remembering a word Gerald had said during the drive home.

" . . . and Rich?"

She turned when she heard that name, though she missed the rest of the thought. "What was that?"

"What's going on with you and Rich? I saw the looks between the two of you."

Denise rubbed her face, before she opened her car door, pulling her coat tighter around her. It had snowed the night before, and her shoe slid into the four-inch blanket of white, freezing her ankles. "Rich and I won't work out. There's too much in my past to lay on him . . . We're just over before we really began. That's all. Come on, Mom and Dad will be wondering what's keeping us, and it looks like Paige and Cliff are already here."

Gerald gave her a skeptical look and appeared to be trying to decide whether to say something, but wasn't given a chance to question her further since the front door opened and Paige beckoned them in.

Looking into the beaming face of her sister as Paige showed off the new, sparkling ring on her finger was almost more than Denise could bear. She gave Paige a big hug and offered her congratulations, then excused herself to the bathroom to be alone.

The cool, wet washcloth soothed her face as Denise took deep breaths and forced herself to calm down. It didn't make sense to feel this tight fist of jealousy in her belly, the breath-stealing ache in her chest. Cliff seemed to bring out the good qualities in Paige. They were good for each other. It was Denise's certainty that she would never be able to enjoy the same happiness with Rich that caused her pain.

It took ten minutes for Denise to feel back under control again. She returned to the living room where she was able to give Cliff a hug as well. He messed with her hair, teasing about how she would be his little sister now.

"What do you mean? I'm older than any of you," Denise said.

"Yes, but I'm taller than any of you. So that makes me the biggest, right?"

"I guess I could handle having you as a brother, if I don't have any other choice." Denise rolled her eyes and let out a long, exaggerated sigh.

"Speaking of brothers, I ran into Curtis at the bookstore in Logan," Gerald said to Cliff. "I thought he was you."

"Yeah, we get that all the time, being identical twins, and all."

"Well, I guess it's a good thing I made birthday cake, since you'll be a member of the family soon, anyway," Jennette said as she brought out a tray of sodas to share around.

Denise looked at him in surprise. "When's your birthday?"

"Tomorrow." Cliff took a soda from the tray and handed it to Paige before grabbing one for himself.

"Congratulations. You'll be twenty-two, right?"

"Yeah."

She looked him up and down. "Funny, you don't act that old. I'd've put you at fifteen."

He stared her down. "Are you really asking for another noogie?"

She laughed and shook her head before Jennette pulled her into the kitchen to help with dinner.

Denise returned to work that Monday feeling better than she had in days. She managed to avoid Rich again Sunday night and felt she was starting to get a handle on her feelings for him. On Monday night, Lily grilled her.

"Denise, what's going on?"

Denise hung up her keys and walked to her room. "What do you mean?"

"I thought you and Rich had something going on. Now you're treating him like a leper. What happened between you two?"

Her hand gripped her wallet for a moment. She loosened her fingers and let the wallet drop onto the dresser. "Nothing. And nothing is going to happen between us." Tears threatened to fall.

"There *is* something between you. He's good for you. I can see it."

Denise didn't glance in Lily's direction, focusing instead on the clothes she was pulling out for the next day. "Rich is a great guy, a really great guy, and I'm really lucky to have had a chance to get to know him."

"Oh, no you don't. I hear a *but* in there and I don't buy it. The man's totally in love with you, and you have feelings for him too. Don't give me the baloney about how you work together because you didn't let it come between you a couple weeks ago."

Denise's fingers tightened on the hanger, but she continued to move around her room. "I put in my notice Friday. I got hired somewhere else and I'll start while Gerald's home for Christmas. The good news is, I'll get the whole week of Christmas off to spend with family and get ready for the holiday."

There were two seconds of silence before Lily spoke, confused. "But you love your job."

"It's just a job. Yes, I enjoy it there, but I'll enjoy it at Frandsen Computing too. The money is a little better and . . . ."

A tear slid out of her eye and trailed down Denise's face. She held back the curse that formed on her tongue. She'd thought she had it licked until she felt the wetness on her cheek.

Lily reached out and wiped it away. "The whole situation's killing you, isn't it?"

"Everything in my life is kind of haywire right now. I can't deal with Rich and our feelings, try to find family members and get to know the new ones I have, placate my adoptive family, and change jobs too. I wish more than anything we could make it work, but I can't. Please, Lily, I need your support right now."

"You know, things wouldn't look so bleak if you just let yourself trust once in a while." Lily's voice was brittle, making it clear she wasn't happy with Denise's choice. "Rich loves you, I love you, your family loves you, and your Heavenly Father loves you, but if you don't let anyone share the load you're carrying, you're going to break your back."

Denise turned to see Lily shutting the door to the bedroom behind her as she left Denise alone. She knew Lily was right, but to trust was to give up control, and she felt she was barely holding on with her fingernails as it was.

She lost herself in programming and most of Tuesday passed before Joan came in and stood in front of Denise's desk. "What's this I hear about you leaving us?"

Denise looked up and flashed Joan an easy smile. "Yes, I've been hired by Frandsen Computing. I start right after Christmas."

Joan stared her down. "Can I have a word with you?"

"Sure." Denise tried to look unruffled.

Joan led Denise to the conference room again, and pointed to a chair, shutting the door behind them. "Now what's this all about? You admit you have feelings for Rich, you have a little . . . whatever you want to call it in the office a couple weeks ago, you've barely looked him in the eye since, and now you're quitting? I would say congratulations, but you don't seem happy."

"This is a good opportunity."

"Don't feed me that bull. What's up with you and Rich?" Joan took the seat around the corner of the oval table and looked her in the eye.

Denise leaned in, crossing her arms on the table in front of her. "It is a good opportunity, but, as you said, there is more to it. No, Rich hasn't been harassing me; there's no problem here for Donaldson."

"I didn't think there was." Joan lifted a perfectly shaped eyebrow at Denise.

"The only problem for Donaldson is the fact that I have feelings for my boss, and he has feelings for me. That doesn't work even without the no-dating rules. Even if we did work it out, it's not a good mix for the office."

"So are you going to work things out?"

"I don't think so. And no, it has nothing to do with what you walked in on a couple weeks ago. Not really. I'm not upset about that." Denise shook her head and settled her temple on the palm of her hand. "It was time to end things."

"You talked about what a good man he is."

"He is, really good. Too good, actually. Because of my past, a relationship with me entails a lot of trouble, on both our parts. I'm not ready to deal with it, and he doesn't deserve it. I'm going to miss you like crazy, Joan. You've made a difference in my life here." Denise fought back tears that pricked her eyes. It disgusted her that she was crying so easily these days. Under normal circumstances, she hardly ever cried. "Now, I have work to do, and I don't think those phones answer themselves."

"Sure they do, that's what voice mail is for." Joan's voice was light, but the sheen on her eyes said she was near crying, too.

None of the guys talked to Denise when she came back to the office, but when it was time to clock out, they were still there. Denise shut down her computer and grabbed her lunch box.

"So, Denise, you're leaving us, huh? Who are we going to have to clean up after us when we screw up?" Mick asked.

"You'll have to learn to take care of yourselves. You're all big, strong men, after all." The comment was light and teasing. It was a long-standing joke that as the woman in the office, she was there to mop up the messes, but the truth was, they all helped each other out. There had been several messes she needed their expertise on too.

"So once you leave here, the no-dating policy will be null and void. Does that mean you'll finally go out with me?" Jake asked, his grin making it plain he was joking.

"Jake, what would your fiancée say? I could call Candy and ask her," Denise offered, intentionally screwing up the woman's name.

"It's Cathy, not Candy." Jake stood from his own desk. "And I don't think she'd have a problem with me grabbing a bite with someone who's like a sister to me." He reached out to noogie her hair, and she backed away.

"No way you're touching this head today." Denise went around the side of her desk but didn't make it to the door before he grabbed her shoulder and ran his knuckles through her hair. "Oh, you are so in trouble." She reached out and tickled his ribs, causing him to release her.

"What's going on here? End-of-the-day celebrations?" Rich asked, his arms crossed in front of his chest and a wry look in his eyes.

"You bet. One less day to deal with Jake," Denise said as Jake released his hold on her and adjusted his shirt. She tried to hold back her smile, but couldn't quite manage it as she ran her fingers through her hair to straighten it out.

"Sorry, boss. The kids haven't learned to grow up yet. We're heading out," Mick said, passing behind them and turning toward the front door.

Denise felt almost branded as Rich's eyes swept over her. The amusement in his eyes faded until he looked tired. "See you later, boss." She turned and hurried out behind the others.

CHAPTER TWENTY-ONE

Hundreds of miles away in the state of Virginia, a tall, fair-haired man sat at his desk, a white sheet of paper with a short message written on it in his hands. He had sat like this every night for the past two weeks, but he still wasn't sure what to do. There had been a time when he wished to get a letter like this, but now . . . he wasn't so sure.

His marriage to Daphne had been tempestuous at best. They'd known each other two weeks and he'd been blinded by his devotion to her, agreeing without more than a second thought when she suggested driving to Vegas to seal the deal. The next few weeks were good, then he started to realize there were some major problems.

Pete stood and walked over to the window, looking into the dark backyard and watched the trees and bushes groan under the onslaught of a wind storm. Marriage had never been a light issue to Pete. He may have jumped into it blindly, but he took his vows seriously once they were made. Three months into the relationship, he learned that half the time she said she was at work she was in another man's arms. When his mother passed on, every reason he thought he had for staying disappeared. Even now he shook his head over it as he held his daughter's letter in his hands. His and Daphne's relationship was doomed from the start, but he'd been too wrapped up in his fantasies of what it could be to realize that.

His fingers tapped on the glass as he remembered his resolve to make the most of it. It had only taken two more weeks for Daphne to refuse his love and bolt. Pete tracked her down a couple months later to get divorce papers signed, and it was over. He left Utah and traveled east to get away from the pain and memories. He realized, once he had some time and space between them, that his feelings for Daphne were never as strong as he had thought. But that didn't make his feeling of failure easier to bear.

His eyes fell on the family picture, and he zeroed in on his wife. He and Renee had met a couple years after his divorce finalized. He was nearly ready to pop the question when the letter from Daphne arrived. She called him every name in the book, told him she was mad he ran out on her, and asked what she was supposed to do about the brat he saddled her with. She wanted money, lots of money. Even now he remembered the worry, fear, excitement, and wonder he had felt when he realized he had a child. Renee had urged him to go get his daughter and bring her back with him. Everything Pete knew about Daphne said she shouldn't be raising a child.

Pete answered the letter, saying he would be out to verify that it was his daughter and to discuss custody arrangements. The memories of that time had been relegated to the back of his mind for so long. Dredging them up now was painful. But he couldn't forget arriving back in Utah to find Daphne had disappeared with the little girl.

Pete hired someone to track Daphne until his money ran out, but he never heard anything again, though he tried again a couple of years later. He often wondered about the poor little girl Daphne was raising, wondering if she was his daughter, and if she was being taken care of. Renee had been heartbroken to lose the chance to parent Denise. It had only grown worse when they had trouble conceiving.

About the time he figured his daughter would turn eighteen, Pete tried to track her down again, but had no more luck. Ned's family had been able to tell him she was adopted from foster care and hadn't known until it was too late. Pete kicked himself for never putting in a police report, for filing something that would have caused the state to alert him when his daughter came into custody.

Now, years later, he had a letter from a woman who thought he was her father. Nerves assaulted him. What if she ended up not even being his? What if this Denise only wanted to find him so she could ream him out for deserting her? He wouldn't put it past Daphne to tell their child he was a deadbeat who had never cared.

Renee seemed apathetic about whether he contacted Denise or not, leaving it in his hands, once he agreed to a preliminary background check. Now it was his decision whether to respond or not.

His fingers shook as he opened up a word processing program on the computer and started writing. The sounds of his daughter playing the piano in the other room and the television going in his son's room came through the doors. Pete had never told them about Denise. How would they react?

Thursday at work, Denise watched Jake reset his Room Defender by the doorway again. She shook her head and went back to writing code. The toy was his favorite, second only to the electronic box that sounded like someone was passing gas. She would never understand men, she figured, though she couldn't help but like his current toy. She had taken her turn activating the Defender on more than one occasion.

It was getting to be lunchtime, which meant she was growing anxious again, watching the clock as she wondered if today would be the day her mailbox would hold a letter from Pete. Again she worried about why she hadn't heard from him. Maybe he was sick or dead, and his wife was opening his mail but didn't know about Daphne and assumed it was junk. What if she never found him and spent the rest of her life wondering?

She heard the telltale sound of the Room Defender activating and saw Mr. Murphy standing in the doorway. Two foam disks lay at his feet.

The man sighed and turned irritated eyes on Jake. "You need to stop this thing. It's a hazard, and someday it's going to cause an accident."

"Sorry, sir, I thought I had it on remote only. I would never intentionally have it hit you or a visitor, sir. It won't happen again." Jake looked embarrassed; to Denise's surprise, his face was taking on a slight pink tinge. She decided this was one for the record books, Jake blushing.

Mr. Murphy mumbled something under his breath and dropped off some papers on Mick's desk. He turned to leave, getting more foam disks shot at him. "Today, Cornwall. Today."

Unable to help herself, Denise allowed a quiet laugh at the sight of Murphy receiving a direct hit. It was an image she would carry with her for a long time.

"You think that was funny DeWalt?" Jake asked. "I'll show you funny." But he settled back at his desk without more than a murmur.

Denise checked the clock again and decided the best way to be productive would be to go check her mail. When she got back, she could settle down again, so though it wasn't quite noon yet, she saved what she had done and hurried out of the office, ignoring the disk that hit her on the way out.

She'd given up on pretending that she was going out for lunch, when she was checking her mail. Of course, she told the others she had an errand, if they bothered to comment on the fact that she wasn't eating lunch at her desk anymore. Personally, she wanted this whole thing to be over for more reasons than just her mounting frustration. She also wanted to end the mid-day distraction; it was cutting back on her productivity. And she was having to fill her gas tank much more often.

She pulled into the parking lot and headed straight to her box. After more than a month of making these trips, she had given up on getting too nervous. But there was still a bubble of anticipation in her stomach when she slid the key into the box and turned it.

A small package, something she'd ordered online, lay on top of what looked like sales circulars. She wondered if others actually looked at them. "Do you know me?" she muttered as she glanced at the ad of a child kidnapped by a family member. She wondered if her life would have been different if Pete put an ad in for her all those years earlier. She flipped it into the garbage along with an auto parts ad. She might be pretty self-sufficient, but she drew the line at changing her own transmission fluid. She flipped over the next letter expecting junk but found Pete's name in the return address. She paused less than a second before turning back to her car.

This time, she didn't wait to drive somewhere else before tearing into the envelope. She opened it before she got the door unlocked. Denise pulled the paper from the envelope as she slid into her seat and closed the door behind her. She unfolded the sheet printed from a computer.

Denise,

I'm Pete Sumner, the one who was married to Daphne Callister. That was her maiden name anyway. I spoke with Ned about you, when I first learned you existed, but your mother had taken off, and I never found her again. All I really know is that you're about twenty-six and Daphne's daughter. I hope you don't get offended when I question whether or not you're my daughter as well.

I hoped for many years to get in touch with you, but now that you have found me, I don't know where to go from here. If you don't mind, I would prefer to have a DNA test done, to verify if you are my daughter. I will pay for the test if you can send some sample hair to the address listed below.

I have wondered about you for the past two decades, wishing I could be with you and worrying about the kind of life you've been living with Daphne. There's so much I want to say, but I don't know where to start. I don't know if you have access to email, but if so, write me at the address below.

Pete

Tears flowed down Denise's cheeks. She wasn't any more certain what to think about all of this than he was. *I can't blame him for wanting the test, but please, please let him be the one. I can't go through this again.*

She read the letter again and slid it back into the envelope before returning to work. Her hands shook as she wiped her face before getting out of the car. The drive gave her a few minutes to get excited and a bit jumpy, a good feeling after the depression that had been bothering her lately.

Denise walked to the front desk where Joan sat. "Could I steal a blank envelope and buy a stamp?"

"Of course." Joan handed them over to her, and Denise paid for the stamp. She returned to her car to include some hair samples and fill out the envelope. She wrote a short note, sealed the envelope, and drove it directly to the post office. She was afraid if she waited, she might get cold feet and not get around to sending her hair in, and she needed to know.

Rich found her in the break room a while later and pulled some left-over pizza out of the refrigerator while sending her a curious look. "You're eating early. Did you already run your errand?"

Denise smiled despite herself. "Yeah. It was a good mail day."

A couple of women from advertising came in; one was talking about her date the night before, but Denise caught Rich's eye and knew he understood.

"That's great. I hope to hear more about it later." His look said he would try to track her down to get all of the details, one way or another.

Denise wasn't sure what else to say. She was trying to keep some distance between them, but his concern warmed her, and she couldn't help but smile at it. She wasn't sure she would have made it (sanity intact) without him.

CHAPTER TWENTY-TWO

That evening Denise was back at the gym, working off some of her nerves and excitement on the court. What if Pete wasn't her father? Where would she go from there? And would Daphne even know who the father was? Denise doubted it. What she did know about her mother's relationships indicated that the woman hadn't been terribly picky or kept careful records. Even if she had the guts to write Daphne and ask, she doubted Daphne could answer.

Denise hadn't found anyone to challenge to a game of one-on-one, so she covered the ground herself—practicing different moves, keeping herself going—hoping the physical exertion would help her deal with everything.

"Hey, sis, what's up?"

Denise's shot went wild, and she turned to find Cliff standing on the sideline. "Not much, just working off some energy. Care to play? I promise to go easy on you." She retrieved the ball and walked over to him.

Cliff shook his head. "Fine, but I'm not going to go easy on you." He lunged forward and stole the ball from her, and the game began.

Neither of them bothered to keep score, so when they were both exhausted and feeling worn, they came to a stop, walking to cool themselves down.

"So how are things going on the family search?" Cliff asked after a minute.

"Slowly but surely. I heard back from someone I think is my dad today. He requested DNA testing to make sure I'm really his daughter.

That's part of why I'm so anxious tonight, I guess."

"That's great, isn't it? You must be thrilled."

"Thrilled and terrified. What if it isn't him and I never track him down? What if it is and we end up not liking each other very much? Or what if he's wonderful, and I spend the rest of my life feeling cheated because my birth mom kept me from him?" She shook her head. "I'm sure it sounds crazy to you."

"Not at all." Cliff looked over at her and rubbed his chin for a moment. "I've thought once or twice about checking into finding my birth family, but there are complications with that. I have a lot of the same concerns. What if I look but when I find them they aren't interested? A couple of my siblings aren't interested in finding their families. They understand that I might be even though my oldest brother had a bad experience with his birth family once he tracked them down. I'm afraid of hurting my adoptive parents, and then there's Curtis, my twin—he's flat out against searching. If I find my family . . . that's a direct lead-in to him, especially with the basketball stuff. It would be hard for him to stay anonymous."

"That makes sense. It must be frustrating to have someone else to wonder about, and wonderful too. Most of my life has been spent in a family where no one else looks like me. No one else shares my DNA, or even my blood type."

He looked over at her. "A negative."

She smiled. "Me too. Guess that's one thing that will change with the wedding. Someone else in the family will share my blood type, at least. They're all B positive."

He chuckled. "If you ever need a blood transfusion, I can help out."

"And vice versa." She looked into his blue eyes and let out a wistful smile. "I'm sorry you've been caught in the middle of things with Paige like this. It must be twice as hard for you, being caught in this one and with your brother."

He shrugged but dropped his eyes and she could tell it was bothering him. "She'll come around. Paige's just trying to get her bearings in this whole thing. She cares about you, and I think she's feeling like you're looking for a replacement for her family. She won't talk about it; she doesn't want to think about it, but if you hang on, she'll come around."

They wandered over to the benches on the side of the track and lounged down on them. "You're pretty great for Paige. I'm glad she has you," Denise said, her heart twisting painfully in her chest.

It was getting late when Denise returned home, but though she knew she ought to head directly to her own place, she paused as she passed Rich's door. She debated for a few seconds, shook her head, and turned back toward her own apartment. She couldn't approach him. It would be too hypocritical.

Two steps later, Rich came around the corner, heading from the direction of her apartment. "Denise, I was just at your place."

She stopped and looked up at him, allowing herself a moment to enjoy his broad shoulders and brown eyes. She felt her heart squeeze painfully at the sight of him. "I've been at the gym."

He smiled. "I should have guessed. I've been wondering about your letter all day. Come in for some hot chocolate or something?"

Despite her resolve, she felt herself weakening. She ignored the fact that she would regret it later; she wasn't anywhere near ready to go to bed, and Lily would be leaving for work any minute. "Okay."

His tentative smile broadened, and he pulled out his keys and turned toward the door. "I thought maybe you were still in avoidance mode."

"I was but decided I can't pass up a cup of cocoa. Do you have marshmallows?"

He dropped his keys on the kitchen counter, pulled a teapot out of the cupboard, and began filling it with water. "My packages of cocoa do. Loads of them. Can you get out the cups?" He pointed to a cupboard nearby before turning off the water and reaching to put the pot on the stove.

Denise opened the cupboard to find his dishes, what few there were, including two mugs. She pulled them out and set them on the counter. When she turned to lean back against the counter, Rich was closer than she expected.

He reached out and touched the tips of her hair, rubbed it between his fingers, and drew back. "I've missed you."

"Rich," she protested.

"Sorry. You're here now. Tell me about your birth dad," Rich said, taking her hand and leading her to the sofa.

Denise sat across from him, her pulse not quite normal. She filled him in on the letter and her response.

"How does it feel to know you almost have a complete family?" Rich's free arm stretched across the back of the sofa, his hand played with the soft fall of hair around her chin, brushed against the exposed skin of her neck.

Denise felt a shiver go down her spine and pulled away before she gave in to instinct and moved closer. "We're not complete yet, but it's getting more that way as time goes on. I still have to find my other sibling. That won't be easy, especially if Daphne doesn't give us a birth date and gender. I'm glad to have my parents there to support me, though. Mom was supportive, if not ecstatic when I called her, and Gerald seemed happy for me. Paige will be another thing."

"That's great you've had your parents be there for you when your birth family couldn't be." Rich looked her in the eye and brushed his fingers against her neck again, causing her to shiver, only this time she didn't pull away. "I know you have two families who will be there for you now, but I'm glad you decided to share some of it with me. I'll be there for you too. If you'll let me."

Her stomach tightened in a hot ball of pain as she realized what he must think of her. She hadn't meant to give him hope, but she could see she had. Nothing had changed between them. Nothing could. "Rich—"

She was cut off when the teapot began to whistle in the other room. Rich stood, holding out a finger to tell her to wait a moment. She silently berated herself while listening to him pour the water and open the cocoa packets. Why did it have to be so difficult? Why couldn't she just have a normal life, put it all behind her? He came back, offering a cup of cocoa to her. "Rich," she continued after a sip of the creamy drink.

"Now, where were we?" he asked.

Denise placed a hand on his shoulder, preventing him from moving closer. She took a fortifying gulp of her drink and scalded the back of her mouth. Angry with herself, she set the cup on the table and fisted her hands in her lap. "We've talked about this before. I'm glad to have you as a friend, you've been very important to me. But I can't offer you anything permanent. I don't have it in me."

He shook his head and set his drink beside hers. "I don't believe that. I don't need anything from you that you can't give. Everything in my life seems to be better with you in it, just the way you are."

Feeling his fingers in her hair again, undone by the soft urgency of his voice and the deep response in her heart, Denise pulled away and stood up. "I can't give it to you, Rich. You're a great friend, and I love being with you, but I can't promise you more." She turned and hurried toward the door.

Before she reached it, she felt his hand on her shoulder. He didn't restrain her, just touched her. She stopped short and turned to look him in the eye.

"Then let me be your friend. I can wait on the rest as long as you need me to."

Denise bit her bottom lip. "What if I'm never ready?"

Rich's eyes scanned her face before he dropped his hand. "You're in the middle of a big change in your life now. When things settle down, you may feel differently. I can be patient for now." He stepped back and gave her a half smile. "I've got eternity, how about you?"

"Good night, Rich." Denise opened the door and hurried out, hearing his "good night" before the door closed behind her. Her first tear fell before she reached the door of her apartment.

CHAPTER TWENTY-THREE

Sunday family dinner was growing in importance as it seemed to be the only time the engaged couple could meet with Jennette and Lynn to make plans. The flurry of holiday parties and preparations only complicated things.

Cookie must have heard my car pull in, Denise thought; when she opened the front door the mutt was already jumping around, wagging her tail in ecstasy. "Hey, baby. You're too adorable, did you know that? You must have missed me lots. I missed you, too."

When she entered the kitchen, her face all but buried in her dog's fur, she saw Paige sitting at the table with her mom while something bubbled away on the stove. Cliff was settled in front of the television watching a game with Lynn and Gerald, but it was clear they were having more fun talking about his game against the University of Utah the previous night. "Hey, guys," Denise said.

Everyone turned to acknowledge her, and Cliff and Gerald waved her over to join them.

"How have things been?" Cliff asked. "Heard anything from Ogden?"

"Things are pretty good. I have an office Christmas party, and I'm sure we'll have a jolly old time. I get to bring a date. You're coming with, aren't you, Ger?" Gerald shrugged and nodded. Denise smiled in response. "Good. I heard back from Ned and Sharon, and Kaylee. They're all excited about the news from Pete. I got an email back from Pete too; he's hoping to have results before Christmas."

"Do you have to ruin our day by talking about that?" Paige said, coming up behind them. "It's like you don't even need us with your new family. I wish you would stop rubbing our noses in it. You have a dad, a mom, and a sister—your family will be complete without us."

"*What?* Look, they asked, I told them. I'm not rubbing anyone's nose in anything. And nothing Daphne could do at this point would ever make me consider her a mom again." Denise felt her shoulder muscles bunch as she looked at Paige's retreating figure. Wouldn't she ever let it go? What was the big deal? Denise was here now, wasn't she?

Denise felt a hand on her shoulder and turned to see Gerald looking her in the eye. "Take it from the expert. Don't worry about it. You have to do what you have to do. It doesn't affect Paige, and she'll learn that soon enough."

Lynn pursed his lips while Cliff nodded his head in agreement, and then told them more about the annual Christmas party to which his parents had invited their entire family. Denise sighed in frustration. She turned her eyes back to the game the men were watching, though it took most of the quarter before she relaxed enough to enjoy it. Could Cliff be right about Paige feeling like she would be replaced? And what was with her father's response?

When Denise picked up Gerald for the company party Wednesday night, she was dressed in a sleek, black velvet dress—the only thing she had purchased since high school that would be appropriate. It was a formal affair, something she wasn't very comfortable with. The weather had cleared after the previous day's snow storm, and Denise looked over at her brother when they reached a stoplight. "This is the big time, buster. Something for you to look forward to in your old age."

"Oh, yeah, you're practically decrepit now." Gerald smiled at her, and she eased on the gas as the light turned green again.

"Better watch out, it tends to sneak up on you."

"You're one to talk. Twenty-six already? How do you even manage to get out of bed in the morning?"

Denise laughed at the note of mock concern in his voice. "I've missed you, Ger. It's good to have you home."

"Don't get too used to it. When the semester starts again I'm going to have to go back to school."

"That's such a pain," Denise teased.

"Yeah." Silence stretched as only the sound of tires on wet cement and other cars on the road penetrated the distance between them. "Denise, what's going on with you and Rich?"

Denise straightened in her seat. She didn't want to talk about this. "There's nothing going on."

There were two heartbeats of silence. "Why not? He seems interested and I got the impression from," he paused for a moment, "various sources that maybe you were a little interested too."

"Cliff, Rich, Mom? Who talked about me?"

"All of the above." Gerald had the decency to look mildly embarrassed.

She pushed away the annoyance. "He wants to get serious, but I don't think things are leading where I can let them go. He's a great guy, but I don't think we have a future." Her voice was final, and Gerald seemed to understand that the conversation was over, whether he agreed with her or not.

The party was bright and colorful, the tables close together and stuffed with chairs. Music drifted over the party goers, and the food tasted great. The only problem Denise could see as she lingered over dessert was the fact that Rich managed to finagle the seat next to hers. Their elbows touched every few seconds as they moved their knives and forks. His laughter rang in her ear as he responded to one of Jake's jokes. His fingers brushed over hers beneath the table on one occasion, making her heart pound, yet she couldn't move away without causing a scene.

The real problem: she didn't want to move away. They were friends, and even more under the surface. It had been years since Denise thought herself in love, and now that she felt it again—only ten times stronger— she wasn't sure she trusted herself.

When the music started and people filled the dance floor, Denise found herself maneuvered into Rich's arms for a slow song without being completely sure how she had gotten there. Her heart raced as he pulled her close, the velvet of her dress whispering against his dark suit. His breath on her cheek sent tingles down her neck, and the scent of his aftershave made her stomach tremble.

"I've missed you," he said after their bodies began swaying in time. "I miss your laugh. I miss the way you lift your brow when you're trying to look annoyed in spite of the fact that you feel like laughing. I miss the feel of you in my arms and the light touch of your hand on my shoulder."

Denise felt her barrier begin to crumble, and she hurried to build it back up. "Nothing has changed, Rich."

"I know. I still love you. I'm still waiting for you to stop being too scared to admit why you're scared in the first place. But I can wait. I love your perfume. You smell like summer rain. I would kiss you now, if I wouldn't lose my job. Next year though, I plan to bring you here as my date. We'll leave your brother at home."

"He'll probably be on a mission." Denise caught the change of subject and stretched to wrap it around her in a protective shield. She felt like the city of Jericho under siege. And it turned out her walls were made of water.

The music continued soft and romantic, and stuck where she was, Denise allowed herself to be sucked into it for one song, then another. His nearness made her feel slightly off-kilter, made her heart ache. Made her wonder if she could be happy without him or if her fear would condemn her to loneliness. She knew if she were going to marry anyone some day, he would be the one for her. It wasn't until the evening's MC paused the band to announce another door prize drawing that Denise moved away, pulling herself back together.

After a perky good night at the table and excuses to everyone else, she was leading Gerald back to her car. A lifted eyebrow indicated Gerald had plenty of questions about what he saw on the dance floor, but he kept his mouth shut.

Denise thanked the heavens for small blessings.

Holiday music filled the car as Denise headed home from the grocery store a few nights later. It seemed Christmas excitement swirled around her in the air as she did her shopping—music piped from the speakers, the shelf-end displays were filled with ingredients for Christmas dishes, and bright bows and tinsel hung everywhere.

The one thing Denise couldn't seem to forget, however, was the comment on the radio she had heard on her way to the grocery store.

Christmas was about families, about love and understanding, forgiveness, and coming together in the celebration of Christ's birth. Lately all she could see when she thought of her family, however, was her father's compressed lips, her mother's worried face, and Paige striding away. Family peace had been hard to find lately.

On a whim, she turned toward her parents' house instead of returning home.

The front porch blazed with Christmas lights. The railing was nearly covered in garland and lights and dripped with red velvet bows. The roofline glittered with more lights, and a trio of glowing reindeer grazed on the lawn. Outwardly, the house was filled with cheer.

Feeling strengthened by the holiday spirit, Denise locked her car and strode up the walk, calling out to announce her presence as she opened the door. A huge Christmas tree sat in its traditional corner of the front room, a small pile of presents already growing beneath it. Denise heard her mom's voice and followed it to the kitchen where the counters were filled with cooling racks of sugar cookies.

"I didn't expect to see you tonight," her mother said.

"I stopped by on a whim." Denise picked up a tree-shaped cookie and broke off the trunk, sliding it into her mouth. "Looks like you're cooking for a crowd."

"If you and Gerald don't eat them all, I told Cliff's mom I would take some up with us." Jennette checked the cookies in the oven, and then set the timer on the stove for a couple more minutes. "I guess work has been keeping you busy?"

"Yeah, I've been trying to get this project done before my last day. Good cookies, Mom. Where's Dad?"

"He's out of town overnight for work, and Gerald had a date. The house seems too empty without him." She smiled and pulled the remaining dough from the bowl beside her, rolling it out on the cupboard.

Denise picked up the cookie cutters and played with them while she finished her cookie, watching her mother roll the ball of dough to a uniform thickness. Now that she was here, she wasn't sure how to start the conversation.

"Is something wrong, honey?"

"That's what I wanted to know." Denise began cutting shapes into the dough as she searched for the best way to begin. "I understand that you have some reservations about my searching for my birth family, that you're worried I'll be hurt or something. And I know Paige being so upset about it has added to the stress. But there's something else bothering you, too."

There was no answer for a long moment and when Denise looked over, she found her mother focused on tinting the frosting she had mixed for the cooled cookies. "You've pretty well summed it up. I don't guess there's more on my mind than there was before."

Denise paused, catching the edge of something else in her mother's words. "What's that supposed to mean? Am I missing something here? Something has been bothering you for a long time then, but it's just coming up now? What?"

"It's just more pronounced than it was before. And we did bring it up in the past. You just didn't care." Jennette beat the frosting with a spoon harder, taking her frustrations out on it.

"Mom, what are you talking about?" This behavior was so unlike her mother, Denise didn't know what to make of it.

The bowl slammed against the countertop, and the alarm went off on the stove. After taking a deep breath, the older woman grabbed the oven mitts and removed the golden cookies, then placed a new sheet in the oven and reset the timer. When she turned back around, her face looked calmer. "Am I your mom, Denise? Are we your family, really your family? In your heart and not just on paper?"

Denise blinked and shook her head. "What?"

"We could all have been sealed as a family five years ago, but when I mentioned it, you brushed me off. You didn't want to belong to us forever, and now you're all excited about your birth family. Where do we fit in, Denise? You say that nothing is going to change, that you aren't looking to replace us, but . . . ."

Horror trickled into Denise's gut as she saw a tear slide down her mother's face. Her horror only increased when she felt wetness on her own cheeks as well. This is what she had been worrying about? Denise had mentioned to her family that she wasn't ready to go to the temple, she had no idea her parents hadn't realized that fact hadn't changed. "But we talked about it, at the time. How I wasn't ready. How I couldn't go yet. I thought you understood?"

"I did, at the time. You weren't ready to go to the temple. But I would have expected in the five years since then that you would have told us when you wanted to make that move. But you haven't. So, what is it?

Where do I fall short of what you need?"

The tears came thick and fast now, and Denise wiped at her face, trying to understand. "Nowhere. Nothing. How can you say that after everything you've done for me? You saved me. You couldn't have done better, no one could have. I should have ended up in some gutter, dead, or behind prison bars like Daphne, but you wouldn't give up on me. I owe you everything. How could you think you weren't enough?"

"You didn't want our family. You didn't want to be part of us, and even now you keep yourself separate. No matter how hard we try, you hold a piece of yourself back from us. I try to understand, try to be there for you without suffocating you."

"This isn't about you!" Denise knew she was raising her voice, but the thought of her mother blaming herself for Denise's inadequacy was more than she could bear. "I feel privileged to be part of this family. I don't deserve it, I don't belong, but you all accept me anyway."

"What do you mean you don't belong?" Her mother's voice was low, surprised.

Denise wiped her face with the back of her hand. When she spoke again her voice was calm, though her hands shook. "Did I say that?"

"Yes."

Trying to catch her breath, Denise leaned back against the cupboard. "I hardly realized I felt that way. You thought I didn't want the family because I haven't been to the temple yet?"

There was a long pause while her mother's eyes narrowed. "You haven't been yet? As in, you haven't been at all? Not even for baptisms for the dead?" Her mom led her around the counter and motioned to a chair at the table.

Denise sat, sniffled, and pushed the hair back from her face. "No. I haven't." She took a quick breath. "I don't belong there. There's nothing I want more than to belong to someone. Really belong to someone. If I felt good enough, I would love to be sealed to you." Tears were pouring down her face again, but Denise didn't bother trying to stop them.

"What do you mean? Honey, this isn't about what happened to you as a kid, is it?" Jennette's face was pale as she swiped at her own damp cheeks.

"How can I forget it? It's part of who I am."

"It wasn't your fault. None of it. And even the trouble you caused in high school, the Atonement wiped it all away. Don't you understand that?

You were as clean as a newborn babe when you came out of the font when you were baptized."

"I know the drill, Mom. I just have a hard time applying it to myself. I'm sorry I've been holding back from the family. That's how I am, I can't change it. There's no one I share more with than you. All the people I love most are in this family." Rich came to mind, and she flicked her eyes away, blinking. Her feelings for him might be as strong as those for her family.

"I think there's someone you're leaving out in that statement. But we'll leave that till later. I'm both worried and relieved now I know why you haven't been to the temple with us. Honey, you aren't to blame for the horrors you went through as a child. The Lord would never hold you responsible for the evil things that were done to you. You have to accept that for yourself if you want peace."

Denise nodded but said nothing more, and the subject dropped.

They finished baking the cookies together, decorated them, and talked well into the night. Though Denise still wasn't able to let go of her past when the night ended, a great weight had been lifted from her shoulders and she returned home a little less stressed.

After the long discussion with her mom and letting the problem with Paige eat at her for nearly a week, Denise left work and made a beeline for her sister's apartment. The hurt and anger that had existed between them for fifteen years was too much of a burden. If she could work things out with her mom, she could do the same with Paige. After Paige's blow-up at dinner Sunday, she knew she needed to clear the air, if only to make Sunday dinners bearable again.

Unfortunately, that meant dealing with the unpleasantness and a possible scene. Paige may not be receptive to the conversation and if it went badly . . . Denise didn't want to think about that. She just wanted to have a little more peace in her life.

She found an empty spot to park on the street—a minor miracle in its own right, she figured, making her way around the brown brick building to Paige's door. Her stomach trembled as she waited for someone to answer her knock, and she sent up a prayer that Paige would be home. She hadn't called first, hadn't known what to say over the phone.

When a perky redhead answered the door, Denise wondered when she last visited Paige. Too long if she didn't recognize her roommates after a full semester. "I'm Paige's sister, Denise. Is she home?"

"Yeah, come on in." The girl indicated a sofa for Denise to sit on while she ran upstairs to get Paige. Some hip-hop music boomed through the apartment, and Denise wondered why the music wasn't against the honor code. Anyone with good taste would know that wasn't real music, right? She caught herself and muffled a laugh. Her mom would have said the same thing about some of the music she chose to unwind with. It took all types, after all.

When Paige came around the corner of the room, she lifted her eyebrows in disbelief. "Slumming are we, Denise?"

Denise winced. Obviously it had been far too long since she reached out to her sister, and Paige wasn't in a good mood. She forced a smile. "I was thinking, if you don't have any plans, maybe we could grab a bite to eat. I know Cliff's out of town for a game."

Paige's expression asked if Denise thought she could be an adequate substitute for her fiancé, but she nodded. "Let me grab my coat and purse." She turned and walked back upstairs, and Denise let out a breath of relief.

First step down.

The short drive to the burger joint passed in silence as Denise tried to figure out how to begin the conversation, and Paige eyed her warily.

With their order in, they took a seat in the back of the restaurant, thankful to find a seat at all during the holiday rush. They sat sipping their drinks for a moment before Denise was able to bring herself to begin. "I know I don't go out of my way to spend time with you or to work on our relationship. I'm sorry. I know I was a pain to live with when I first moved into your house."

"We all grow up, don't we," Paige said, her expression blank.

"Thank goodness. Look, I realize you don't understand what's going on with this search I'm doing. Maybe I should have discussed it more with you, maybe then you would understand—"

"What I understand," Paige interrupted, "is that you don't need us anymore. That after years of being included in the family, despite the trouble you were as a teen and the heartache you caused my parents, you've decided we aren't that important after all."

"Oh," Denise let out a whoosh of air. "That's not true. That's not what this is about at all. I don't want to lose you guys. I have no intention of losing anyone. You and Gerald, Mom and Dad. You're the only real family I've ever known. You're the only reason I've had the strength to turn out even a little normal.

"Do you know how I used to long to belong to a family, a real family? With parents who loved each other, and me, who didn't hit or scream. A brother and sister to play with and to be there to share with? Every day that I lived with Daphne, I wished I could have the kind of life you grew up in, with the kind of family you had since birth. I can't tell you how jealous I was when I first moved into your home, how desperately I wished I could be *you*."

Paige snorted, and Denise steeled herself for the rest of the conversation. "Paige the pretty one, Paige the one everyone loved, the one who hung with the cool kids, who got all the dates. I know I was a brat. I was a major brat. Because I was so afraid of opening up my heart and having to move again, being ripped away. It had already happened twice before I met you. Besides leaving my . . . Daphne's house."

"Your adoption was finalized and you still caused trouble, maybe more than before," Paige countered.

It hurt Denise to think of that, of the way she pushed and prodded her parents after they proved that they were willing to stick to her. "Yeah. I figured I had you all fooled. Mom and Dad seemed to think I was worth something, made of something good. It terrified me that some day everyone might wake up and realize they were wrong. Do you think kids who are adopted never end up back in the system again? It happens. Believe me, it does. Every time I closed my eyes, I could see it happening to me.

"And I guess a part of me wanted to claim responsibility for the adoption failing. I didn't want to have it just happen to me, not again. If everyone was going to reject me, I was going to give them a reason for it. It made the rejection less personal. You have no idea how many years of therapy it took for me to realize that."

Though she hadn't said anything, Paige's eyes narrowed, as though she wasn't sure if she believed a word Denise said. Taking that hesitation as encouragement, Denise continued, though it wasn't easy to admit. "If I didn't give you a reason to hate me, and you did anyway, that would mean there was something about *me* that was wrong or bad. If I caused trouble, it wouldn't be me, it would be the trouble. The only thing I didn't count on was Mom and Dad not giving up on me. I was sure they would, that I would find myself in another home. I knew you would never get sent on. I envied that."

Paige's face showed disbelief. "You can't be serious? I mean, sure, I had a normal family, but you're so smart. I felt like I was always trying to keep up with Smart Denise. You were so strong inside, so perfect. You never left a mess around the house." She wiped at a tear on her cheek. "You never . . . well, I was going to say got into trouble, but that wasn't true." She laughed, and Denise laughed with her, relieved at the mood breaker.

"No, especially the first few years. I was in trouble all the time. I found myself in the perfect home, with perfect parents, and they weren't mine. They were yours, and I couldn't be in my own home. I was so afraid of being hurt again. I couldn't believe it would last because nothing good ever lasted for me before. When I was ready to make things work . . ."

"I was impossible to live with." Paige shook her head. "I figured you hated me already, otherwise you would have been my friend. So I gave you reasons to hate me. Guess we're more alike than we thought." A ghost of a smile slid onto Paige's face, and though everything wasn't better, Denise thought they'd made a good first step.

CHAPTER TWENTY-FOUR

Denise had planned to take Rich to Kaylee's concert, since her younger sister had wanted to meet him, but their current relationship made that the wrong choice. She was glad to go, though, needing to be somewhere she didn't associate with Rich.

After a long, slick drive, Denise enjoyed the concert and was glad she came. Kaylee wore a black velvet dress and looked like a professional on the stage, somber and focused while she played, nothing but smiles when she finished. Tears came to Denise's eyes as she watched her sister play. She'd been denied this for so many years, but now it had been restored. That was one blessing in her life she couldn't deny, and Kaylee didn't ask more than Denise could give.

Sue sat beside Denise during the concert, squeezing her hand when they sat again after giving the students a standing ovation. "That's my baby," Sue said, her pride evident.

"She's sure something," Denise agreed.

"She's going to go all the way. The finest musical training, the largest concert halls. Some day she'll be headlining all over the nation. My girl." She turned to Denise and beamed for a moment. "How have you been, Denise? We didn't have time to talk when you arrived. I heard you found Pete."

Denise filled Sue in on the latest developments, but neatly sidestepped a question about Rich. "You don't know anything else about the other baby, do you? Kaylee mentioned in her last email that you were scheduled to visit Daphne this week," Denise said.

The bustle of people standing and making their way out of the auditorium filled the room with noise. Sue glanced at her husband and back to Denise. "I told her you were searching, that you wanted to find your last sibling. She smirked and said she would tell you. But you have to go visit her if you want to know."

The breath whooshed from Denise's body, and she gasped for breath before she could answer. "She wants to see me? She expects me to go visit her there? I don't know if I'm ready for that yet. After everything she did to me, she wants me to come visit?" Denise had considered meeting Daphne again some day, but not yet, not now. How could she when she didn't know what to say, or even how she felt about the woman who had given her life and then terrorized her?

"It takes a month or more to get clearance to visit. And once you get clearance, you don't have to go right away. If you want to take some time to work up to it, you'll have it." Sue took Denise's hand and pressed it between her own.

Denise held on, grateful for the anchor. She felt as if she were in a hurricane, buffeted by the wind and waves. She wasn't ready for this. "I . . . can't she just tell you what she knows?"

Sue shook her head. "She won't tell us. We shouldn't have told her it was you who wanted to find your other sibling. She wouldn't even tell us if it was a girl or a boy. Daphne insists she will only tell *you*, face-to-face. You can put the visit off, but you won't be able to track down your brother or sister until you talk to her."

Derrick set a hand on his wife's shoulder, since she sat between Denise and himself. "Daphne isn't all bad. I know she put you through some horrible things, but she's clean now, and I'm sure she has a lot of regrets. The choice is yours, but if you want to start the paperwork, let us know and we'll have her request it."

The crowds were thinner now. Everyone had gone to the entryway to congratulate the students, and Denise followed Derrick and Sue out of the auditorium as well. Her mind whirled and her stomach turned as she tried to decide what to do. She pushed it aside and focused on smiling as she gave her baby sister a hug of congratulations.

The last day at the office was a sad day for Denise. She finished up her project in the morning and spent the rest of the day troubleshooting smaller issues. When she returned from lunch, she started having trouble with her keyboard, she kept hitting the 'M' key and getting an 'N' instead, and vice versa. It took less than a minute to figure out who the culprit was.

"Jake, have you been 'fixing' my keyboard?"

His look was one of complete innocence. An expression she learned to mistrust more than a year earlier. "What are you talking about?"

"Had to pull one last prank. That was a pretty good one. It had me going for a few seconds. It would be even more effective on the new guy Rich just hired to replace me. He wouldn't know you were responsible for everything that goes awry in this office." She gave him his due respect, even if he did exasperate her sometimes.

He grinned back at her. "Thanks for the suggestion. I think I'll try it, as a sort of initiation."

"I believe they call it hazing in school," Mick said without looking up.

"Naw, we'll take it easy. Nothing serious, and I'll give him a whole day to adjust before I initiate him." Jake rubbed his hands together and grinned evilly.

It made Denise laugh. "There's no one else like you, Jake. You're one in a million. And thank goodness for that—it means it's unlikely I'll have to deal with someone like you in my new office."

Late afternoon she was working on a particularly complex string of code when Joan came in the door holding a cake. A dozen or more people filed in behind her, including Rich. Joan's eyes glistened with moisture.

Denise had to hold back the tears as she realized the cake was for her.

"We're going to miss you. Frandsen doesn't realize how good he's got it," Joan said.

The promise of something more shined from Rich's eyes, so Denise avoided his gaze.

The ice cream cake was cut and pieces carried off to all corners of the building. Words of well wishes and requests that she stay in touch assaulted her from every department. This surprised Denise. She hadn't realized how many people even knew her name. Of course, she realized as she held back a grin, people become really friendly when there's food involved.

A wave of nostalgia came over her later that afternoon as she added her box of orange spice tea to the bag already holding her family picture and other personal items that accumulated in her desk after more than two years. Her desk had begun to feel a little like home, and the few trappings she allowed herself had been her way of surrounding herself with things she loved.

A few minutes before she began to log out, she received an email from Rich.

STOP BY MY OFFICE ON YOUR WAY OUT.

That was all, one short sentence, but it made her heart beat faster and her stomach tighten in knots. After today he would no longer be her boss. She wondered if she had chosen right. The change had been so fueled by emotion that she second guessed it more than once.

She finished packing her personal effects and shut down her computer for the last time. Denise stood and walked out of the room, her bag of belongings still sitting by her desk.

Her stomach flipped when she looked into Rich's office. He sat bent over some paperwork, wrinkles forming between his eyes as he concentrated. The window behind him showed the glow of the parking lot lights. It was nearing the shortest day of the year, and darkness fell early. Too early. She watched him for a few seconds as he picked up a pen in his big hands, the muscles of his arm shifted as he reached across the desk for another when the first one didn't write. Knowing she needed to stop staring, Denise knocked on Rich's doorjamb.

His eyes flitted to hers, the brown softened, and the slight frown he'd been wearing loosened into what might have been the beginnings of a smile. "Come on in, Denise, and shut the door."

She hesitated for a moment, then kicked at the door blocker and allowed the door to close as she walked over to the chair across from him. "I'm all logged out and packed up."

He studied her face, his eyes seemed to take in every curve, every feature. He swallowed hard. "I know I could have done this at your place tonight instead. But as my last official act as your boss I've been told to extend an offer to come back anytime. Murphy was livid I didn't fight for you more, offer you a raise. You're a valuable asset to this company. We're sorry to lose someone with your skills, work ethic, and ability to get along with others." He rubbed a finger across his bottom lip. "I, of course, have other reasons I'll miss seeing you each day. But . . ." His expression filled in his hopes without another word.

"Rich—" The protest she was forming in her head never made it all the way out.

"No. We understand each other. I hope someday you'll feel free to discuss what it is that's holding you back. Until then," he reached behind his desk and pulled out a large box wrapped in green paper. "The company wants to present you with this and offer you luck."

She opened the gift before standing, unwrapping a duplicate of Jake's Room Defender. She fought tears again and looked up into his face. It was a good thing the big wooden desk sat between them, or Denise was certain he would have broken company policy and pulled her close for a hug. But he could always do that tonight at her place. If she was there.

She focused back on the gift on her lap, not daring to meet his eye. "Thank you. I've enjoyed working here, and I'll feel free to suggest to others that they'll find fair employment here. You've done good things for this department, and I'll be sorry to miss seeing what else you'll accomplish."

She stood and walked to the door. She gave him one long look as she held it open and walked out, letting the door close behind her.

CHAPTER TWENTY-FIVE

Denise returned to her parents' home that night and stayed over in her old room so she could spend extra time with Gerald. That was her excuse to everyone else, anyway. She spent half the evening scrubbing every nook and cranny of her mother's kitchen, and though her mother gave Denise knowing looks, she kept her own counsel.

On Saturday morning, she went Christmas shopping with Gerald, and they stopped at Paige's to pull her away for lunch. Since Cliff was already at home getting ready for the party at his parents' house, Paige was available and more than a little bored.

The crowds were out of control, the lines interminable, but the three of them stood around laughing and joking, as if the tension that had been between them had never existed. Denise knew the tension might return eventually but hoped the time they spent together would help keep it to a lower level. She and Paige were both making an effort, and it was paying off.

After they finished shopping, Paige went with them to their parents' house to get ready for the party. She talked with Denise about school and roommates, her job at a clothing store in the mall, and how miserable her finals had been.

By the time they reached the Werner's house in Ogden, Denise was feeling loose and relaxed. She had no one to impress. She put her family search problems behind her for the night and Rich out of her mind. She laughed with Gerald as they made their way up the walk and through the front door to find Paige already in a lip lock with Cliff.

"Guess we found the right place," Denise observed. She smiled as Cliff pulled away from her sister, then leaned in and whispered something to Paige. They had been apart most of the week, with his four-day basketball trip and return home. To see them together now, Denise wondered how they'd survived so long without each other. If a tiny ache squeezed its way into the corner of her heart, she ignored it. Tonight was a night to talk, laugh, and have fun.

She turned to find a carbon copy of Cliff at her elbow and blinked in surprise. "Wow, you must be Curtis, I heard you two looked alike, but I never even guessed. Are you identical?"

Curtis nodded and smiled, looking deep into her eyes. She felt a strange tug in her chest and blinked in surprise, nearly missing what he was saying. "You must be Denise. Cliff told me all about how you surprised some of the guys on his team with your basketball playing." When his eyebrows drew closer together, and he drifted off at the end of his sentence, she wondered if he felt the same things she did.

"Yeah, it was fun. I enjoy playing with someone who can give me a run for my money again. Heaven knows Gerald can't. He's almost as pathetic as—" Denise caught herself, realizing she was about to say, "as Rich," but she didn't want to go there tonight. "As playing Paige. Well, no. No one's as pathetic at basketball as Paige. But she enjoys watching, so I suppose they'll be happy enough."

Curtis grinned down at Denise and then led her into the room, introducing her around to family and friends, exchanging insults with Cliff when they got close enough to talk, and keeping Denise more entertained than she ever expected.

Most of the night was over before Denise realized Curtis hadn't left her side. They talked about everything and anything, exchanged a few good-natured insults of their own, and laughed until her sides ached. Curtis finally turned her over to his mother, Martha, so he could drive an elderly neighbor home.

The two women spoke for several minutes about Cliff and Paige before Martha turned the conversation. "You look like you've been having fun."

"I have. You've raised a couple of great men there. This evening was just the distraction I needed, and your party is so fun."

"I'm glad you think so, and thank you. This is one holiday tradition I can't quite seem to give up, despite the hassle, and none of the kids would let me if I tried. We've been doing it since the twins were in diapers."

After more small talk, Martha looked over the top of her punch glass and took a sip, watching Denise. "I hope you don't mind if I ask. Cliff mentioned you've been searching for your family. How's that going for you?"

Denise felt her happiness deflate just a bit, but she smiled anyway. The woman had several adopted children, so she was curious. It was only reasonable. "Mixed results, I'm afraid."

"My kids all came through private adoption. Except the youngest, she was a medical miracle. But you didn't have that advantage, I understand. Forgive me if I'm prying."

Denise shook her head. She seemed to be getting a lot of practice at talking about her past lately. The fact that she was even considering sharing with this virtual stranger was a testament that she was letting go a little. "I'm always curious about adoptions, the situation, how they happened. I think part of it is a search for answers for my own situation. Because of the circumstances surrounding my removal from home, there are a lot of extra issues to deal with."

She held off the anger at Daphne, this wasn't the time or the place, but she could feel it boiling just below the surface. "Someday I'm going to have to face my birth mother. And when I do, she'll have a lot to account for. I'm trying to work through a lot of anger and frustration first. And I'm hoping to find all of my family members, whether the reunions go well or not."

"I'm sure it's difficult. My kids have had mixed results."

"Hey, let's have no talk about that nonsense, it's so depressing." Curtis's cheeks were rosy from being out in the cold. "Come dance with me, Denise. They're doing the Jitter Bug."

"I'm not sure I'm the right partner for that one," Denise said with a smile as he took her hand and waved good-bye to Martha. She followed Curtis out onto the dance floor and followed his moves, surprised to see how well he knew the dances, and what a good teacher he was.

When her father came looking for her to go home, Denise was laughing and out of breath from several energetic dances. Curtis helped her with her coat, donned his own, and walked her out to the car.

"I've had a lot of fun with you," he said, burrowing deeper into his coat. "How is it you're not dating anyone?"

Not for lack of his trying. "Relationships and I don't get along. Thanks for keeping me distracted tonight, it was just what I needed. Maybe I'll have to try and catch the game when you come down to play Cliff in a few weeks. If you're that good on the dance floor, I can't wait to see you on the court." The initial snap in her chest when she met him had dulled through the evening, melting into a comfortable friendship.

"That would be great."

Denise could hear Cliff and Paige talking behind them, bringing up the rear of the family as they sought the shelter of the car. When Cliff and Paige walked around to the other side of the car for their good night kiss, Denise found herself in an awkward moment with Curtis. She had fun, laughed and joked, but it felt almost datelike, with the two of them floating around the room together, though there was often a third or fourth in their group. She felt so instantly comfortable with him, so easy. It confused her, and when he leaned in toward her, she worried for a second that he was going to kiss her, but his lips only skimmed her forehead.

"I'm sure I'll see you again. I'll call you or something," he said as he moved back.

The door shut on the other side of the car, and Cliff came around the back to where she still stood with Curtis. "Hey, watch out for my woman, will ya?"

"Sure. I'll watch her walk right off a cliff." Denise laughed at her own pun and poked him in the side. She slid into the car, grateful for the interruption. *He's going to call me? What's going on?* She waved good-bye to the twins and sunk back into the seat of the car, more tired than she had realized, but her mind wouldn't quit.

The thought came to her again that she had been so comfortable with Curtis, without the pressure she felt when she was with Rich. There was an undercurrent between them that she didn't understand. She worried now that she had time to consider it. How could she feel that way about Curtis if she was in love with Rich? What did it mean? Or was she just going crazy?

Pete's hands trembled as he opened the letter from the test lab. It was December twenty-second, three days till Christmas, and he had gotten the results of the DNA tests he requested for himself and Denise. Now he would learn for sure if she was his daughter, if Daphne had deprived him of that relationship for all these years, or if it was all a hoax.

The question was, would learning that his daughter had been kept from him be more heartbreaking than finding out she wasn't his after all?

He pulled out the white sheet of paper with the lab's letterhead across the top. His eyes scanned it until he read the words that confirmed it. He was her father. Pete dropped the letter onto his desk at work and stared out the window of the car dealership he'd bought from his uncle a few years earlier. The reality was hard to believe, nearly impossible to swallow whole. His kids had a sister. He had another daughter. How would he explain everything?

Tears came to his eyes and he allowed them to fall, allowed himself to mourn the lost years. This woman he was getting to know through emails was a bright, energetic person. Her life had been hard, mixed up, and crazy for so many years, but she appeared to be doing something good with it, to be a whole person. And he'd missed out on that.

Now that he had proof of paternity, he wanted to see what she looked like, to talk to her on the phone, and learn her voice. To see her in person and see if she'd picked up any of the family mannerisms, the way Jesse's mouth cocked when he grinned, the irritated flip of hair Olivia performed when she didn't get her way. The mischievous look in Beth's eye when she was putting together a plan. Would she share any of these traits?

The pain of all he lost poured over him. Everything he had been cheated of because of Daphne's vendetta. He knew his daughter hadn't been cared for, at least not under Daphne's hands, or Denise wouldn't have been removed from her home and adopted by someone else. He ached knowing that he could have been there for Denise. He and Renee could have raised her. He wiped his face and tried to put together a plan.

First, he needed to figure out how to tell his other kids. He had always been honest about everything. Except this. He cringed as he thought of how it could affect his family. What if Denise didn't stick around? That scared him most of all.

After everything he had been through, after the difficulties he and Renee had faced, Pete didn't want to risk their hearts again. Renee and the kids were settled in their lives, happy with the status quo. If it had been only himself, Pete knew he would have responded to the letter the same day and hung the negative consequences while he tried to determine if she was his, but he couldn't take those kinds of chances with his family.

A salesman came in and distracted Pete from his train of thought. He had a buyer who was ready to go. They needed to finalize paperwork. Pete put the letter down on the desk with a promise to himself to call Renee as soon as he had a chance. They would sit down together and tell the kids. He needed to email Denise too. The direction their relationship would take remained to be seen.

Renee had taken the initial contact news calmly. She'd read the emails Pete and Denise exchanged without comment, and wholeheartedly supported the idea of the DNA testing. So Pete had every expectation of finding her happy about the news.

"Already? You heard back already? Are you sure they checked carefully enough? Maybe there's a mistake." Renee stood from the bed where she had been folding laundry when Pete came in. She walked to the window and then whirled around. "Maybe they should check again."

"What? They checked carefully enough, and it took a little longer than they expected." Pete couldn't understand what had gotten into his wife.

She pushed the dark curly hair back from her face and stalked over to him. "Maybe they sent you the wrong results. They could have been mixed up in the lab. You should be tested again."

Pete settled his hands on his wife's shoulder and looked into her brown eyes. "Renee, Joe took care of this personally. He promised to take extra care with it. The results are right. What's going on?"

She pulled away and took a few steps toward the window again. The silence stretched while she came up with the right words. "Once, twenty-two years ago I let myself get excited about the possibility of raising your daughter. I would be a mother. You went to Utah, and I was sure you would bring her back with you, even if you had to give that hag of an ex-wife some money to satisfy her. But you came back empty-handed. It shouldn't have been such a big deal, but it was. Losing her when I thought we had her about broke my heart."

Pete remembered how she'd silently mourned for his daughter and the struggle they dealt with as it took four years after they married for her to get pregnant. He crossed to her and settled his hands on her shoulders again, this time kneading gently at her back muscles, trying to inject some comfort. "I know, honey. If it was hard for you, it was even harder for me. I always wondered about her. Worried about her. But now we have the chance to get to know her."

"What if she isn't the kind of person we want the kids associating with? What if she's more like her mother than her father? The kids are all at that age where anyone but their parents knows best."

Continuing to sooth his wife's tight muscles, Pete leaned down and spoke into her ear. "She doesn't sound much like Daphne in her letters. How about if we give her a chance? The other report came back clean."

"I don't like it. I don't know if I trust her, but she's your daughter, and I won't keep you away."

Frustration welled up inside Pete. After everything they had been through, why had she waited until now to voice a concern? It was completely unlike his usually placid wife to overreact like this. Feeling trapped, he turned his wife around and looked into her eyes. "Can we still tell the kids? They deserve to know they have another sister."

It took a moment before Renee met his gaze; she pursed her lips and nodded. "They'll never forgive us if we don't tell them. I just don't want to see any of us hurt."

And understanding that she was as worried about herself as anyone else in the family, he pulled her into a hug. "Me neither."

CHAPTER TWENTY-SIX

Pete faced his three tow-headed kids that night in the family room. Dinner had been eaten and cleaned up, homework done for the holiday break, and now the three of them watched him with curiosity. It wasn't often their father called a full family council.

He clutched Renee's hand and looked into three sets of eyes, two blue, one brown. "You all know I was married once before, don't you?" They nodded their heads in agreement. His middle child, fifteen-year-old Olivia gave him a shrewd look, and he glanced away. His seventeen-year-old son, Jesse, slumped back in his seat, his arms folded over his chest. Eleven-year-old Beth only nodded. He wondered how clammy his hands had grown and felt a slight pity for his wife who was stuck holding one.

"A couple years after the divorce, I received a letter from my ex-wife asking me for money. Child support for a child I hadn't known she was carrying." That was the worst part, watching the incredulity slide across his kids' faces. He forced himself to continue before they could respond. The whole story tumbled out while the kids sat silently listening.

"Daphne was never faithful to me, so I had no way of knowing if the girl was actually mine. Since no one seemed to know how to reach her, and no word came to me over the following years, I determined it must have been a hoax. Her family said there was a child, a little girl, but they were no more certain of the paternity than I was.

"I admit, the idea of there being a child out there who might belong to me, but who I couldn't track, hurt. But I could learn nothing." This would be the sticky part, admitting how long he'd known where she was.

"Denise tracked me down a few weeks ago."

"You heard from her and didn't tell us? How could you not tell us?" Of course Olivia was the first to break the silence, the first to express her indignation. He expected it to come sooner but was grateful that shock seemed to have bound her tongue until now.

"I wanted to be sure. We both submitted hair to a DNA test, and I got the results today. She is your sister." He let that sink in and didn't wait long to hear the results.

"So now I'm really out numbered," Jesse said. Though his words complained, his look said he was more intrigued than upset.

"Am I going to have to share my space with her if she comes to visit?" Olivia asked. "I shouldn't have to share a room again just because she wants to take over our family."

"Cool, I have another big sister? Tell me she's not like Olivia, please," was Beth's reply. "If she moved in, Olivia wouldn't be the boss anymore."

"We've been outnumbered for years, son. I don't know if she'll come out to visit anytime soon, and we'll have to work that out when it happens, but I doubt she's got any intention of taking over. And Beth, she's twenty-six. I don't imagine she'll be moving in." Jesse shrugged, Olivia crossed her arms in front of her chest and pouted, and Beth sighed at the loss of her illusions. All three responses were typical, Pete figured.

He pulled out the letter Denise sent, along with printouts of the emails he had received from Denise during the wait for the test results, and passed them around.

"You should have told us sooner. We deserved to know," Olivia said again when she finished reading the letters. "You didn't tell her where we live, did you? She's a stranger; she could be a psycho. Why didn't she look for us sooner? Maybe she needs money or a place to hide from the law."

That's Olivia, Pete thought, *always the drama queen, always the one to come up with ridiculous scenarios*. If there was anything his middle child loved most it was being the center of attention. "Liv, I think you're overreacting. I didn't have to tell her where we lived, because she found me, not the other way around. It sounds like she doesn't need any money, and," not wanting to admit that he had his own doubts, but feeling the need to reassure, he added one more point, "your mother and I hired a private investigator to check her out."

Olivia looked at him, too intrigued to continue her argument.

"Do you mean like 007?" Beth asked, her eyes as big as hubcaps.

"Did you think she might be desperate?"

"What do you know about 007?" Renee asked, her sharp eyes turned on their youngest.

Beth folded her arms in front of her and hunched down in her seat, pouting. "Not much. You won't let me watch it."

Pete ran a hand through his thinning hair and looked at each of them. "I didn't want to risk exposing you kids to someone who could be out to hurt us. I called a PI, and he checked her out before I ever wrote her back. Her record is clean—she got good grades at the University of Utah, works as a computer programmer, and spends a lot of time at the gym. She also seems active in her singles ward."

Denise's eyes fluttered open and she stretched lazily in bed. It was Tuesday morning, two days before Christmas. The previous day she had taken the time to do a little shopping, picking up a few things for Kaylee.

Spending hours at the mall was not her idea of a great time.

Now she had little left to do for the holidays besides pick something out for Rich, if she had any idea what to get for him. The strange relationship they shared made her question whether she wanted to get him anything at all, but she knew he would get her something and wanted to reciprocate. The question was what she could buy that wouldn't be too personal.

Her first move of the morning, after slathering a toasted bagel with cream cheese, was to pull out her laptop and log onto the Internet. Her inbox held several messages, so she opened the first one, a note from Rich sent the previous evening.

DENISE,

THE OFFICE SEEMS SOMEHOW EMPTY WITHOUT YOU IN IT. I DON'T KNOW HOW MUCH WORK I'M ACTUALLY GETTING OUT OF THE GUYS. WITH THE HOLIDAYS DRAWING SO NEAR, THERE SEEMS TO BE A LOT MORE HOLIDAY CHEER FLOATING AROUND THAN WORK. I HOPE YOU'RE ENJOYING YOUR WEEK OFF. I MISS YOU. I'LL TRY TO STOP IN TO SEE YOU TONIGHT.

RICH

She missed him too but wasn't sure she was ready to see him again. She had kept busy shopping and, in an attempt to give herself more time, had been at her parents' house a lot. She was also enjoying her new relationship with Kaylee, who was getting excited for Christmas. Kaylee told Denise that Sue seemed to be softening up on the hair dye issue and Kaylee hoped to get what she wanted before school started again in January.

The next email was, surprisingly, from Curtis. It was short and a little awkward, but chatty about what was going on. He hadn't mentioned how he had gotten her email address, but she figured a phone call to her parents would have solved that issue. Or he could have gotten it from Paige. She debated for a long moment before she shot back a reply telling about her shopping trip—how much she hated it—and making fun of last-minute shoppers. She wished him luck in his upcoming game and sent it off.

The next two were junk mail, and the fifth was a note from Pete. She felt butterflies in her belly as she opened the note, wondering if he had heard about the tests.

DENISE,

    I GOT THE RESULTS BACK FROM THE TEST TODAY. IT WAS POSITIVE. I GUESS I'M STILL TRYING TO TAKE THIS ALL IN, TO FIGURE OUT WHAT I WANT TO HAVE HAPPEN FROM HERE. MY WIFE AND I ARE GOING TO SIT DOWN AND TALK TO OUR KIDS TONIGHT ABOUT THIS WHOLE THING. I'M SURE BETH, AT LEAST, WILL HAVE A THOUSAND QUESTIONS FOR YOU. SHE'S ALWAYS BEEN MORE CURIOUS THAN A MONKEY. BEFORE I LET THEM SEND EMAILS THOUGH, I WANT TO BE SURE YOU WILL WELCOME THEM. I DON'T WANT MY OTHER KIDS HURT IF YOU HAVE JUST BEEN FILLING YOUR CURIOSITY. I WOULD LIKE TO SEE YOU, TO GET TO KNOW YOU. LET ME KNOW HOW YOU FEEL ABOUT ALL OF THIS.

PETE

He included a post script with their home phone number. Denise sat back, her stomach turning over as she tried to decide where to go next. Three more siblings. At the rate things were going she would have a family big enough to fill a basketball team. She hurried to write back.

PETE,

    THANKS FOR THE NOTE. IT'S BOTH A RELIEF AND A LITTLE SCARY NOW TO KNOW THE TRUTH. NED AND SHARON TOLD ME A LITTLE ABOUT YOU, AND YOU SOUND LIKE A REALLY NICE GUY. THAT MAKES ME QUESTION YOUR SANITY

SINCE I CAN'T SEE HOW A NICE GUY ENDED UP WITH DAPHNE, BUT SHE MAY HAVE BEEN A DIFFERENT PERSON THEN THAN SHE WAS WHEN I WAS TEN. I'M SORRY FOR ALL THE HEARTACHE SHE PUT US BOTH THROUGH, BUT MOSTLY FOR YOURS. I CAN ONLY IMAGINE WHAT IT MUST HAVE BEEN LIKE TO KNOW YOU HAD A DAUGHTER FOR TWO DECADES, BUT NOT TO KNOW HOW TO HELP HER.

I'D BE HAPPY TO HEAR FROM YOUR OTHER KIDS. BETH SOUNDS GREAT, AND I HOPE THEY ALL ACCEPTED THE NEWS OKAY. I WILL UNDERSTAND IF THEY NEED MORE TIME TO GET USED TO EVERYTHING. I START A NEW JOB NEXT MONDAY, SO IT MAY BE A WHILE BEFORE I CAN ARRANGE TIME OFF TO MEET YOUR FAMILY.

DENISE

She shut down the computer with feelings whirling through her chest. Things with Pete looked promising, and she hoped and prayed that they would turn out okay. Her feelings about Curtis and Rich were another story.

After reading Curtis's email, and remembering the laughter in his eyes, the comfort of being with him, she'd started to second guess her feelings for Rich. Though she'd been feeling like there was something very special between them, something she never expected to find elsewhere, there was something about Curtis she couldn't completely ignore. Why was this happening to her now?

Surely she couldn't have met two men with whom she could be happy. Her feelings for Curtis were nowhere as strong as her love for Rich. But, if Rich was the one for her, as he was so sure he was and as she had begun to believe, why the connection with Curtis? Why was she finding herself even more torn now? And why, after all of the years she'd spent with no interest in a romantic relationship, did she find herself faced with two men pulling those kinds of feelings from her?

CHAPTER TWENTY-SEVEN

Rich finally found Denise at home while she was filling out the paperwork required by the prison to visit an inmate. Denise had been concerned that she had to give Daphne her address. The inmate had to request the paperwork be sent out. But Denise had received the paperwork three days before and hadn't received a letter from Daphne yet.

"Are you really going to do it?" Rich asked. He sat beside her at the counter.

"I don't know. I don't have any choice if I want to find out about that other pregnancy. She hasn't even said if it was a boy or a girl. It could have been stillborn for all we know. That's what bothers me most. She's got all the cards and is manipulating me into doing what she wants." She looked over at Rich and caught the compassion in his eyes.

"You'll make the best decision, I'm sure."

She noticed for the first time the rectangular Christmas package he had set on the counter when he sat beside her. It was a little over a foot long and about eight inches wide and deep. Denise eyed the package for a moment, and then looked back at him.

"Yes, that's for you. But you have to wait until Christmas to open it."

"I sent yours over with Lily."

"I got it. I'm sure I'll love whatever you got me."

It was an Angel Moroni tie tack. Denise finally gave in and purchased the trinket when she couldn't find anything more appropriate for him. Besides, he didn't seem to have a tie tack, and his ties were always flopping around. Still, she was disappointed she hadn't been able to find the perfect thing, instead of just a filler gift. She looked at him again and suddenly wished he wasn't leaving in a couple minutes to start the long drive to California to visit his family.

"There is," he said after a brief pause, "one thing I want more than anything. One gift only you can give me."

"Yeah?" Denise felt her mouth go dry as he leaned closer. The protest she was trying to form halted when, like a whisper, he buzzed his lips over hers, then came back for more. Unable and unwilling to stop him, she allowed her eyes to close.

Denise leaned into the kiss, enjoying the sensation while it lasted. Her heart pounded and her hands grew shaky, but she let the gentle touch of his hands on her shoulders, and the softness of his lips run over her for a moment. Just a moment she promised herself. Being in his arms felt so right, and she had missed him, more than she wanted to admit.

When Rich pulled away, it took a moment for Denise to re-engage her mind. "Well," she said, unable to come up with more of a response. She pushed against his shoulders, and he backed off without hesitation.

"Merry Christmas," she said as she stood and went to the cupboard for a water glass.

"I'll have my cell phone if you want to talk. I'm never more than a phone call away," Rich said as she finished swallowing a full glass of water. "And we'll only be a few days. Neither Lily or I could get off work for long."

Denise snorted. "More like she couldn't stay away from John for more than a few days."

Rich's eyes flitted over her. "She's in love. Who can blame her?"

Feeling hot and knowing she was blushing, Denise looked away. She refilled her glass from the tap. "Love is fine and good, but the man hates me."

"He doesn't hate you—what are you talking about? He seems nice enough." Rich came around the counter and stood beside her.

"He's nice as can be if you only look at the veneer. John thinks I'm trash because I was in foster care. You should see the way he looked at me when Lily mentioned I was adopted. He puts on a good front of friendliness. If that's what a loving relationship is supposed to be like she can have it. He doesn't care if she's happy. Condescending, egotistical—" she didn't get a chance to finish her thought since Rich silenced her with another kiss.

"I'm crazy about you, Denise DeWalt. Have a great Christmas." Rich pressed his lips to her forehead, and then moved away. As he opened the door he called over his shoulder, "I'll talk to you in a few days."

Denise leaned against the counter wondering how she could resist wanting to be with him always, and why, if her feelings were so strong for Rich, was Curtis even a question in her mind?

Christmas phone conversations were awkward. Cliff called to talk to Paige when she and Denise were visiting their parents, and he passed the phone to Curtis so he could talk to Denise for a few minutes. Rich called from his parents' house. And there were emails from Pete's family, except from Olivia. From some comment Beth made about her sister, Denise got the impression that Olivia was struggling with the issue more than anyone else.

Jesse seemed curious about life in Provo since he planned to attend BYU the next fall. Beth peppered her email with questions, filling in around the edges with silly details about her holiday vacation and what she got for Christmas.

Denise was enjoying getting to know her biological siblings better, but something still felt wrong.

Her mind went to the paperwork she had popped in the mail on Christmas Eve. No doubt it wouldn't get looked at until after the new year, but having it out of her hands, unable to change her mind, made her tense. If there was one thing Denise hated, it was not being in control. Her nightmares hadn't stopped, but continued at least once a week, and it was really getting to her. Denise stayed at her own place at night except for Christmas Eve.

On Christmas Eve she stayed up late giggling with Gerald and Paige until they all crashed on the living room floor beneath the Christmas tree. Then the horrible images struck again.

Denise sat up, breathing hard, terror washing through her. She lifted her arms to protect herself. Then she heard Gerald's voice, "Hey, Denise, it's okay, it's just a dream."

When she lowered her arms and looked at him, she realized it was her brother, and that she was in the family room with colored lights blinking on the Christmas tree and piles of gifts tumbling underneath it. The run-down, moldy apartment of her dream, and its inhabitants, were far away.

"It's okay, everything's fine." His voice was barely more than a whisper, and he rubbed a hand up and down her arm, comforting and calming her.

Denise glanced around and saw Paige curled up in a ball beside her, still sleeping peacefully. "I'm fine, I'm fine." But she didn't feel fine. She felt shaky, her nerves were firing, and adrenalin was pumping through her. The clock above the television said it was only two in the morning.

"That must have been some nightmare." He pressed a hand to her cheek.

Denise tucked her feet beneath her and forced a smile. "Yeah. Some dreams seem very real."

"You want to talk about it?" His hand moved from her cheek to her shoulder.

"No, it was nothing."

"It wasn't nothing. Whatever it was, it was definitely something. It reminded me of when I was little, and you first came to live here."

Her eyes flashed to his face. How could he possibly remember? He couldn't have been more than three at the time. His eyes narrowed. "You still have that old nightmare, whatever it was?"

"How do you know about that?" She hugged her blanket close.

"My room was next to yours. You would cry out in your sleep. I heard you sometimes."

"I don't usually get them often, but they've been a bit more regular lately. They're more memories than dreams, really." She tried to pretend she wasn't worried about their frequency, but she could tell he didn't buy it.

Eventually she managed to settle down to sleep again.

Denise enjoyed the long Christmas day with her family, but was grateful to be back at her own apartment in the silence. She set an armload of gifts on the sofa. The few other items she had received for Christmas were still in the trunk of her car, but she figured they could stay there for now. The small Christmas tree she and Lily had decorated held court gaily on the corner table next to the sofa and, beneath it, the shiny gold packaging of Rich's gift winked at her.

Denise could have taken his gift to her parents' house to unwrap like she had Lily's, but whether it was a premonition, or more likely, the desire to prevent too many extra questions, she'd decided to leave it.

Now it sat taunting her, and she crossed the room to pick it up. The package was heavier than she expected and larger than she remembered. The wrapping job was far too perfect to have been done by a man.

She pulled off the card that read 'read me second,' and started to unwrap the gift. The box beneath the flashy paper was plain brown with only a company name and a part number stamped on the outside. Beneath that, two pieces of Styrofoam cradled the contents. When she pulled the packaging away, a porcelain statue of Christ on a wooden pedestal gleamed at her. His hands were outstretched and welcoming, the piercings in his hands evident, and on the base was a brass plaque.

Matt. 11:28–30

Come unto me, all ye that labor and are heavy laden, and I will give you rest. Take my yoke upon you, and learn of me; for I am meek and lowly in heart: and ye shall find rest unto your souls. For my yoke is easy, and my burden is light.

Tears formed in her eyes, and she reverently placed the statue on the table beside the Christmas tree. She picked up the card.

DENISE,

SOMETHING CALLED TO ME WHEN I SAW THIS, AND I KNEW YOU HAD TO HAVE IT. I PRAY THAT YOU CAN FIND REST. THE SAVIOR IS THE REASON FOR THE SEASON AND OUR ONLY HOPE FOR SALVATION. I WANT YOU TO KNOW THAT I HAVE A TESTIMONY OF THE GOSPEL AND THE ATONEMENT OF CHRIST. I LOVE YOU.

MERRY CHRISTMAS,

RICH

She laughed hollowly to herself. How like their relationship. She got him a tie tack, and he bought her a symbol—something with meaning to both of them. An utterly beautiful symbol. She was touched and felt even less deserving of the man who loved her. Catching sight of a candid picture of Lily and John that sat on the coffee table, Denise compared the relationships. Rich, like Lily, did all of the work, it seemed. He held the relationship together. He was their glue.

On the other hand, that was where the similarities ended. At least, Denise hoped they did. John seemed to expect Lily to change to fit his lifestyle. Denise would never do that to Rich. She thought he was great just the way he was.

A second thought came to mind, and she realized she expected too much, and maybe not nearly enough of him. His testimony warmed her, made her realize once again how much he loved her. Denise wasn't sure if he loved her enough for her to be completely straight with him. And did she love him enough to take that final step?

Denise stood inside the front door at Frandsen Computing four days later. She gripped her lunch box like a nervous first grader and took a deep breath before continuing around the corner to the front counter. The office manager, Keith, smiled as she came in and directed her to her new desk.

In no time at all, Denise was given her directions for the day and put to work. Used to having a work routine, Denise found herself floundering, trying to adjust to the new way things worked, the new pecking order, and the stress of working with all new clients. As the day progressed, she felt her tension increase.

When she left at six, Denise breathed a sigh of relief in the freezing air and hoped her stress headache would melt away with the pain medication she had swallowed. She missed a beat in her walk when she saw Rich wrapped in a dark green coat, leaning against her car in the lamp light.

"How was the first day at your new job?"

They hadn't seen each other since his kiss good-bye before Christmas. "Not bad. It'll take me a little while to adjust, but I'll manage." She stopped in front of him, less than a foot away, and tugged the collar of her coat tighter around her neck.

"Good." Rich reached out and cupped both her shoulders with his hands, pulled her close, and kissed her.

Denise trembled at his touch. She needed reassurance, a friendly face after her crazy day. "What are you doing here?"

"I thought maybe you could use a good meal and friendly conversation. I know I could. Care to join me?"

The thought flickered through Denise's mind that she shouldn't. She should break things off with him for good—and stick to it—but she needed him. "Follow me home so I can leave the car in our lot?"

"You bet."

Denise joined Rich in his car fifteen minutes later.

"Heard from your family?" Rich asked.

"Not much since Christmas, but I got an email from Kaylee today. She's anxious about a solos and ensembles piece she's preparing for a competition this spring."

"Yeah? I bet it'll be a real kick to hear her perform. I always liked the cello myself, it's got class."

"That's my main concern in life, you know. Class."

Rich smiled back as he heard the laughter in her words.

Dinner was casual and comfortable. The food was good, and the restaurant quieter than usual. Most of the college students were still home for the break, and the Christmas rush was over. Snow fell outside the windows of the restaurant, and Denise found herself teased into a light mood as they talked over their meals. Here there was no pressure or expectations.

Back at her front door, Rich leaned in and slid his mouth onto hers, making her brain switch off and her toes curl. He slipped his hands inside her coat, placed them on her hips and pulled her closer.

When Denise began to step back, he followed her and she found herself leaning back against the door, blocked in as his lips slid from hers and began to nibble up the length of her jaw. "You smell incredible—lilacs, and fresh snow, and Denise."

"Rich. That's enough." Denise was surprised she could think straight enough to say the words. The warm halo of romance slid around her, covering her mind and distracting her. But something leaped within her as he kissed her pulse point, and she pushed him away, a trickle of fear running through her when he didn't respond immediately. "Rich, that's enough."

The panic in her tone must have caught his attention, because he backed off but trained searching eyes on her face. "What's wrong?"

"I'm tired. I want to go inside." She turned and fumbled for her keys in her pocket.

Rich reached out and put a hand on her shoulder. His touch was firm, yet gentle, asking her to stop without demanding it. "Please, Denise, don't turn me away. What did I do?"

The longing in his voice stilled her hand on the knob and made her pause and consider what she owed him. The truth. When he walked away, she would at least know she had been fair with him. Besides, it was obvious nothing else would explain her stance on their relationship. And she seemed unable to stick to her own resolve to keep her distance. She turned the key in the lock, stepped inside, and gestured for him to join her.

Chapter Twenty-eight

She watched Rich remove his coat, put it on the hook next to her own, and then take a seat on the sofa. Denise began pacing. "There's nothing wrong with you, Rich. You haven't done anything wrong." She ran a hand through her hair and turned to look at him. The eight feet between them gave her strength. She needed distance to talk about this. "It's not your fault I can't—"

"Don't say that," Rich broke in, his voice thick with irritation. "I don't believe it. You talk as if you aren't capable of having a serious relationship. Like there's something missing in you. I can't see that."

Denise clenched her teeth and pushed away his words. "Living with Daphne was a nightmare most of the time. There were good days too. Days when she laughed and smiled, and we went out for ice cream. Days when the sun shone, and she was happily in love with her newest man. But most of the time, at least during the last couple years I lived with her, things weren't happy. The latest man never made her much happier than she had been before, and they didn't last long.

"When she was sober and alert, Daphne was a nice person. Mostly. She wasn't quick to anger, unless she was high or getting jittery for her next fix. She threw parties, though who paid for them I never knew. She never seemed to hold down a job for long. Ned said Daphne had always been a social butterfly. Plenty of friends and no problems spreading the joy around. The thing was—" Denise turned away now and swallowed hard, stealing herself for the unadulterated truth. Needing something else to focus on, she walked over to the counter and ran a finger around the edge of a striped plate Lily had left on the counter.

"When she was angry, I spent a lot of time in my room. A lot of time. I missed a lot of school or I showed up late, and for the last year or so, I seldom had much clean to wear. Daphne's fists flew when she got angry. If her fists didn't connect, if I moved away, the beating got worse." She fought the images that came to mind, the smells and tastes of her former life that she couldn't forget, no matter how much she wanted to. Her fear was almost tangible, and at the same time, she wanted to hit the image she held of Daphne, to strike back for all the pain she had lived through. "Soon I stopped trying. The safest thing for me was to hide in my room and hope she forgot I existed until she woke in the morning."

She didn't hear Rich stand and walk over, but he touched her shoulder, his fingers light as they trailed down her arms to her elbows, and back up again. "I'm so sorry about all of that, Denise. I hate that she did that to you. But it's been nearly two decades. Don't you think it's time for you to put it behind you?"

Denise shook her head. "You don't understand. I've dealt with most of that, or I thought I had. But you want me to be something for you, Rich. You want a wife and children, and part of the reason that I can't be a part of that, is where I came from. It's not you. I haven't even considered marriage in years, never wanted it the way I do now, not really. Yeah, there was a time when I dated someone a few years back that I thought about it, wondered if it was possible, but I had my doubts, worried how I would make it work. You're the first one to really make me question my conviction that I would never marry."

He seemed to take that as an affirmation of his hopes and slipped his arms around her waist.

She lifted her arms in protest. "No. Don't. Please don't. Please sit back at the couch. I'm not done."

He pulled his arms away and moved back across the room. "Are you afraid you'll turn into your mother? I'm telling you, you couldn't."

"I thought for a while I might, but I know better now." She pushed away the recurring nightmares and got back to the main subject. "There's more than that, much more. If only the bruises had been the biggest problem." Tears pooled in her eyes and fell onto the counter, her throat closed up, and she wondered how she would tell him. How could he ever understand? "The men, her boyfriends. She wasn't always around and when she left," Denise took a shaky breath, trying to put those horrors into words.

"she left me alone with them a lot." She couldn't go on, her throat closed up again; the words wouldn't come.

There was a long strained silence before he spoke, as she couldn't get a sound around the lump in her throat. "Are you saying you were sexually abused?" His voice was soft and strained.

Her heart constricted. She was grateful he'd found the words first; it was easier not to say it out loud. Denise nodded as the knot in her throat loosened. "She had a few friends who watched me sometimes, or they would come party and wait until she passed out. I told Daphne once but she didn't believe me. She beat me for even suggesting it. That wasn't the last time it happened, but we never talked about it again. Pretending it didn't happen was easier for her than facing the fact that she was failing. She was always trying to convince herself that she was doing fine, that there was nothing wrong."

"She knew and she just let that happen to you. Let them . . ." His voice was angry now and she heard him stalking back and forth across the room, muttering things she never thought to hear from him.

She didn't turn around to face him. She couldn't look him in the eye now. Not now that he knew the truth. In her head she knew it wasn't her fault. She was a victim. She had been told so dozens of times, but she couldn't quite get her heart to believe it. Her shame was thick and heavy. After a long minute, she heard him walk up behind her, saw his hand rest on the counter beside her own, but he did not touch her. She wasn't sure if she was disappointed he kept his hands to himself or grateful. Denise longed to be held, for him to make it all better, to be told it didn't matter. But it did matter to him. She knew it would.

"Denise, I—"

"Don't try and find some nice platitude to smooth things over. Don't try and empathize. I've heard it all. I've had therapy, talked about it in embarrassing detail, kept journals that I promptly burned so no one would find them. I've gotten through things enough to be held, to allow a few kisses, but I don't know if I'll ever be able to let go enough to have a normal marriage. That's part of me that I can't get rid of, no matter how hard I try. Those memories won't stop haunting me. And searching for my family has healed something inside me, but it has also torn this wound again, making it all seem like it happened yesterday. Those images are fresher than ever. They haunt me every step of the way."

She felt him touch her hair, running his fingers down her head. He rested his left hand on her shoulder. "I wish there was something I could say, something I could do. But I don't believe the Lord wants us to stay apart forever. He brought us together for a reason. You're part of me now, Denise. I love you."

She wanted desperately to believe him, but she couldn't. "I don't see it happening. You've been good for me. You've helped me through rough patches, and I hope you'll continue to help me, to be my friend. But I can't promise you more. Please try to understand. I do love you, and I do want to be with you. But I can't."

Silence circled around them. He didn't make any other attempts to touch her, except to squeeze her shoulder a few times—a symbol of his support, but it wasn't enough. Not nearly.

Finally, Rich moved away. When Denise caught his eye for the first time in fifteen minutes, she could see he had been crying. "Please understand, you're the best man I've ever known. I wish things could be different."

His lips moved as though he were trying to say something. After a moment, he turned and pulled his coat from the hook. "I'm down the hall if you need me. Please call me anytime."

"Thank you."

She was left staring at the door after he closed it between them. Feeling the finality of his exit, her heart broke. Then, feeling restless, she turned on her CD player and drowned out her reeling emotions to the heavy chords of her favorite ballads.

With nothing else to do, she got out an old tooth-brush and attacked the shower grout.

The next twenty-four hours were unbearable. Finding himself unable to sleep, Rich took a page out of Denise's book and spent a few hours scrubbing down his apartment. To his disappointment, while it wore him out, it didn't help him think any clearer or feel any more in control. He finally slept a few hours before his alarm reminded him of the coming day.

Work was a welcome respite from Rich's inner turmoil the next day, though his talk with Denise kept intruding as he moved through the motions. He was grateful when the clock said it was time to leave.

Back in his own apartment, Rich began pacing and reliving the conversation. He didn't know what to do with the revelations Denise had hit him with. Sure, it had crossed his mind that something like sexual abuse could be part of the problem, but he figured when she got around to talking about it, they could work it out. Now it sounded as though she almost didn't want to work it out.

Her reason for thinking they didn't have a future wasn't something he could just brush aside or fix and put away. It would be between them for as long as she couldn't let it go. How did he accept this?

He needed to talk to someone. Anyone. But who? She would hate him for discussing her problems with someone. Rich sent up a desperate prayer and immediately received an answer. A surprising answer, but somehow right.

Desperate, he fumbled with the phone book, hoping it wouldn't take long to find the right number. Finding only one listing under DeWalt, he picked up the phone and began to dial.

While the phone rang, Rich tried to figure out what he would say. How did one bring up the conversation? And would Lynn even want to talk to Rich about it? It wasn't like Lynn DeWalt had ever met him. He hadn't thought it through very carefully first, maybe—

"Hello," a male voice answered.

Too late. "Hello, is this Lynn?"

"No. Hold on a minute."

Rich realized it must be Gerald as he heard him call for his dad. Rich's palms grew sweaty, and he rubbed them on his pants while he waited.

"Hello, this is Lynn."

"Hello, this is Richard Jensen. I'm . . . a friend of Denise's."

"Denise? What can I do for you Richard?"

Rich heard Gerald in the background, saying something and Lynn came back on the line. "Ah, that Richard. Sorry. Is everything all right?"

"No and yes. Look, I know this is strange, but I need to talk to you. Would you be able to spare me some time tonight? I can come there, or you can come here. Whatever works for you. I don't know who else to talk to."

"Sure. Gerald says you live in her building, right? What apartment?"

That was easier than I expected, Rich thought when he hung up a couple minutes later. *Now, how to broach the subject?* Denise said her parents knew her whole history, but he didn't know how many details Lynn had. Rich hoped all that training Denise said her parents had taken had paid off.

The ten minutes he waited for Lynn to show up seemed to take forever. Given enough time, Rich was starting to wonder again if he had been rash. Should he have waited, kept it to himself? No, he needed to talk. Lynn DeWalt would understand.

The doorbell jolted Rich from his thoughts, and he walked across the room to answer the door. Standing on the other side was a man who looked much like Gerald, only a little fuller around the middle and with graying hair. "Hello, sir. Thanks for coming over on such short notice. I appreciate it. I'm Rich."

Lynn smiled and took Rich's hand in a firm shake, returning his greeting. He came in and took the seat Rich motioned to on the sofa. "Now, what's this all about? You sounded pretty upset over the phone."

Rich forced himself to sit and face Lynn. He sat for a moment, his hands opening and closing as he tried to form sentences. "This must be strange for you, I know we've never met, but Denise talks about you and your wife all the time."

"I understand you've been helping her a little as she searched for her birth family," Lynn said with an easy smile that belied the curiosity in his eyes. "And that there's something a little more than friendship going on between you."

Rich forced himself to look the man in the eye. "I love your daughter. I want to marry her, if she'll ever have me."

Lynn lifted an eyebrow. "So it is serious. What do you mean, if she'll ever have you? Have you asked her already?"

"Not exactly. But she knows I want to. She's having a bit of difficulty with the idea, apparently. Not, I don't think, because she doesn't want to be with me. She told me she loves me, but she seems to be struggling with her past a lot. In fact, last night she told me not only what her mother did to her but what her mother . . . didn't protect her from. The men." The words left a nasty taste in his mouth. Lynn's face grew serious, and he nodded encouragingly but said nothing.

"I can accept and deal with her past, but she doesn't seem to be able to get beyond it. I hate that her mother, the woman who was supposed to protect her, not only hurt Denise, but also did nothing while others violated her." He paused, realizing that he had gotten ahead of himself. And that he was on the verge of tears again. He didn't cry easily, but it was tearing him apart.

"That's okay, keep going." Lynn seemed to recognize what was going on with Rich, how upset he was. "It was horrific. I can't even imagine how it must have been for her. It made me sick when I first found out. We were reading her file, trying to decide whether to take her from the home she was already staying in. I hadn't met her yet, hadn't had a chance to love her, and it made me sick then. I can imagine how it must feel for you to learn now. And she must trust you a great deal if she told you about it." He laid a comforting hand on Rich's arm. "I doubt she's told anyone else, even Lily. Paige and Gerald don't know, as far as I'm aware. Not that part, anyway. You should feel honored she trusted you that much."

"I do. I understand so much more now," Rich said. "But I don't know how to accept that this is it for us. She refuses to accept our relationship could go further. She's so tied up in knots about what happened fifteen, twenty years ago that she can't focus on now, on her future. On our future." He met the other man's gaze again. "Mr. DeWalt, I love her, and I don't know what to do to help her through this."

"Please call me Lynn. I'm glad to hear that you love her, and you want to marry her. Thanks for being there for her when she needed a shoulder to cry on. Denise wasn't always easy to love."

"She doesn't trust herself or others," Rich corrected him.

Lynn smiled. "I know. Even at eleven years old, she was a spitfire. She needed love and support, but she didn't accept it easily. I've seen a change in her over the past few months. She's stronger than she was before she started the search for her family. More sure of herself in many ways, but she's more vulnerable too." He rubbed his hands together, staring down at them, and then met Rich's gaze. "You know, in our foster classes we were taught that grief and healing were like onions. You have to do it in layers. She's done a lot of healing the past few months, and she's ripped through the membrane in a few places, making things harder in many ways. Her pain is fresh in some spots, but I'm sure, given time, she'll be able to get through this layer to the next one.

"I have to warn you, though, we never know how many layers there are. She may work through this enough to marry you. You may have a good life, but somewhere down the road she could trip and accidentally start ripping that next layer. It could be at the mall, at church, five months or twenty years from now. She may be lying in bed and overhear something on the news that will start the next layer of healing. It could be quick and nearly painless, or it could be worse than this time. When someone's been hurt that deeply, you never know."

"So you're saying it's hopeless, that it will come up again, and we'll never be free from it?" Rich sent Lynn a bleak look. "That's not the encouragement I was hoping for."

Lynn laughed softly and shook his head. "That's not quite what I meant. I'm saying it won't be easy all of the time. Triggers happen, and she could relapse. But if you're good to her, if you trust her and she trusts you, and if you work together, a relapse won't have to be like this time. Next time, if there is one, it could be a minor irritation that goes away in a day or two. I just want you to realize that life with Denise, though worth it, won't always be easy. You'll have to accept her for everything she is up front. Because if you hurt her, it will take three times the work to put it back to right than any other woman would need."

"I don't ever want to hurt her, sir."

"Lynn," he corrected.

"Lynn."

He nodded. "Good, she's been hurt enough."

CHAPTER TWENTY-NINE

The next few days passed with little more than email contact between Denise and Rich. She avoided Lily and the apartment as much as possible, avoided her parents' house when she and Gerald hung out, occasionally worked out with Cliff who was back in town for basketball practices, and otherwise hid in her room with movies. She didn't feel like dealing with anyone. If the phone rang or someone knocked at the door, she didn't answer it unless she was expecting someone. Curtis left a message on her home machine. She added his number to her list by the phone but didn't return the call. She didn't know what to think about him any more than she knew what to think about Rich.

Thursday was New Year's Day. She had gotten a message from Rich Wednesday night, saying he wanted to see her. Instead, she watched movies with Gerald at her parents' house. She stayed the night on the living room sofa and woke in the morning to the smell of bacon frying.

"Up and at 'em, sleepy head," Jennette said as she gave her daughter a nudge. Tiny dog paws walked up Denise's back, adding to her mother's insistence. "Everyone's up except for you. You know the Werners are going to be here with Paige and Cliff to plan the wedding in a couple hours. Martha said she was going to try and drag Curtis with her."

"Go away and leave me alone. Maybe next week. Thanks," Denise mumbled, though earlier she had been looking forward to talking with everyone that day.

"No way. You stay up late, you pay for it in this house, like you always did. Besides, it's after nine, and we have things to do. Are you going to get up for breakfast, or am I supposed to let your brother eat it all?"

Denise buried her face in the pillow a little more, but made herself start stretching her limbs out. "Fine, I'll be right there. Don't let him hog all the orange juice."

She heard Jennette's footsteps as her mom left the room, and Denise pulled her face out of her pillow and nudged the dog from her back. She was usually a morning person, but she had been up far too late the previous night.

She leaned over and gave Cookie a back rub in greeting. Then she brushed her hair back from her face. A minute or two later, Denise wandered into the kitchen where Lynn and Gerald sat working their way through a stack of pancakes. "Morning."

"Good morning, Sunshine. Feeling any better?" Lynn asked.

"Sure, Dad, staying up late playing board games with the kid here makes for a great morning. Did you save me some orange juice?"

"We know how you are about your juice," Lynn said.

Gerald nudged the pitcher a little closer to her, and Denise grabbed a glass, filling it almost to the top.

"Rich called to check up on you already. He didn't hear from you last night and was worried." Gerald sent her a knowing grin.

Denise set the bacon on her plate and glanced over at her dad and then looked back at Gerald. Her eyes narrowed as his words connected. "Rich called *here*?"

"Second time this week. I'm telling you, that man's worried about you, no matter what you say." Gerald took another helping of pancakes.

That got her attention. "What? The second time? When was the first?"

Gerald looked over at Lynn, oblivious to the way his father's eyes had grown wary. "Was it Monday night?"

Lynn avoided both their eyes and concentrated on his pancakes. "Yeah, Monday."

Denise wondered why he would have called. "Wait, why did he call Monday night?" The sinking sensation in her stomach did not bode well.

Gerald shrugged. "He asked for Dad."

Lynn looked her in the eye this time, setting his silverware down on his plate. "You want to talk about this here?"

It only took Denise a moment to realize she didn't, not in front of Gerald. "No. Let's go to your office."

A faint smile appeared on Lynn's face. His office had always been the place he took the foster kids when they were discussing actions and consequences. Denise could tell from the look on his face that he hadn't missed the reminder.

As soon as he was in the room, she shut the door behind them. She leaned back against it, not sure if she was angry, irritated, worried, sad, or something entirely different. So many emotions raged in her that she couldn't pick them out. "What's going on?"

"You dumped a lot on the poor guy and then kicked him out. He needed to talk to someone who already knew your history. He called me."

"Wait, hold on. First, I didn't kick him out; he practically ran at the first opportunity. Second, he just picked up the phone for a long chat with my dad? A guy he'd never met? How could he do that? And you talked to him about it? Especially—" She gestured with her hands to indicate her frustration.

Lynn sat on the edge of the desk and folded his arms across his chest. "Actually, I went to his apartment, and we had a long chat there. It wasn't the kind of thing you talk about over the phone. I'm impressed with him. He really cares about you and seems to have his head on straight."

Lynn's straightforward gaze unnerved Denise, and she wondered if she were still asleep. She couldn't be having this conversation. Things like this didn't happen to her. "You actually discussed my . . . history with him?"

Rubbing his forehead, Lynn stood and pulled Denise into his arms. She stood stiff for a moment before accepting the hug. This is what she had needed from Rich and instead he had walked out. This thought had her hugging back. "No, *you* discussed your history with him, I just helped him work through his feelings about that. Denise, he had no one else to talk to. Your mom and I have worried about you lately. You've been so preoccupied with this family search. She mentioned you were interested in someone months ago, but I hadn't heard anything since."

"It's humiliating, having people talk about that. Knowing anyone else even knows about it. I hate that I had to share it with him, but I had to so he would know what he was asking for. I know it disgusted him. He could barely stand to touch me after I told him. Once again, my past catches up with me, and the guy is scared away. Only it never mattered so much before."

Lynn leaned back and looked her in the face, his brow furrowed in confusion. "Scared away? You thought he was scared away? Honey, before I left, he asked permission to marry you—if he could ever convince you to accept, that is."

"He asked you what?" She stood dumbfounded for a moment. Rich had left her needing to be held. Then he had called another man to talk instead of calling her. And asked *him* for permission to marry her. The only emotion she could lock down of the dozens shooting through her was anger. It was also the easiest of the emotions to deal with at the time, so she seized it.

Her father must have seen the look in her eyes because he stood and pressed a kiss to her forehead. "It was the only thing he could do, under the circumstances. I'm running late for my meeting, but you ought to have a chat with your young man." After giving her shoulders a squeeze, he turned and left the room, leaving her standing in shock and anger.

Denise walked to her room to gather her bathroom items and a clean set of clothes. She couldn't believe Rich had called her father. How could he think that was fine? *How could Dad talk to Rich about it? But I told Rich; he did know, and I do appreciate Rich not discussing it with a new person, if he had to talk about it.*

She set the shampoo she preferred on the edge of the tub. *He should have asked me first, shouldn't he? He hadn't met my parents. How could he call like that? And what was this about asking Dad's permission? Yeah, he mentioned he wanted to marry me, but he never asked me.* Flipping on the hot and cold water, she adjusted them to the right temperature, then continued her inner rant. *I even told him I couldn't marry him, but here he was, blithely making plans for our life together without discussing it with me. And if he asked permission to marry me, does that mean my past doesn't bother him all that much? Why didn't he tell me instead of Dad?*

Denise hadn't come up with an answer by the time her shower was over, but she'd pushed it far enough back in her mind to function again. She decided to finish the breakfast she had left. It could be a long day otherwise. And the last thing she wanted to do was spend her day obsessing about her father's discussion with Rich.

When she returned to the dining room, the table was still piled with food. Her half-finished glass of juice sat in front of her plate, bacon lay cold on the edge, and a plate of pancakes stood nearby. Her heart hurt as she ate the food without tasting it. Things seemed so mixed up. She didn't know what to think anymore.

After she finished eating, Denise carried the dishes into the kitchen and put the leftover food away, cleaning up and loading the dishwasher. Jennette came in to help at the end, and then she began preparing food for the guests that afternoon.

"You know," Jennette said after a long silence. "Rich needed someone to talk to. Someone who would understand how devastated he was, how devastated you were. He picked the right person to talk to, under the circumstances. And it couldn't have been easy for him to call and talk to your dad when they'd never even met before."

"Yeah, I know. I just don't know how I feel about it yet. My head and my heart haven't been able to agree when it comes to Rich. I'm not ready to deal with it." Most of her anger had burned off, but confusion still seethed under the surface.

"Well, if you need a distraction," Jennette gave her a wry grin, "Curtis will be here this afternoon. I just got word from Martha."

Denise smiled despite herself. "Just what I need, more confusion. Whoever invented guys, anyway?"

"I thought you two got along great at the party."

"Fabulously. So well I hardly know what to do about it. My confusion about Rich went through the roof after I met Curtis. If my feelings for Rich are real, how could I have feelings for anyone else?"

Jennette threw back her head and laughed. "I shouldn't laugh at you, but I bet you never thought the day would come when you had two guys after you." She patted Denise on the shoulder. "Don't worry, honey, it'll all sort out in the end. Now, I know you've scrubbed the house to near sterility, but there are a few things left to prepare for this afternoon."

Denise stuck out her tongue at her mom and then pitched in.

It was almost one in the afternoon when the doorbell rang. Cliff and Paige had arrived half an hour earlier and sat snuggled on the living room sofa. Denise walked by them and to the front door.

"Welcome, it's good to see you," Denise greeted Cliff's family. She was surprised when Curtis set a hand on her shoulder and gave it a friendly squeeze, like he didn't quite dare give her a hug, but a handshake wasn't personal enough. "I heard rumors you might come down."

"Yeah, somehow I managed to be game-free today and hoped you might be up to showing me around your turf, if you don't have anything else going on. Everyone else will be totally wrapped up in wedding plans." He rolled his eyes.

"My only plan is a friendly game with your brother and his pals later. He said you were up for it too."

Curtis smiled and followed her into the kitchen.

After ten minutes, the food was on the table. The first order of business for the afternoon was to fill their stomachs. Paige was happier than Denise had ever seen her, Cliff and Curtis laughed and exchanged friendly insults at every turn, and Denise found herself feeling more part of a family than ever before.

After lunch, Curtis agreed to go with Denise to her apartment for a while. They made plans to meet up with Cliff at the gym in two hours to practice with some of his friends.

"Wow, quite the labyrinth you've got here," Curtis said as they made their way through the hallway to her apartment.

"Yeah, the building's a little crazy, but the apartments are really decent." Denise glanced at Rich's door as they passed it but didn't stop. Considering the way she felt right now, she hoped she wouldn't run into him, especially not with Curtis at her side. She pulled out her key and let them into her own apartment, wondering what Curtis would think of it.

"Pretty nice. Homey too, a lot more than I expected." He ran a finger over a floral arrangement on the wall.

Denise picked up a note by the phone that said for her to call Rich and stuck it in her pocket. "That's my roommate's. I like it though. Someday I might break down and buy a few homey decorations for myself. Lily works graveyards at a toy store, and I know she worked last night so she's probably asleep." Denise showed him her room and was glad, once again, for her almost obsessive need to keep the place neat.

"Do you actually live here, or is this a front? I've never seen a room so clean," Curtis teased her from where he stood in the doorway.

"I've always been a bit of a neat freak." She reached under the bed for a large plastic container that held most of her CDs.

"Wow, what's this you listen to? Led Zepplin, AC/DC? I love this."

"Don't forget the Beatles, my church music, and other stuff."

"Yeah, but you expect that kind of thing. You like this?" Curtis looked impressed.

"It's my mood music. When I get worked up, it brings me back down to level. I always used to listen to it before a game. It kept my blood pumping without letting me get too shaky. My mom hates it."

"So does mine." They shared a grin. "Queensryche is my favorite before a game."

"I've got that in the car." Denise was surprised to realize how much she had in common with Curtis. Granted, she listened to the hard stuff selectively; she copied off a few favorites from each CD and never listened to the rest, knowing no matter how much she liked it, most of it wasn't going to promote the spirit she wanted, even if it sometimes helped her mood. They moved to the living room and sat on the sofa. He flipped through a scrapbook of her basketball days, and they discussed their war stories while the Beatles played low in the background.

The hour and a half they spent flipping through pictures and talking about important events in each of their lives was strange and comfortable for Denise. When she looked up to find Lily standing in her doorway, watching them talk about basketball tournaments, she saw that her roommate was glancing uncertainly between them. Lily still wore the pajama pants and oversized T-shirt she usually slept in, and her hair was in mild disarray, though she ran her fingers through it to smooth it out when Denise met her gaze.

"Hey, who's this?" Lily asked, her voice bright, a little too bright to be genuine.

"Curtis, Cliff's little brother." Denise grinned teasingly. She remembered Lily had never met Cliff. "And this is my roommate, Lily."

"Hi, I'm the older twin," Curtis corrected Denise, turning back to her. "You know I'm going to have to whip you on the court for that comment."

"Promises, promises. That extra eight inches you've got probably won't hurt," Denise pointed out.

"Height is secondary to skill, babe."

Denise rolled her eyes and looked back at Lily. "He's a prince among men. We're going to have to leave soon if we want to catch up with the guys at the gym. Did we wake you?"

"No, you're fine. I've been asleep since seven. Going back to school is going to kill me." She smiled despite her claim.

"Student teaching is a necessary evil and a good exercise," Denise said. She caught Lily sticking her tongue out at having her words thrown back at her.

"Yeah, I know. Denise said you're studying landscape architecture at Utah State," Lily said, turning to Curtis.

"Yeah, it's a good school. Are you going to the Y?"

"UVU."

Denise glanced at the clock and noticed the time again. "We're going to have to go, Curt. Cliff will be waiting for us."

Curtis shrugged apologetically at Lily. "It was good meeting you, anyway."

"You too." Lily disappeared back into her room. Denise and Curtis put away the scrapbooks before heading off to the gym.

CHAPTER THIRTY

"Your roommate seems nice," Curtis said as they took the stairs down to Denise's car. "She's really cute."

"Yeah, she's my best friend. She's helped me through some crazy times this past year, while I've been searching for family." *She and her cousin.* "She's getting married in May."

"Hmm." He pursed his lips for a moment and glanced over at her. "Cliff was always my best friend. I know it sounds cliché to say so, but it's true. He's the only one who had the same genetics as me. He'd been through all the same things, understood me almost better than I understood myself sometimes. He was also my fiercest competition. We would have driven each other crazy if we played on the same college team. We both got offers at several schools."

"So humble." Denise unlocked the car doors and slid into her side. "Did you each go where you wanted to or would you have rather come here, but didn't because he was?"

"I always liked Logan. It was my main goal from elementary school. Cliff was never so sure about it. I think we both ended up where we were supposed to be. Did you like it at the U?"

"Yeah, it was good for me. I needed a little space from home for a few years, I think. But not too far to come home when I needed to. I was still trying to figure out who I was, what I was doing, dealing with the past and future. By the time I graduated, I'd settled down a lot. I bet your mission helped with that." She glanced over as they pulled onto the road.

"Some, but I always felt pretty centered, pretty sure of myself. My parents are responsible for a lot of it. I knew if I wanted to search my background, they would support me, and if I didn't, they wouldn't push it. I always knew who I was, as much of where I came from as Mom could tell me, though I have the feeling she may not have gotten the full story." He fingered the zipper pull on his coat. "I've had few insecurities about who I am. Mostly they've been about having my own identity, being part of Cliff-and-Curtis instead of just being Curtis. But even that hasn't been so bad."

"I almost envy that. I always got along great with Gerald, but he's almost eight years younger than I am. That's a big difference. Paige and I never got on that much, not until recently. I think when I first came along, she didn't think of me as anything more than one of those kids who come and go all the time."

Denise flipped her blinker light and switched lanes, surprised they were both being so forthcoming, but grateful she felt so comfortable with him. "When her parents decided to keep me, she resented me, thinking I was trying to take over her family. It wasn't until recently I found out she hated the distance between us as much as I did, that she felt like I didn't want her in my life. That was a revelation."

"You seem comfortable at home." His response was surprise.

"Yeah, it took a long time to grow into that. I didn't make things easy on my parents the first few years I lived with them. It was bad enough they got me for the rough teenage years without having all of the garbage left over from Daphne and switching homes to add to it all." Denise paused and waited for a break in traffic to turn left into the parking lot of her gym. "My birth mom was a real peach. I'm glad you and Cliff didn't have to go through that."

Curtis didn't talk as she found a parking spot and pulled in. They both got out of the car, and he met her on her side. "You turned out pretty all right anyway."

"You too." Denise punched him on the arm. "Rat nose."

"Egg head."

"Frog face."

"Hey, that's my insult, you can't have it."

Denise nudged him with her elbow as he opened the door and let her in.

"Watch those pointy objects, will you?" he said as he rubbed his side, though she hadn't nudged him that hard.

The redhead behind the counter greeted them as they came in and she gave Curtis a confused look when he pulled out his wallet. "But you have a membership, don't you?"

"No, I have the membership, this joker is just down to visit," Cliff said from behind them.

"Wow, two of you." The girl looked at Denise and lifted an eyebrow. "How did you ever get to hang with double-trouble here?" Her voice was a little flirty; her smile when she looked back at Curtis was a lot flirty.

"Family connection." Denise smiled and headed to the dressing room with her gym bag.

When she came out again, Cliff and Curtis had both changed into some clothes Cliff brought with him and were warming up on one end of the court with Rooke and the others.

"Hey there, gorgeous. Ready to go out with me yet, or is that guy still keeping you to himself?" Rooke threw an arm over her shoulder.

Denise smiled but held back the laugh that bubbled up at the thought of dating someone who barely looked old enough to be out of high school. "He's a tyrant, man. But I'll let you know if I can ever sneak away. You're just so adorable." She patted him on the head, though it was a long reach, and held back a smirk when he winced at her choice of words. "You know, I have a sister not much younger than you."

Rooke put on a wounded look, and Denise shook her head.

"Come on, we've got a practice to get to," Cliff said, tossing a ball at Denise.

She grabbed it, slipped from under Rooke's arm, and ran for a lay-up.

They played around for a few minutes, warming their muscles, stretching and getting ready for a little three-on-three. Denise ended up on the team with the twins with the other three guys playing against them. Though the teams were well matched, Denise's team pulled steadily ahead throughout both games, reaching fifteen with the other guys trailing a few points behind.

"Twelve-fifteen. Man, I don't think I want to play you guys again," Rooke said, wiping his forehead with his arm.

Curtis plopped an arm on Denise's shoulder and grinned down at her. "Half-pint here packs a punch."

"I've experienced worse," a familiar voice said.

Denise turned to see Rich standing nearby, his hair wet from a shower and a gym bag in his hand. He looked as though he had been there for hours, though she didn't remember seeing him until now.

"You're pathetic at this sport. Don't try and make excuses." Usually Denise would have smirked as she said that, but she had been avoiding him for days, and it was hard to smirk through her discomfort. The fact that Curtis was holding her close added to the awkwardness.

"No excuse, I'm a lot faster on a keyboard than the court." His response was a lot more casual than hers, but still a little stiff as his eyes drifted toward her companion.

"Not to rush this, but we need to be heading out. Our moms are going to be wondering what happened to us. I hope we're done talking flowers and cakes and stuff," Cliff said. "The two hours we talked about it lasted for days."

The other guys lifted a hand and waved them away. Denise turned to Curtis. "Hey, why don't you go home with Cliff? I'll catch up with you guys back at my parents' house."

Curtis took a long look at Rich and then glanced back at her. "You're sure?"

Denise nodded. "Yeah," though she wasn't sure at all. She fell into step with Rich.

CHAPTER THIRTY-ONE

"You didn't call me back last night," Rich said when they were alone. His voice was strained, and she avoided his gaze.

"I didn't get your note until this afternoon, and then I had Curtis with me."

"Have a hot date last night?"

"Yeah, with Gerald. We sat up and watched movies, played board games. We fell asleep in the living room. It's been crazy today too, with Cliff's parents and Curtis coming down to coordinate wedding plans. Not that Curtis has gotten sucked into that. We've been hanging out." She grabbed her gym bag and slung it over her shoulder but didn't look at Rich.

They headed outside before he continued the conversation. "Are you mad about something, or is this just guilt because you're dating someone else on the side?"

Denise thought of her reaction this morning when she found out about Rich calling her dad and the memory of him walking away Monday night. "Irritated and confused, yes. A lot of confused, but we'll have to get to that later. I'm expected at home now."

He stopped her with a touch on her arm. "If you're upset with me about something, maybe we ought to talk about it now."

She met his eye for the first time that day. "I don't have time for it now, and I have no idea what to think anyway. I have plans with my family."

"And your date?"

She looked away again, and then back at his eyes. "It's not a date, exactly." She knew the line between a date and what she had been doing all afternoon was a fine one. Needing to be honest, she pushed on. "I feel so comfortable with him. It's confusing and . . . I really have to go." If she stayed any longer she was going to start crying, she knew it.

Rich pursed his lips and shook his head. "Nothing I do can make me more than a distant second to your fears." He ran a hand through his hair. "I want to be with you, but it has to come from you now. I can't keep working on this relationship if you aren't willing to give something back, Denise. Figure out what you want from me, from him, and from yourself. I'm still willing to wait and see what happens, to give you time to work through your fears, but only if you're willing to try and work things out. The ball's in your court. Come find me when you make up your mind."

He turned away, and then flipped back around and took a hold of her shoulder. "Just remember this while you're discussing cakes and flowers at your parents' house." He pulled her close and kissed her. What should have been angry, if his demeanor was any indication, turned out to be sweet, gentle. His grip on her shoulder softened until she leaned in on her own, pulled in by the love his kiss conveyed. When he pulled away, he settled his forehead on her own and whispered, "I love you, and nothing we discussed the other night can change that." Rich pushed himself away and turned toward his own car, leaving Denise with her head reeling.

When she got a handle on herself, she made her way across the snowy parking lot. Had that just happened? All this time she had been pushing him away, and he finally accepted it? Would that be the end? It wasn't as if she hadn't expected him to break up with her. Except his last words echoed in her head. Her revelation the other night hadn't changed his feelings. She remembered her father saying Rich had essentially asked her father for permission to marry her. So maybe he wasn't like the others— maybe he would stick no matter what. But then why was he letting her go now if he wasn't bothered by her past?

At least she would have a few minutes to get back under control before appearing at her parents' house, she thought as she wiped tears from her face. She'd hurt Rich, though his last actions hadn't seemed exactly hurt. Curtis was obviously confused about what was going on with her and Rich too. Could she say she'd been honest with either of them? But she wasn't dating Curtis—she was just spending an afternoon with him.

When she pulled up in front of her parents' house more than half an hour later, she still wasn't feeling calm. She came in the front door to find Curtis in the front room, leaning against the wall, looking at her. His eyes were wary, and Denise wondered what he was thinking.

"We wondered what happened to you," he said. "Cliff said you've been seeing that guy on and off, but you didn't look too happy to see him today."

"Sorry, I stopped at my place to clean up before heading back here. It took longer than usual. How's dinner coming?" She put on a falsely bright smile, still not sure what she was feeling.

"Not too far away. Are you and that guy dating seriously?" Curtis pushed the hair back from her eyes and tucked it behind her ear.

Rich was one subject she was sure she didn't want to get into right now, but they were on it, and she really did owe it to Curtis before things went any further. "I'm . . . we're . . . Yes and no. Okay, yes, I guess."

His brows lifted over his dark blue eyes. "What do you mean, you guess? Why didn't you say you were seeing someone?"

She met his gaze and tried to form complete sentences. "I . . . We broke up, but we're, I don't know. I'm so confused. We've talked about marriage, but I don't know what to think anymore. There's so much baggage." She slumped back against the wall.

"Do you love him?"

She could see the pulse jumping on his forehead and the way he clenched his jaw, waiting for her answer. "Yeah, I do."

"Does he treat you good? Is he a worthy priesthood holder?" His blue eyes flashed as he bit off the words.

"Yeah, he's worthy and he treats me very well. He's put up with a lot of indecision from me lately. More than he should have to deal with." She felt the tears resurfacing but pushed them back. "I'm sorry if I misled you somehow."

His face softened, and he lifted an eyebrow. "So if he's so great, and you love him, why did you spend the afternoon with me instead of with him?"

She tipped her head back against the wall and stared at the ceiling. "There's just so much baggage. I wonder sometimes if I'm ever going to break free. Where does it end? Where do I begin? I don't think I can trust my feelings." She looked back at him, met his gaze.

Curtis reached out and wiped away a tear from her cheek, seeming to understand what she wasn't saying. "I felt it too, at the party. We just clicked."

She let out a low laugh, devoid of mirth. "Too bad you're a twin."

"Why's that?"

"I've heard of adoptees having an instant connection with birth siblings, from the first time they meet. But I'm just looking for a brother or sister, not a set of twins. You'd even be about the right age. I think."

Curtis leaned against the opposite wall in the hall, a couple feet between them as they faced off. He shrugged like an embarrassed, little boy. "You're pretty cool, for a girl. If I had to have a bio sister, I guess I could do worse."

Relieved to have come to some kind of understanding, she grinned back at him. "You're a pretty good basketball player—for a frog face."

He tweaked her nose, slid a friendly arm back around her shoulders, and headed toward the kitchen.

Martha smiled at them when they came into the kitchen area. Now that the air had been cleared, Denise felt their relationship to be more of friends than a romantic interest. It still confused her that she felt such a strong affinity for Curtis, and she wondered what it meant, but it was clear he'd given her the go-ahead signal with Rich, one way or another.

If only she could give the same signal to herself.

Rich spent the next few days wondering if he had made a mistake in the parking lot. As he shuffled papers at his desk, he wondered if maybe he should have given it more time before telling Denise she needed to decide if she was in or out of the relationship. After that big revelation, she probably needed more reassurance that he wasn't bothered by her past. He glanced at a memo about an upcoming meeting and made sure it was logged in his PDA.

Okay, so he was bothered, not that it was a breaking point for the relationship. He loved her and wanted to marry her just the same now as he had before. Nothing that happened to her as a child could change that. But still, he could picture the thin little girl hiding in her room, and it bothered him. It made him angry and upset, haunted his nights and kept him from sleep. He ached for her.

He ignored his blinking email and shuffled some papers again, looking for that form he had in his hands only moments before, and then let his mind lapse back to his personal worries.

Still, the ultimatum, since that was the only way he could really view it, had been long overdue. Other than exchanging greetings with Denise at church, he hadn't seen her at all in the past few days. He missed her, but she had to make the decision, had to become active in the relationship, or back out of it entirely.

He had to back off completely. It was agonizing, but he had little choice left.

For just a moment, he closed his eyes, hoping and praying the relationship wasn't truly over. He would have to work on getting used to a life without Denise, if that was what she chose.

In some ways, it was almost a relief not to wonder if Rich would be over to talk that evening. When Denise realized that first weekend that he was serious, that Rich really wasn't going to keep working on the relationship if she wasn't willing to meet him partway, a small part of her, the part that had been telling her to call it quits, had howled with relief.

Unfortunately, that part of her was so tiny, Denise could hardly hear it anymore.

A full week went by without more than a friendly hello in passing, though she noticed he seemed to be watching her as much as she watched him when they were in the same room together. His final kiss and words still echoed in her head.

He loved her, and her past didn't matter to him, not in the ways that had worried her. Things at her new job began to even out as she became accustomed to her new surroundings. Gerald returned to school, and Denise spent more time online with other adoptees. Lily started her student teaching and put plenty of hours every night into completing her teaching certificate and preparing her lessons, when she wasn't out with John.

Time passed far too slowly.

On Friday night, more than a week had passed, and Denise was home alone, staring blankly at an old movie to which she wasn't paying any attention. She missed Rich. Was her life better without him? She couldn't say it was. Was she really better protected, would her heart hurt that much less to lose him now than to lose him later? Probably not. And why was she sitting alone, miserable, when she could be enjoying his company? Why wasn't she soaking up every drop of happiness available to her? How could she be wasting this precious time?

With a clarity she hadn't possessed before, Denise realized she had been her own worst enemy. Nothing was certain, but Rich didn't seem to care about guarantees. The only thing he wanted was her promise to try and make things work, to work on herself, and to let him be a part of her life without pushing him away constantly.

How stupid could she be?

CHAPTER THIRTY-TWO

The next morning, Denise knocked on Rich's front door at 9 AM. Rich wasn't known for being a terribly early riser, but she figured he would be up by now. She had been up for a couple of hours herself, unable to sleep, worried he might have changed his mind.

He answered the door in jeans and a T-shirt, but Denise had the distinct feeling he had pulled them on only moments before. His face was creased from his pillow, and his hair stood on end. It was endearing and made her smile.

"Denise, what are you doing here?" There was far more hope than hostility in his words.

She wet her lips and tucked her shaking hands into her pockets. She opted for the direct approach. "Did you mean what you said, about my past not mattering? That it doesn't make a difference to you?"

He lifted an eyebrow and his eyes seemed to clear, as though her question woke him up completely. "It'll always matter, because it's what made you what you are. Aside from your tendency toward martyrdom, I happen to like you a whole lot. What impresses me most is that you could make yourself into someone so amazing when you've been through so much."

Her heart lightened, and she managed a smile. "In that case, I'm offering to take you to breakfast. I believe we have a few things to talk about."

He smiled back. "Could you give me fifteen minutes to shower and change? I'll meet you at your place."

She nodded and returned to her own apartment. She spent the entire fifteen minutes pacing the living room, unable to settle down.

When Rich arrived at the door, she wondered if he really looked more handsome this morning than ever before, or if it was her imagination. He tipped his head toward the hallway and she smiled, following him out to his car.

They drove a few blocks to Denny's and slid into their seats with no more than general talk about their respective offices. When the waitress had taken their orders and brought them their milk and juice, Denise looked at Rich. There was one thing she had to clear up right away. "I'm not dating Curtis. We're not going out. He knows about you, even seemed to think I should just marry you if we feel so strongly about each other."

Rich grinned. "Smart man." His smile slid away. "What about that connection you said you felt with him?"

"I don't understand why it feels so real, so strong, but it's not as strong as the way I feel for you, or even as strong as I felt the first time I met you. Look at that grin on your face. I shouldn't be encouraging you like this." She felt a grin sliding onto her own face in response.

He laughed, took both her hands in his, and gave them a squeeze. "You had me worried. It feels good to know he's a problem we don't have."

"I'm so sorry I've been acting like a terrified child. A wishy-washy one at that. You don't deserve it."

"So we'll go on from here and look back only long enough to be sure we won't make the same mistakes again."

The fact that he didn't gloss over her mistakes stung less than she would have thought. He was right; it was past time to pretend her problems weren't there or to blow them out of proportion. "What mistakes have you made?"

"I've made some. Enough I was starting to worry you wouldn't come to me after all. Last night I was sure you would never stop at my door again. I've been trying to convince myself staying away was the right move."

"It was. I needed some time. Thanks for giving it to me." The waitress brought a fresh pitcher of maple syrup and a bottle of ketchup, and they waited until she left. When they were alone again, Denise saw Rich open his mouth and then close it again. "What is it?" she asked.

Rich shrugged. "I was just thinking, wondering when your nightmares started again. Lily mentioned that she never used to hear them but does all too often now."

"I used to have them all the time, but they grew less frequent over the years. There were months between them before everything started happening again." Denise reclaimed one of her hands to twist her glass of juice on the tabletop, watching the curved glass. "They started up again shortly before we met." She played with her straw, stirring up the ice cubes. She looked up through her lashes at him and saw the worry on his face. "No, it had nothing to do with you. There were some other events that brought it all back to me. Thinking of Daphne will do that to me, sometimes. And they haven't gone away because of the family search."

"So you think you're having nightmares because you looked up your family?"

She debated that thought for a moment and looked him in the eye. "No, I think it's because I *haven't* looked up Daphne. I hate to say it, but she was the reason I started the search. Things are starting to come together with the rest of the family. I found a sister, Kaylee, who is sweet and adorable, if a little obsessed with her music. I found aunts and uncles, and I found my dad, and his three other children.

"Pete is interested in meeting me, knowing me, and his kids have given me varied levels of acceptance over the Internet, though his wife seems to be holding back a bit still. Beth is every bit as cute as Kaylee, and Olivia's pretty well wrapped up in her own life and doesn't seem all that interested in having an older sister. But I think it could be fun, if she lets herself like me. Jesse is planning to come to the Y next fall, so he might be close by. He was awed when I told him Cliff was marrying my sister. He made me promise to introduce them when he comes here for school next year." She grinned to herself at the thought. It wasn't everyday you went from being nonexistent in a sibling's world to being the means of them meeting a hero, after all.

"I think things are going well with my family, it's . . . ." She sighed and tucked her hair back behind her ears. "As much as I'm not sure I want to talk to Daphne, or see her face again, I want to know why she put me last. Why she couldn't care about me enough to do the right thing for me. Kaylee and the other child, they had a good life with families who loved and cared for them from the start. At least I think that's true. Why did this all happen to me? And why can't I let go of it? I'm so angry with her, and I know I have to forgive her if I want to be happy, but it's so much harder than it sounds."

Rich wiped away her tears with one hand. "Oh, honey, don't blame yourself. It doesn't help to ask how or why. It happened. You're a remarkably strong person because of everything you went through. I'm not saying it wouldn't have been better if you'd been able to be adopted by the DeWalts from the beginning, but what you've been through has made you stronger. Don't you think?"

"I know all the pat answers. I've heard them most of my life."

"You don't need me to tell you if this is right; you should pray about it. He'll let you know. I can understand you not wanting to go back to see Daphne, but I'll be there for you if you decide you do want to see her. It has to be your decision. I think you already know what you need to do."

"I'm worried," she admitted after a moment. "I'm going to see her. I have to know anything she can tell me about my other brother or sister, but what if she doesn't tell me? What if the baby was stillborn and she plays with me for a long time before telling me the truth? Or what if she tells me birth information, but it's wrong? I don't know if I can trust her. Yeah, Derrick says she's made some positive changes in her life, but what if he's wrong?"

There really wasn't a right answer to her questions, certainly nothing Rich could give her, so she wasn't surprised when he reached over and squeezed her hand instead.

"So is that everything?" Rich asked a moment later, when they were both feeling calmer.

Denise shook her head. "Actually I still feel a little weird about you calling my dad about our conversation. I guess I've been keeping things to myself about you and me. My parents know about you, though they still haven't met you, or at least hadn't until Dad came to see you a few days ago."

Rich had the decency to look a bit apologetic. "It was a little odd."

"It made me uncomfortable to know you discussed something so personal with him. Something I hadn't discussed with them in years. Yet, as Dad pointed out, who else did you have to talk to?"

He laced their fingers together on the table, studying her face. "It took me a while to decide what to do, where to turn. I couldn't bring up a subject like that with just anyone. Even if Lily had been around, I wasn't sure how much you told her, and I wasn't about to divulge that kind of secret. But you said your parents knew everything, and when I prayed about it, Lynn was the only person I could think of to talk to."

The waitress brought their breakfasts. They both thanked her, giving her a smile before Rich turned back to the subject. He picked up Denise's hand again. "I knew you might get irritated, but under the circumstances, I thought it was my only resort."

"I can accept that and deal with it." She grasped his hand back, knowing she had reached a bend in the road. "I want to be with you, Rich, but I don't know that I can promise forever."

"Offer me now, and we'll let forever work itself out later."

She smiled, relieved at his words. "I think I can do that."

He ran his thumb over her knuckles and gave her hand a squeeze before releasing it so they could eat.

It had been three weeks since her talk with Rich, and Denise was grateful for the change in their relationship. They loved each other and the fact that she was no closer to being ready to commit didn't seem to bother him—or at least not much. She decided to quit pushing and enjoy their relationship while it lasted, and she found her life fuller for having him in it.

Lily started student teaching, and both she and Paige were planning like crazy for their spring weddings. Denise found the bitterness she had been feeling over their plans reduced to an occasional soft pang as she grew closer to Rich every day. With a goal worth striving for, she began a regimen of daily prayer and scripture study, and even spoke with her bishop a time or two as she worked toward becoming emotionally ready to enter the temple someday. If not with Rich, then with her adoptive family.

Daphne's block for visiting time came up on a Wednesday from 6 to 8 PM. Denise considered getting permission to leave work early to go visit, but decided she didn't need a full two hours anyway. Visiting time had already started on the day she arrived at the prison.

Her stomach began to quiver as she showed her ID and was ushered through the first set of gates. She parked her car, double checked to make sure anything of value, including her wallet and most of her keys, were locked in the trunk. She removed the single car key from the ignition, sliding it into her pocket. The rules were simple and direct. Bring nothing except a key, ID, and any change you might need for the soda machines. Be prepared to wait.

She went through another gate, down a walkway with a wire fence stretched high on each side, and pushed a button to let the steel door open. Denise refused to believe her hands were shaking as she reached for the slip of paper in the eight by eight room on the other side. She entered her name, Daphne's name, and an ID number, then walked over to the window where Ned had told her she would need to submit the paper and ID. She pushed a button, and a box like the one at her bank's drive-through window slid out. She placed the documents there. After a long moment, the paper was returned, and she sat to wait.

Two officers came in a few minutes later and began letting people go through the metal detector, and Denise got in line. She placed her coins in a clear plastic bag and put her key and her belt on a half wall beside the machine, walked through the machine, and collected everything again. She could feel her pulse scramble and hoped she wouldn't pass out. Denise wondered at her sanity in coming alone. Why hadn't she waited until Ned and Sharon were coming again? She reminded herself of the unknown sibling and strengthened her resolve. This was important, even if it was difficult.

When three other people were ready, the officer buzzed them through the last door, which led them to the room where the soda machines sat. Denise could hardly handle her change as she slipped it into the machine. Despite her general aversion to soda, she had the feeling she would need something to do with her hands while she spoke to Daphne. She put in some more change to get one for Daphne as well, hoping to soften the woman up a little. With a deep breath, she smiled at an old man beside her. His returning smile was reassuring.

"It's not such a big deal. You'll be fine," he said. Though she was certain he thought her fear was about being surrounded by security, she felt strangely reassured anyway. Denise reminded herself that she was supposed to be here, that Daphne couldn't hurt her anymore, and that her need for peace of mind had demanded she come.

Everyone was directed down a short flight of stairs into a room full of square tables with four chairs. It reminded Denise of a cafeteria from her middle school. About ten minutes later, the inmates began to arrive. She watched each face as they entered the room, knowing Daphne would be changed.

By the time five or six inmates had entered, Denise felt faintly ill. She looked at the soda in front of her and wondered if she would be able to drink it. The door opened again, and Denise looked into a familiar face.

Daphne hadn't aged gracefully. Her hair was full of gray, her cheeks sunken. The extra weight Denise remembered Daphne having years earlier had fallen off until she was much thinner. Denise imagined Daphne was probably corpselike when she came into the system and had since filled out, but only a little. Her skin looked stretched. Her gaze floated across the room, alert, touching on every face until her eyes met Denise's. One eyebrow lifted as she looked at her daughter. Daphne studied her for a long moment, and then she sauntered across the room.

CHAPTER THIRTY-THREE

Daphne sat across from Denise, an air of vague curiosity filling her face. "Denise, I wondered if you'd show up."

"Daphne." Though her stomach was rolling, Denise affected as casual an air as her mother. She pushed the extra soda across the table.

Daphne raised both her eyebrows this time and then lowered them. She scowled at the drink, and Denise wondered if it was because there was no caffeine in the soda, but then Daphne picked it up and took a few swallows anyway. "So you've returned to the fold." Daphne crossed her arms on the table and leaned in, more to support herself than to get closer, Denise thought. Denise nodded in response.

"Took long enough." Denise shrugged and Daphne continued, "So what've you been doing?"

"I'm a computer programmer. I program Internet software."

"Got yourself a fancy education an' fancy job. Think you're better than the rest of us." Daphne pushed back her hair and narrowed her eyes.

"I am what I am. I found something I enjoy, something I'm good at, and it pays decently. That's all I ask."

Daphne snorted. "So what's it pay?"

"Enough." Denise swirled her soda slightly in the bottle. She had been told to leave the cap behind in the other room and hadn't taken more than a swallow from it yet, so she couldn't roll it much. The one swallow had made her feel even more ill.

"Seen your sister?"

A smile flit across Denise's face. "Kaylee's great. She's so bright and happy. I went up to her recital a few weeks ago. She plays the cello, you know. She's really good at it. Sue thinks she could go pro, and I can't argue with her."

"I heard." Daphne took another long drink.

Denise took a few swallows of her soda and felt even sicker than before. She pushed the growing nausea away and focused on the woman who'd given her birth. "You told Sue you would only tell *me* about the other child, that I needed to come here to find out. I'm here now."

"Haven't seen you in fifteen years and only thing out of your mouth is you want something from me?"

"You manipulated me into coming before I was ready to see you. I wanted this information. That's why I'm here." Denise was picking up on the breakup of Daphne's language—her sentence structure was falling apart. Sue had warned her that drug addicts went through this, so she wasn't surprised. Denise was more surprised that it seemed so mild.

Daphne looked her over. "What if there wasn't another baby, I miscarried, and that's why you don't remember?"

"I'd say you brought me here on a lie. If there's no other child, it's time for me to go." Denise could feel the anger welling up in her chest.

"Gave you what I had. Raised you best I could, put a roof over your head, food on the table, clothes on your back. Took care of you. Least you can do is visit, get me out of the stinking cell once in a while."

Denise nodded. Daphne wasn't going to apologize, admit that she was wrong. It wasn't too surprising, though Denise had hoped for better. She still had a chance to have her say, she reminded herself. She would have to take it now. "Sometimes. Sometimes there was food. There were clothes, a few of them were my size, sometimes they were clean. Mostly not. Took care of me . . . that one's debatable, but the state already covered that issue well enough." Denise leaned back in her seat and folded her arms over her chest. "I have to wonder why you ever made an effort to get me back or to keep me from my birth dad in the first place. I obviously wasn't as important to you as you were."

Daphne's eyes blazed and one finger pointed in the air. "I did my best by you. And don't bring up that no-account. He didn't deserve time of day."

Angry, Denise watched her words carefully and moderated her tone, but said what she wanted to say. "Pete is a successful business man, remarried with three great kids. He's a good man, and you kept me from knowing him."

"He wasn't a good man then. Controlling, vindictive. I couldn't let you go to him. That's why I never told the state about him. They'd've found him. I cared about you. You belonged to me."

Denise sighed as the tightness in her stomach began to ease. The scary woman she remembered, the tyrant she'd grown up with, was no longer a threat. She was pathetic. Though Denise still felt vaguely ill, it was for different reasons. Daphne had never been a real mother, one who loved and cared for her child, and though Denise felt pity for her, she couldn't bring in a stronger emotion. Her anger disappeared. She actually smiled at that realization, feeling free for the first time in ages. Not that there weren't still chains holding her down, but they seemed to have lightened considerably.

Denise had no plans to use that pity to bring the woman into her life, to let her children meet her. Children she could almost imagine having now. With Rich. "You didn't care about me. Not really. Oh, sure, a corner in your heart somewhere cared, but not like a mother should have. You cared about your booze, you cared about the next hit, and sometimes you cared about your latest man. A woman who cared about her child wouldn't hit her hard enough to send her flying halfway across the room when the child told her what her latest man had done while she was out. You were blind and self-serving. Scared." Denise laughed lightly at herself. "Guess that one's genetic."

Daphne let out yet another snort. Denise wondered if her mother had any other defense mechanism. "So that's how it is? You're blaming me for your imagination."

"Not my imagination. There was physical evidence, in case you forgot." Seeing the stubborn look come back into Daphne's eyes, Denise curbed a sigh and stood. "Never mind. I won't waste my time with you again. I hope you keep believing those stories. I don't know how else you could manage living with yourself."

"You always had an imagination, girl."

Curbing her disgust, Denise looked into her birth mother's haggard face. "Don't you feel even the slightest remorse for everything that happened, everything your choices cost your kids?"

Daphne's dull eyes hardened. "Selfish child. You only cared about yourself. You haven't asked what it's like living in this hole." Daphne glared around her. "Having everyone watch your every move."

"You're the one who got yourself here, Daphne. No one made you take those drugs, rob that store. Your choices got you here, so you could say you chose to come to prison. I'm sorry it got this far, that you couldn't have made something of yourself instead. I'm sorry you don't seem to have learned from your stay here. Nothing to make your life better, anyway. I hope you enjoy it here, I understand you'll be here a while longer." Denise turned and took a step away.

"Denise, don't you want to know about the pregnancy? Didn't you come here for answers?" Daphne's voice was desperate, loud enough to turn heads.

That stopped Denise, and she turned back to look at Daphne. Did she trust the woman? Was she telling the truth now? Would she get the truth at all or was it a desperate attempt to continue manipulating Denise? Unable to walk away if this was her only chance, Denise decided to listen, at least for a moment longer. She walked back to the table and sat again. "What do you have to tell me?"

Indecision flashed across Daphne's face before she spoke. "Guess I started this wrong." Her hands twisted on the table, and Daphne stared at them. "Remember when you were six, we lived in Oklahoma, and we had a picnic at the park. A river ran through it, and we stopped to feed the ducks." She spread her hands out until her palms both lay flat on the table. "Shoulda done that more. You'll think I'm making it up. I wish I gave you more good memories—and fewer bad ones."

Feeling the brittle shell around her heart begin to crumble, Denise scrambled to shore it up. There was no reason not to believe she was being manipulated. "Sorry if I don't pause for a moment of silence. You had your chances. Do I have a sister or brother?"

The dark blue eyes dimmed and sadness filled the woman's face. "You're so cold. You always so cold? I made mistakes. I'd get involved with men, but always worried they didn't really love me, so I pushed 'em away. Put up a barrier to block people out, it hurts less. Therapist says so anyway."

Denise blinked as she realized she had done this time and again with Rich. *Genetics or conditions?* she wondered. She pushed the question away and focused on the reason for her visit. "It's heartwarming that you can open up to me after all this time. Do you remember a birth date?"

"So impatient." Daphne sighed.

"I'd like to believe that the first part of this visit was you acting and this is the real you, but I don't have much reason to trust you right now. When you finish, I have to hurry home and start researching. I don't know that I believe a word you're saying, and I won't take anything you say at face value. You manipulated me as a kid. You manipulated me when I was in foster care, and I refuse to allow it any more. I'm done being your pawn. If you have information, tell me."

Daphne leaned back in her seat and clapped, obviously making fun of her performance. Just as Denise had decided she might as well leave, Daphne leaned in. "You have identical twin brothers, born at LDS hospital. Don't know why I came to Utah for the birth, maybe 'cause Mormons are easy to manipulate. I wanted the money. The couple who adopted the boys already had some, but they wanted the babes, wanted them bad. Their birthday is December 8. They are twenty-two."

Could it be true? Was Daphne being honest this time? Denise didn't know. "How do I know it's true?"

"If their adoptive family kept any paperwork, it'll have my first name on it." Daphne hesitated, seeming unsure whether to complete her move. "I watched you, you know. When you played basketball in college, your team in the playoffs. Saw your games on TV. Never told Ned why I watched. I had to see you. You were great. When you hurt yourself, I heard about it. And when you couldn't play again, I mourned."

Tears prickled at Denise's eyes. She wished she could be sure she believed Daphne, but it was too far-fetched to be true. Ned or Derrick must have told her about the basketball thing. They must have. She shook her head. "No. That's not true. You didn't care about me. I was just an inconvenience, someone to shut in the other room while you had your parties. Don't lie to me."

"I'm not lying, Denise. This time I tell the truth."

Almost panicking, Denise pushed back from the table, but Daphne's hand snaked out and grabbed her wrist.

"Quit lying to me." Tears started to fall, and no matter what she did, Denise couldn't hold them back.

"I have. I quit. I'm sorry, sweetheart."

"I'm not your sweetheart." The words came out in a sob, but Denise stopped trying to move away from the table.

An officer walked over and asked if there was something wrong. Denise covered her mouth with a hand and shook her head, desperately trying to hold back the sobs that threatened to come out. Daphne's hand loosened and her touch became almost comforting. The officer studied them a moment and then turned away.

"I never stopped caring for you," Daphne said.

After a deep breath and a long moment to pull herself together, Denise was able to reign in her emotions enough to ask, "Why didn't you stop the drugs? Why wasn't I important enough for you to stop?"

"I don't have an answer. I screwed up. The pull was strong, and I knew I'd never kick it, so I gave in. I always loved you."

"Bull. That's a cop-out. Do you know how I found you? I had to check back on my original birth certificate and track down Loren Miner. He's the one who directed me back to my family. *My family.* Don't you get it? All those years I sat in foster care, bounced from home to home with no one who really cared about me, I could have been with Pete. I could have been with Ned and Sharon. I could have been with someone, *had* someone who cared about *me.* Why didn't you share that with the state?" Denise grasped her soda again but didn't lift it to her mouth. Instead she tightened her fingers around it, desperately needing something to cling to.

Tears poured down Daphne's face as well, and Denise wondered how much of it was an act. "I . . . I couldn't have you go to Pete. Knew he'd do better than me. He knew it from the start. That's why he tried for custody before. Yes, I knew he wanted custody. And he'd've been better than me. I couldn't admit I was failing. It was easy to believe I was okay if you were there. If you left, I'd prove a failure. You have a good family now, don't you?"

Denise closed her eyes on the tears that kept falling. "Yeah, my family's the best. They saved me when I was so lost; it's a wonder I found my way to sanity. I hardly deserve them." She saw the pain flash in Daphne's eyes and was surprised to feel a moment of sympathy. "They've been wonderful for me, but I wasn't always easy to live with. . . . The men. It really happened, regardless of what you want to believe."

The feel of Daphne's fingers tightening on her own brought Denise's attention to where their hands were clasped together. She wasn't sure how it happened or how she felt about it. Daphne seemed to be struggling to speak, but after a long moment she nodded. "I think I knew that, didn't want to believe it. I have terrible taste in men, honey, always have."

Though Denise didn't know if Daphne really believed it or was just pretending to, she felt vindicated by the admission, and she felt one more bolt unlock in her heart.

"The first time I saw you on TV, I knew it was you," Daphne said. "Wasn't sure at first, then you hit a three-pointer, and you smirked, like you did as a kid. I knew it was you, no question about it."

"Why didn't you ever try to contact me, if you knew where I was?"

Daphne snorted. "Would you have talked to me, come and been my buddy?"

"No." Denise nearly laughed at the idea. Of course she wouldn't have. Denise would have been mad, said her piece, and told Daphne never to contact her again. She probably would have moved and changed her phone number. "No, I wouldn't have. I don't know that I can be your buddy now, Daphne. I might forgive you, but that won't make us friends."

"I don't expect it. I don't expect forgiveness. I screwed things up, and I'm here now." She looked around the room, as if resigned to the decade ahead of her. Daphne looked back at her daughter and gave Denise's hands another quick squeeze. "I brought up basketball because, it's a theory, but your brothers play college ball. I think."

Suddenly all of the details Daphne told her about the brothers came back to her, and Denise had an unerring certainty in her chest about the answer. "No, not the Werners. You don't mean the Werners." Even as the words escaped her, Denise knew it was true. That was why she felt so comfortable with them, why they had clicked so fast. She had heard plenty of other adoptees experienced similar feelings. It had to be, but it couldn't.

When her mother nodded, Denise pulled her hands away and thought about the shared blood type, the similar chin and eyes, a strange feeling of rightness invaded her chest.

"Is something wrong with them? You know them?"

"Oddly enough, I do." Denise looked back in Daphne's eyes. "Are you sure? I mean, it could be a coincidence." *Except for the birth date, the fact that we're all basketball players, the older adopted siblings, the rightness of it.*

"Spittin' image of their father. Suppose they'll want to track him down?" She pursed her lips, as though not sure she wanted to do that. "Never told him. He was married, had another babe on the way."

Denise processed that information. It had all kinds of ramifications. "No, well, maybe Cliff. Curtis—" She realized that he hadn't been interested in meeting his family, that he'd held Cliff back, but it was too late now. Now they would have everything he didn't want. He'd said once that she would be pretty cool for a sister. Did he mean it? "Why are you telling me this? You seemed determined to be difficult when I arrived, but you changed your mind. What's in it for you?"

Daphne looked as though she were trying to appear offended. Denise stared her down, and Daphne relented. "Guilt, I guess. I messed up your life, and you could've been happy. Like Kaylee. Like the twins seem to be. This place ruins a person. I might never get out, but you have a life. Live it. Don't let the past ruin your life. Tell the boys to forget me. They're better off."

"How do I even know you're telling the truth about them? You haven't told me anything you couldn't have gotten from a sports cast."

"My name'll be on the paperwork. A first name. Lawyer's name . . . can't remember anymore, but he was old, probably dead now. There are blood tests. We were all A negative, me, you, the twins, and Kaylee. Learn the truth." The officers announced that visiting time was about to end and Daphne stood from the table. "If you think they'll care, tell the twins I watch their games when I can. Their dad, his name was Alex Fields. He's a bit older, married, will have a kid or two. Son, daughter, don't know. We met in Evanston, Wyoming. Don't know anything else. It's a start."

"You remember his name?" Denise asked, standing as well.

"Yeah, I wish I could say the same for Kaylee's dad. Have a good life Denise. You owe me that much."

Denise watched her mother turn to walk away and spoke up. "I don't owe you anything, Daphne, except my thanks for giving birth to my siblings. They're wonderful, they're so great. My life is so much better with them in it. They are a precious gift to me. Thanks for that."

"Will you visit me again?"

Denise tipped her head to the side and considered her answer for a moment. "I don't know. How about if we start with letters and go from there?"

Daphne smiled and nodded before she continued to the door where she was patted down by an officer.

Denise left the room, making her way back through the maze of doors and hallways, picking up her ID as she left. Then she was back out into the fresh air, breathing it in with great gulps. Her lungs burned with the cold and her eyes stung with tears. She had done it. She was done with it.

Daphne had been so much the same, but so much more pathetic than Denise remembered. She shivered when she remembered the look in the old woman's eyes, the anger, the refusal to accept the truth, and then the way she broke down and bled out her heart. It was freeing. Denise would never know if the story about watching their basketball games was true, or if half of what Daphne said was true, but she would know about the twins.

They were her first order of business.

CHAPTER THIRTY-FOUR

When Denise walked into her apartment half an hour later, she found Rich and John sitting at the kitchen counter with Lily, eating what looked like chicken and rice casserole.

"Hey, Denise," Rich stood and joined her halfway between the door and the table. He leaned in and gave her a brief kiss. "How was your visit?" His eyes studied her face, looking for any indication of how she felt.

A shrug was her first response, followed by a slow smile. "It was good. Really good."

Rich looked surprised. "Are you going to see Daphne again?"

"Maybe someday. Not right away. We'll work on letters for now, if things pan out." Denise went to the board where she kept her friends' phone numbers without any more explanation. She had written Curtis's number down but had never used it. She picked up the phone and dialed, her heart pounding. The phone rang half a dozen times, and went to voice mail. Not knowing what to say, she hung up and looked for Cliff's number. When he didn't answer his cell, she tried his landline. Luckily someone answered on the second ring. "Hello, is Cliff there?"

"No, he's not sweetheart," a male voice answered on the other end of the line. "But you know he's getting married. Me, on the other hand— I'm totally available."

Denise rolled her eyes. "You should be Rooke's brother," she muttered to herself. "Look. Do you know where he is or when he'll be back?"

"He's at practice. The coach has them tied up all the time. It'll probably be a good half hour or more before he gets back. You can try his cell, but he keeps it off during practice."

"Do you know which building they practice in?"

The man on the phone told her, and she thanked him and hung up. Denise turned to where Lily and Rich were watching her closely. "No time to explain, I'll fill you in later." On impulse, she gave Rich a big smacking kiss and then hurried out the door.

It took over twenty minutes to reach the gym where the guys were practicing.

Denise pulled into a parking space and barely remembered to lock the door behind her as she got out of the car. It was well after dark by now, and Denise wrapped her coat closer around her to block out the January cold. The hallway seemed longer than she remembered from the couple times she was in the building in the past, but she could hear the sounds of basketballs pounding against the floor, running, and a whistle blowing. A man called out directions, and the sounds started all over again. She reached the doorway and hung back to watch.

Cliff passed the ball to another guy, who took a shot but missed. A third player picked the ball up under the basket and passed it back to Rooke. They practiced in a circular pattern, each player practicing every position, blocking, passing, shooting, until the coach called an end to it. Denise's stomach knotted up more and more as time passed. She wondered if this was a wild goose chase, or if, miraculously, she'd found her brothers.

When the practice ended, Rooke turned and caught her eye. "Hey there, beautiful. I knew you would get sick of the geek and come back to me some day." He walked over to talk to her.

"Forget it, Rooke. I'm not giving you my sister's address. She's way too young for you anyway." She sent him a cheeky smile, since she knew he wasn't after the address.

Cliff glanced over and sent her a puzzled look when she beckoned to him. "What's going on, Denise?"

"Sorry, young lady," the coach said as he walked over to the growing group around her. "This is a closed practice."

"Aren't you done? I wouldn't want to get in the way, but I have to talk to Cliff when he's finished." Denise turned her attention to the coach, and though impatient, she tried to act deferential.

"I'm sure you don't understand this, young lady, but we're serious basketball players here, not Junior Jazz," the coach said. "You can flirt when time's up."

"I understand about conditioning and weights; I played on the women's team at the U a few years ago. And I'm not here to flirt. I just need to talk to my brother when you're through with him."

The coach looked at Cliff. "I never heard your sister played at the U. Why didn't I know that?"

Denise bit her lip and looked at Cliff. "He hadn't met me yet, sir. He only knew his adopted sisters." Her eyes swiveled back to Cliff's, and she sent him a pointed look. His eyebrows lifted, and he looked like he wasn't sure what she was saying.

"Well, I guess practice is over. But don't make it a habit to show up. He needs to stay focused," the coach said with a grimace.

"Of course not, Coach. It's kind of urgent or I wouldn't dream of coming here during practice."

The coach walked off, but Rooke stayed on, his attention riveted.

"What day is your birthday again?" Denise asked Cliff.

"December 8," Cliff said. "Is that what couldn't wait?"

She shook her head. "And where were you born?"

A look of uncertainty crossed Cliff's face. "Salt Lake—LDS Hospital, I think. What's going on?"

Denise laughed and tried to catch her breath. "I think I just found my brothers."

A slow smile made its way across Cliff's face. "I thought there was only one baby?"

"Apparently Daphne had a secret or two." Denise watched his face split in a wide grin. "But," she stopped him before things got too out of hand. "Would your parents still have your adoption paperwork? I mean, I want to check one more thing, just to make sure. Daphne hasn't always been well known for her honesty. It's possible she got her information from other sources."

"Just a minute," Cliff held up a finger and rushed to the locker room. In a minute he returned with his cell phone already out.

Denise bit her bottom lip and started pacing back and forth in front of the bleachers while he dialed home. When she walked past him the third time, Cliff reached out and grabbed her shoulder. "You're making me nervous," he told her and then spoke into the phone. "Hey, is Mom there?"

Denise played with her car keys while he waited for his mom on the other end of the line.

"How am I going to ask her this?" Cliff turned toward Denise and a panicked look came over him. "It's all happened so fast, I didn't even stop to think. Hey, Mom. I . . ." He rubbed his palm over his forehead and sat on the bench. He reached out for Denise's hand, pulling it to cradle against his chest as if he needed the moral support. "I have a question for you. There's no easy way to say this . . . Are you sitting down?"

Denise thought her heart would burst as she waited in silence while he filled his mom in.

When he finished, he paused and then laughed. "I told you to sit down. Do you know where the paperwork is? She has a few facts. I don't know about the rest of it." He looked over and moved the receiver away from his mouth. "She's going to go look. My parents are so organized it's virtually impossible for her not to find it in ten seconds." There was a pause and he laughed. "Yes, Mom, it's completely true."

The silence stretched for over a minute before Cliff spoke again. "What does it say?" He turned to Denise. "Daphne, no last name."

Denise let out a breath of air she hadn't realized she was holding. "That's her."

Cliff's eyes met hers, and he nodded. "That sounds right. Look, this doesn't change anything, right? No, Mom, I don't plan to contact Daphne anytime soon. What I do know of her, well, isn't impressive."

"She'll be in prison another ten to fifteen years anyway," Denise told him.

Cliff's eyebrows lifted, and he shifted the phone further from his mouth. "Paige never mentioned that."

"I never told her. You want to know why?" Denise's voice was sarcastic, she knew, but the wry grin he donned showed he understood completely.

"Sounds like Daphne's out of reach for a decade or so anyway." He ran a hand through his sweaty hair. "Look, I'll call and tell Curtis. He's going to have to decide what he wants, where he wants to go from here, and I need to catch my breath anyway."

Denise watched while he wrapped up the call, promising to call again the next day and turned back to her, her hand still clutched in his own.

"Wow. I think I gained two sisters and a whole family." He blinked, still in shock. "You aren't sitting down? How is it you can still stand?"

Denise smiled. "I got over my big shock earlier. So I really am your big sister."

"Little sister, you mean." He hooted and scooped her up, twirling her around. When he set her down on the floor, they were both breathless. Cliff lifted his hands to cradle her face. "I should have known. We even look alike. You have my chin."

"No, I'm the older one, remember. You have *my* chin," Denise corrected him.

"What's going on here?" Rooke asked, but Cliff and Denise just stood and stared at each other in shock for a moment.

Denise started to explain first. "You see, Cliff is marrying my sister, Paige. You've probably met her." Rooke nodded. "And I'm adopted. So are Cliff and his twin, Curtis. Until today we thought my next youngest sibling was a single birth, but I learned today it was twin boys. Cliff and Curtis, to be exact. Our younger sister was adopted by our aunt and uncle, so that makes her our sister and our cousin."

"And I'm marrying my sister's sister," Cliff said with a laugh.

Denise looked over at him. "Man, that's redneck."

Cliff picked Denise up in a hug one more time and then set her back on the floor. "I have to hit the showers, but I'll call you when I get done."

"You better! Wait until my parents hear about this. And Curtis."

Cliff's face fell a little. "And Curtis. Look, I'll call as soon as I can. Half an hour or so. Don't call Curt before you talk to me."

Denise nodded. "I'll be home."

He hadn't said not to call the rest of the family, so as soon as she got home she picked up the phone and called her mom. Jennette answered the phone, and Denise asked for her father to be brought on the line too. Considering it was nearly 10 PM, Denise was glad he was still up. Her father wasn't known for being a night owl.

Looking up at Lily, John, and Rich, who were listening in on the conversation, she made eye contact, inviting them in. "I have some news for you."

"You're getting married?" Jennette asked.

Denise snorted. "No. You know I was visiting Daphne tonight." It struck Denise that this would be a difficult thing for Jennette to deal with, and she wished she had used a little more care with her lead-in. Things were moving so fast she hardly had time to breathe. But they had known she was visiting that night, so they had probably been waiting for her to call or stop by.

Her mom said she knew about the visit.

"She had twin boys, not a single birth. Cliff and Curtis are my brothers. Cliff already checked."

"Are you sure?" Jennette asked. "Really sure?"

"As sure as I can be without a DNA test." She ran through her whole encounter with Cliff at practice. She could see Rich straining to hold back his own questions when he took her hand and gave it a squeeze. Denise and Jennette talked for a few more minutes about what it meant for her and how happy she was.

The half hour Cliff promised passed while Denise filled the others in, and the hour drew toward a close. John left, and Lily went to work. Even Rich said good night and left after a few minutes, but Cliff didn't call. Denise was agitated and couldn't sit still, but she didn't dare leave the phone for fear she would miss Cliff's call. Shortly after Rich left, there was a knock at the door, and Denise opened it to find Cliff on the other side.

He looked more subdued than he had earlier. She invited him in and asked him to sit down.

CHAPTER THIRTY-FIVE

As soon as he collected all of his things from practice, Cliff hurried home, anxious to get cleaned up and call Denise. By the time he finished his shower and was ready to call, he knew he had to call Curtis first. Denise would want to be in on the phone call, but Curtis had been adamant about not wanting contact with his biological family. Cliff knew Curtis might not respond well.

He stared at his cell phone for a long moment and then got up the courage to dial. Nerves rattled through him as he tried to imagine how Curtis would handle the news. Curtis picked up after the second ring.

"Hey, dork, I heard your game went well yesterday." Clearly, Curtis had looked at his caller ID.

"You, too, bonehead." Cliff smiled; it was a term of endearment for them. "Not too shabby. Better watch out, you might catch up with me on point totals."

"And you might have a chance at blocking half as well as I do. What's going on, dirt bag?"

Cliff cleared his throat and wrapped his fingers around the back of the chair. "Here's the thing, I hadn't planned to go out and search. I thought about it, but—"

"Are you talking about the birth parent thing again?" All the joking had left Curtis's voice as it went flat. "You know how I feel about that. It's fine for Denise, if she wants, but I don't want anything to do with it."

"I know. I wasn't going to search because you feel like that, but—"

"You did anyway?" Curtis's irritation bounced along the phone line.

"No, I didn't. Would you listen for three seconds? I was talking to Denise; she got some new information today, and we put the pieces together. Curt, Denise is our sister."

There was a long pause. "What do you mean?"

Cliff stood and paced the room. "I mean all the dates and locations match up. She had twin brothers, not a single birth like they thought."

"She said . . ." Several seconds passed in silence. "So what do you want me to do about it?" Curtis's voice was defensive, little more than a growl.

Cliff dropped his head into one hand and closed his eyes. This would kill her, after everything she went through to get the information. "Nothing. I know you've never wanted it. I can tell everyone you don't want any contact. If that's what you want."

"What about the birth mom?"

"She's in prison, so I doubt she'll be much of an issue for now. We were lucky, Curt. Denise . . . you don't want to know what she went through growing up with that woman."

"No, I don't. I don't want to know anything. As far as I'm concerned, Denise isn't even our sister, she's Paige's sister." Curtis's voice grew raspy, but hard.

Cliff shook his head, even though he knew Curtis couldn't see him. "Man, I don't care what you do about everyone else. But if you cut Denise off now, it'll kill her. After every—"

"No. I need some time to go over this in my head. I don't want anyone to call or write me. I just want to be left alone." There was panic in his voice now, seeping around the edges of the hardness. The panic was signature Curtis.

If he had been in the same room, Cliff would have been tempted to pound on his brother, as he would have when they were five. As it was, he still wanted to hit something. "Fine. I think you're making a big mistake. You connected with her, she deserves—"

"Don't." Curtis took a ragged breath. "I gotta go."

The phone clicked in his ear, and Cliff shook his head. He should have told Curtis in person where he might have been able to read his twin enough to work around the panic and nerves. But they both had such full schedules with school and basketball that they wouldn't be face to face for several more weeks.

How would he tell Denise?

He couldn't tell her over the phone. She couldn't be alone when she found out Curtis was being such an idiot about this.

She was still all smiles when she opened the door to him, making him feel even worse.

Denise was happy to see Cliff, but she couldn't figure out why Cliff's attitude had changed. "Have you called Paige yet?" she asked.

"No, I haven't had time." He sat on the sofa and pulled her down beside him. "I called Curtis, though."

"Why did you call him without me?" Denise looked at him in surprise and felt the bubbles of joy inside her deflate as she realized what that meant. "No, please tell me he didn't say. . . . He told me on New Year's Day. He told me he wouldn't mind being my brother. He felt that click of connection the first time we met. He *told* me he did. How can he change his mind now?" *How can he not want me?*

"Look, I'm sure he's just freaking out. Before long he'll realize what a jerk he's being, and he'll calm down. Don't let it get to you. He's scared. He's always been scared, and even though he knows it doesn't make sense, he still has this irrational fear. Mom's always thought it was because he thought he would be rejected, like our older brother was when he tried to contact his birth family. But I think it started before that, when we were kids. He can't help it."

Denise looked away. "I understand all too well. Fear like that is impossible to break. And it seems to be genetic. What if he never changes his mind?" She stood and began pacing around the room. *What goes around comes around.* She'd hurt Rich, was bound to hurt him worse if she couldn't let go of this fear. He was being very patient with her, but it wouldn't last forever. Now she had to feel that rejection from the other side. *Just penance,* she told herself. *Just penance.*

Cliff didn't stay much longer. Denise wasn't paying much attention anyway, she was too caught up in her anger at herself for being every bit as irrational. Maybe if she had been raised by Pete instead of Daphne, Denise would have had a chance at a healthy relationship with Rich. Maybe the slap of rejection from Curtis wouldn't have been so harsh.

Maybe.

It was too late for maybes.

When Denise spoke with Lily the next morning, she still hadn't regained her equilibrium.

"So what's wrong? You sound like you just lost your best friend," Lily said. "And you look like you didn't sleep at all. I should know; I didn't sleep at all." She smiled faintly and gazed down at the ring on her finger.

"Cliff called Curtis and told him about it. Curtis was not so sure about his feelings. He doesn't want anything to do with me now." She turned to look Lily fully in the eyes. "I was fine twelve hours ago, but now I'm related to him, forget it. He's not interested."

Lily's jaw fell. "What? Is he crazy?"

"He never wanted to be part of his birth family. He's just not interested. Cliff said he was scared, something from childhood. It's irrational, stupid, and petty, but I can understand him." She shrugged and allowed a bitter smile across her lips. "I can't even blame him."

"I can. That's ridiculous. You're great pals as long as you're not related, but the second he finds out there's a blood bond, it's over?" Lily let out an irritated huff. "He's a jerk, plain and simple."

"No. Just scared. I understand scared."

"Yeah, you should. You live it." Lily's words were barely more than a whisper, a censuring thought.

Denise felt Lily's eyes on her as she grabbed her lunch and headed for work. She didn't need anyone else to beat her up; she already felt pretty well pounded.

Denise didn't talk to anyone else about it. She knew she could get angry at Curtis, rage and bellow about how he had feelings for her, wonder how they were friends, and how could he just wipe that away now, but she wasn't a hypocrite. It was no different than loving Rich and pushing him away. *Is there any way around it? What can I do? I don't want to live like this for the rest of my life,* she thought.

"Why haven't you brought that young man home to meet me yet?" Denise's mother asked when she called midweek.

"This Sunday I'll invite him, okay?" Denise almost felt guilty about putting it off so long. It wasn't that she was ashamed of him or of her family. They had all met, pretty much, anyway. The main reason she hadn't invited him over sooner was the fear of making things too permanent. Inviting him to Sunday dinner was akin to announcing an engagement . . . well, it had never been that serious for Paige, but Denise had always felt that. She hadn't taken Brian home until they were getting serious.

"Your father and brother seem to think he's nice enough," her mother continued teasing. "I suppose he must not be too scary if your dad likes him. And you have been dating for quite awhile, longer than most guys you've been out with. Do you think it will jinx the relationship or something?"

"It's not that, Mom, I just . . . ." And maybe that was her other worry, as irrational as it seemed—that even though things were now going great with Rich, it wouldn't last after she took him home. That week she'd told him everything—more of everything than he had known before, anyway. What if she brought Rich home and he suddenly decided he didn't like her? She scoffed at herself for even thinking it, but she knew something in her believed it.

You're being stupid. "I'll bring him. You'll love him, and he'll love you too. How could he help it?" *How indeed?*

They showed up at her parents' door fifteen minutes earlier than expected the following Sunday. Denise hadn't been able to settle down, too worked up by the thought of bringing Rich home, so they left her apartment early.

"Hello, sir." Rich said as he extended a hand to her father to shake.

"Your Southern manners are fine, Rich, but if you don't start calling me Lynn, I'm going to get offended."

Rich smiled and turned to Cliff.

"It's good to see you again, Rich. Apparently my sister recognizes quality when she sees it," Cliff said.

Rich lifted an eyebrow. "Though perhaps your brother struggles with that?" Denise flinched slightly at the comment. He had been more angry about the choice Curtis had made than she was. It made her feel good that he was so thoroughly on her side, even if his anger was a bit misplaced. Cliff's lips thinned, but Denise could tell he wasn't upset with Rich. "Yeah, he's a bigger moron than I thought."

"Come on, guys, let's leave that behind us. What's the latest in the wedding plans, Paige?" Denise moved over to her sister. That effectively redirected the conversation. A few minutes later, their mother called them over for dinner.

After dessert, Denise brought another load of dishes into the kitchen for the dishwasher. Jennette looked over her shoulder at her daughter and smiled. "I'm glad things seem to be working out with your other family. I know I haven't been as supportive as I should have, but I can see it's been good for you, Curtis aside."

Denise smiled as she thought of her other relatives, pushing away the twinge of pain she felt whenever Curtis's name came up. She pulled her mom into a hug. "Yeah, they are great, but you and Dad will always be my parents. I wouldn't be who I am without you."

"I'll try and remember that. Now, Rich seems like a nice boy. I can't help but like him."

"Me either, and I've really tried to dislike Rich, with all my heart, but my heart just won't cooperate."

"That's a relief." Rich entered, carrying the salt and pepper shakers. He set them on the counter and slid his hands around Denise's waist from behind, pulling her back against him. "I really prefer you not win that battle, if you're going to keep fighting it."

Denise turned her face into his neck and dropped a kiss on his skin. How could everything with him feel so right, but terror still keep hold on her? Being in his arms felt more real and solid every day. "I've given up the fight on that one. There are too many other battles to focus on in life."

He smiled and kissed her forehead. "Amen."

Her mother smiled as well. She began humming as she turned back to the sink to rinse some dishes.

The next few weeks passed quickly. Though Denise missed the people she worked with at Donaldson, she enjoyed her work at Frandsen and began getting to know her new coworkers.

She and Rich continued to see each other regularly, and her relationships with most of her siblings carried on fine. Olivia was starting to thaw a little as she learned that Denise wasn't trying to take over her family or destroy her life, but it was an uphill battle.

Beth made Denise smile all the time. She called to say hi, sent regular emails, and even got in touch with Kaylee. While there was no biological or legal relationship between Beth and Kaylee, the two-year age difference seemed nonexistent when they were chatting online. Their parents said they spent hours instant messaging each other every week. When Rich told the girls that they would be considered sisters if they were in the South, they each started referring to the other as "my Southern Sister."

Paige started to drive the family crazy with her wedding plans, and Denise counted down the weeks until the end of the semester when Paige and Cliff would be married and the whole mess would end. Though there had been some discussion about joining the NBA, they had decided to wait one more year and see what happened.

Denise knew Curtis didn't want to hear from her, knew she was asking for trouble, but after waiting for several weeks, she couldn't help but pick up the phone. She'd been sure he would calm down after a little while, be ready to return to a semblance of their former friendship.

For years, she put up with rejection, accepted it as a matter of course. She wasn't going to make it so easy on him. This time she would make him listen, if only for a moment. Not allowing herself time to reconsider, she picked up the phone and began to dial. When a roommate passed the phone to Curtis, she could feel the butterflies whirling in her stomach.

"Hello."

"Hey, Curtis, it's Denise."

There was a long, strained pause while she heard him moving around on the other end of the line, and then she heard a door shut. "I thought I told Cliff I didn't want any phone calls."

She wanted to tell him off when she heard the hard tone on the other end of the line but reigned her emotions in. If she wanted him to stay on the line, screaming at him wasn't the answer. Not yet, anyway. "You did. It's been so long though that I wanted . . ." How did she finish that sentence?

"Wanted to see if I've lost my mind and need someone to fix it for me. Sorry, it's still here."

"Curtis, please, don't hang up. Give me a minute. I thought we were friends. I thought, I thought you were the kind of person who could see past their nose. I could understand you feeling betrayed if I had intentionally kept the truth from you until after you and I met. But I didn't. It was as big of a surprise for me as it was for you. Nothing has changed since we met. Nothing, don't you get it? I was good enough to be your friend until you found out we shared DNA. That should make the friendship between us stronger, not weaker."

A long silence ensued while Denise fought to hold back the tears that threatened to fall. Her hands pulsed with adrenaline from the confrontation and her throat felt tight. Finally, she took a deep breath. "It makes me feel as though I'm unimportant, as though knowing where I came from now, where we both came from, lowers my value as a human being. Like I'm worthless because I came from Daphne."

Denise had about given up on him speaking again when she heard a ragged breath on the other side of the line. "I can't explain. I don't have to explain myself to anyone. I won't. I'm truly sorry that you feel that way. I don't want to hurt you, but I'm not at a place right now where I can deal with this." There was a brief pause, and then Denise heard a click on the line.

Unable to hold back her tears any longer, she turned off the phone and hurled it through the open doorway into the empty living room. In another few minutes, she changed into her gym clothes and headed to work out.

CHAPTER THIRTY-SIX

Denise's words haunted Curtis.

He went through the motions of day-to-day life—school, practice, games. But in the back of his mind was the knowledge that he liked Denise. She had been great, and he'd hurt her.

Knowing he had screwed up didn't change the reasons why he'd done it, though.

As he opened his drafting program, Curtis remembered how excited his oldest brother Aaron had been when he made contact with his birth family years earlier. Though he played it down in front of their parents, Aaron yearned for that blood connection. Curtis knew it. So when the opportunity to meet his birth family came along, Aaron jumped at it.

Curtis remembered the happy, but apprehensive, way Aaron acted when he returned from the first meeting—the hope and curiosity he shared with his younger brothers.

Clicking to create a new project, Curtis shook his head. What he couldn't forget—what was drilled into his memory the most—was the way Aaron shattered when no second meeting happened. When his family decided they had filled their curiosity enough, they cast him off like a shirt with an ink stain. Curtis was still angry at the thought of the pain his brother had gone through. He sat back in his seat and ran his hands over his face.

If he took Denise into his life, and she decided later she didn't want him, would he shatter like Aaron?

When he realized he had, in essence, done just that to Denise, that after all of these weeks she still wanted to have him around, to be part of the family, Curtis knew he needed to fix the problem—one way or another.

Monday evening Denise was online looking up family members for someone in her adoption group. Her concentration hadn't been up to her usual level today, but she didn't think she was doing badly. She had tried journaling again and was starting to feel her current layer of fears drain away. One day, she hoped to settle the worries in her heart and mind.

Though searching for her birth family had brought up difficult emotions, making contact seemed to be helping. Talking with Daphne had made the biggest difference of all. Having her birth mother admit that she knew Denise was telling the truth about her mother's boyfriends had gone a long, long way toward calming those fears. Her nightmares had tapered off, and more than a glimpse of the future was peeking through. A future with Rich.

She smiled at the memory of Rich arguing game stats with Cliff and her dad at Sunday dinner when the phone rang. Without glancing at the caller ID, she picked up the phone. "Hello?"

"Hi, it's Curtis."

All other thoughts fled her mind as her breathing stopped for a moment. She forced herself to answer, but her voice sounded flat to her own ears. "Hello."

She heard him let out a long breath of air. "Just call me a moron and get it over with. I know I deserve it."

His call threw her off balance, made her feel wrong footed. "You're a moron. Is that supposed to be an apology?"

"You're right. I'm sorry I'm such a moron. I don't know what happened when Cliff called me. I just clamped up. I'm glad to find out you're my sister. I'm not sure how I feel about the rest of the family, but I'm glad about you. You took a big risk finding all of our family, and I couldn't make my 10 percent effort to meet you."

"It hurt me, Curtis. I understand where you're coming from, but it still hurt. I thought we had something. Man, I'm such a hypocrite." Denise pushed her hair back from her face. "You and I, we're two of a kind. You know the torture I've been putting Rich through? I don't know why he hasn't given up on me yet. I just can't get past it. I thought after I visited Daphne it would go away, but I guess I still can't give up the control."

"How was your visit with Daphne?" It sounded as though Curtis wasn't sure he wanted to know, not really. "Cliff hasn't said anything about it, though I can't blame him."

"Believe it or not, it went well. Surprisingly well. I could almost forgive her for everything she put me through. Maybe someday I'll succeed."

"You *want* to forgive her?"

Denise laughed lightly. "Not really. Part of me wants to hate her forever. But part of me *wants* to want to forgive her. I figure that's a good starting place. We had a good talk and she said," she paused and considered before continuing her thought.

"What?"

"She told me the name of your birth dad and where he lived when you were conceived."

"I don't want to know." There was no hesitation in his voice.

"No, I didn't think so. I wrote it down. If you ever change your mind, I have it."

"Thanks, I'll remember that."

She smiled, feeling better about things than she had in a long time. "Are you finished being a moron, rat face?"

"Yeah, geek lover. I'm done."

"That wasn't much of an insult. It happens to be true that I'm a geek lover. In fact, I'm a regular geek myself." Denise settled back in her chair, the laptop temporarily forgotten.

"Okay then, manure breath."

"You can't smell my breath from there."

"You know Gerald called me last week and bawled me out for being such a jerk."

"Did he?" Denise found herself inordinately pleased. "Typical Lancelot complex. Rich didn't call you too, did he?"

"No."

"Good, I better tell him you came to your senses before he gets around to it. Too many Lancelots in my life." Despite her words, she smiled at the thought of everyone who loved her. She had never felt so secure before, so much like she had a place where she belonged. Curtis was the final piece snapping into place.

"I'll try and remember that, frog face," he said.

"You can't use that one. I call it for all time."

"You can't *call* insults."

"Sure I can, I'm the big sister. I get to make up the rules."

Denise was busy the next couple weeks talking to or emailing her family, spending time with Rich, reading her scriptures, and praying. It seemed that her life began to come back into focus as she put her problem in the Lord's hands.

After a quick breakfast one morning, she settled on the sofa to read her scriptures. The latest Grisham novel sat nearby, tempting her to switch books, but she resisted. Lily should be coming in soon, and Denise wanted to talk to her. They hadn't had any time to sit and talk lately.

The door finally opened and a slack-eyed Lily appeared, though she seemed otherwise aware. "Hey, Denise, sleep well?"

"Better than you. How are you managing to work and student teach at the same time? You should be dropping dead about now."

"I'm more than halfway done. I'm holding on by sheer stubbornness." Lily flopped onto the sofa beside her and leaned her head back, allowing her eyes to close. "What are you doing up? It's Saturday, you should be in bed still asleep. That's where I belong. Bed." She said that last word softly, like a sweet caress.

Denise laughed silently. It wasn't that she didn't feel for her roommate. It was a rough position to be in, but it was funny the way Lily melted into the sofa, boneless. "I couldn't sleep anymore. Too much on my mind, I guess."

Lily's right eye opened to peer over at her. "You're afraid."

"Of course. Isn't that stupid?"

With a sigh, Lily pulled herself into a full sitting position, folding her legs under her to turn and face Denise. "A couple years ago I had a lesson in institute. The teacher was talking about fear, especially fear to do the right thing, the thing that will make us happy in the end. He said we have to give fear its due respect, but move forward anyway. We must do more than have faith, we must exercise it. You've prayed about Rich. The only thing holding you back now is fear."

"Easy for you to say." The words came out more of a mumble than anything, and Denise realized Lily was right, but it didn't make things any easier now.

Lily shot her a long-suffering look. "God doesn't give the spirit of fear, but the power of love. That fear you're feeling doesn't come from our Father in Heaven. It comes from Satan. You still have the ability to love, to make things work in your life. God's love will help you create the life you need, if you acknowledge the fear and move on."

"It sounds so simple when you say it like that." Denise felt the rightness of Lily's words, but she wasn't quite ready to face it.

"I've watched you and Rich. You're perfect for each other, you love each other, and giving into fear is hurting both of you. I hate to see you hurting because I love you both. Don't let the evil things your mom did to you ruin one more minute of your life." Lily leaned back against the edge of the sofa. "I'm exhausted. If I've offended you, forgive me. It just seems to me that there comes a time when enough is enough."

Denise watched Lily stand and walk towards her room without another word. Her eyes strayed back to the statue Rich gave her at Christmas with its accompanying scripture. She read the line, "Ye shall find rest unto your souls." "It's enough," she said quietly. Lily looked back at her. "Thanks, Lils."

With a nod, Lily closed the door behind her. Denise lifted her Bible and read the verse again. It was true; she had let her fear take over, control her life, make her miserable. And this time it wasn't only Denise who suffered when she let fear grip her. All of the times she pushed Rich away, kept that invisible barrier between them, she had hurt him too. She bowed her head and began to pray, earnest and heartfelt, that she could let her fear go.

Three days later, Denise sat at the bar in her kitchen, flipping through *PC Magazine*, glancing at articles on new technologies, pitting one utility against another, and checking out the advertisements for upgrades when the doorbell rang. Caught up by an ad for a new wireless network router, she grabbed the magazine and carried it with her to the door, looking away from it only when the door was open.

"Rich." A smile slid across her face, and she forgot the magazine in her hand.

He walked in and kissed her lightly, making her lips buzz. "There's a response I like to see. How are you doing, beautiful?"

"Better now you're here. Jake behaving himself at the office?"

"Not a chance." Rich took the magazine from her hand and glanced at the ad with curiosity. He folded it open at her spot and set it on the counter before grabbing her jacket from the peg on the wall. "He got me with the Room Defender again today. I figure he's trying to make up for your loss. Tim is quiet and focused on his work." Rich said, referring to the guy who'd replaced Denise.

"I don't dare set mine up at work, my boss would freak. You might find it running here someday though. I showed it to Curtis, and he and Cliff want to use it sometime on their brother. They would put Jake to shame."

"Good." He took her hand and led her toward the door. "Do you have your keys with you?"

"Yes. Are we going somewhere?"

He set his hands on her shoulders and dropped a kiss on her head. "Do you have other plans for the evening?"

"No. Are you taking care of dinner?"

"Yes. Brick Oven is calling to me."

Denise let him lead her from the apartment with little more than a lifted eyebrow. "What makes you think I want to spend the evening with you? Maybe I have plans with my secret boyfriend."

"He'll have to reschedule. Besides, you always want to have dinner with me. You're crazy about me. That's why you're going to marry me someday."

"I am?" Denise sent him a sideways look and held in a grin.

Rich stopped in front of his apartment door and pulled her into his arms, kissing her breathless. "Aren't you?" he asked when he pulled away. "I've felt the change in you lately, like you're happy with who you are, where you are. Don't you think you'll be able to marry me someday? Preferably someday soon. I love you, Denise."

At that moment, Denise felt the last of her reserves drain away. She knew what she said to Lily was true—it was enough. Just being with him was enough to justify the risks.

Denise slid her arms around Rich's neck and pulled him closer.

"Yeah, I guess I am. How does May sound?"

Rich let out a hoot of joy and then pulled her close for another kiss. "May sounds just about perfect."

EPILOGUE

A warm spring breeze blew Denise's curls and silken veil as she and Rich came out of the temple in their wedding clothes. The simple white dress fluttered, the sun warmed her skin, and the smiles of their families surrounded them. Denise looked around and felt the glow coming from inside her. Lily and John stood to one side, fresh from their honeymoon in Acapulco. Paige and Cliff stood beside them, a more seasoned married couple of three weeks. Jesse nudged Cliff and sent conspiratorial glances toward Denise.

Beyond the flowers at the temple doors stood Pete, Renee, and their girls. Beth giggled with Kaylee, and Olivia stood to the side, shooting glances at one of Rich's cute male cousins. The Virginia contingent had been in town for several days, and Denise had been thrilled to get to know her other siblings better. Olivia was still a little standoffish, but Denise held high hopes.

The only fly in her ointment was the fact that Curtis still wasn't interested in meeting the rest of the family. Not that he hadn't seen a few of them in the temple, or wouldn't be around them at the reception, but he put out the word to give him space. Denise hoped that would melt away in a short while, and decided to leave that for him to worry about later.

Her parents stood to the side while the photographer adjusted his camera for a shot. She had been sealed to them in a special ceremony a few days after Paige and Cliff had returned from their honeymoon and the day after Gerald had received his endowments in preparation for his mission. They were truly a family now, in every way that mattered.

Rich leaned over and kissed her cheek, pausing to whisper low in her ear, "Seems like a dream, doesn't it?"

"I can't believe everyone made it here. I'm so happy."

"I was talking about you, me, and the temple," he whispered, and poked her in the side.

"Oh, yeah, that." She'd known that was what he meant, but found the idea of being surrounded by family almost as amazing as the fact that she was now Mrs. Richard Jensen. Then again, maybe it wasn't nearly as amazing. She looked up in his eyes and knew that whatever the future might bring, he would be there with her. Together, they could work through any difficulty.

DISCUSSION STARTERS

1. When Denise gets stressed out, she resorts to heavy cleaning. How is that a healthy way to deal with stress? In what ways is it unhealthy?

2. Even though she was only a child, Denise still feels responsibility for the choices Daphne made and for not being good enough to make Daphne make different choices. Do you think this is a common phenomenon among both abused children and those from non-abusive homes? Do people often internalize other people's guilt?

3. Despite the fact that Denise had been baptized into the Church and made many changes in her life, she still felt unworthy to enter the temple. In what ways do we, as members, hold onto our guilt and feelings of unworthiness even after we've repented of mistakes?

4. Denise feels like John sees her differently after she tells him that she was a foster child. In what ways do we make snap, and sometimes erroneous, judgments about those around us based on a few details?

ACKNOWLEDGMENTS

There are so many people who were instrumental in the production of this book. My thanks to the people at the About.com adoption forums who taught me so much about adoption and reunion before I ever considered writing this story. I want to thank the awesome people at Author's Incognito who cheered me on, critiqued for me, and were brutally honest when necessary. Special thanks to Mary Greathouse, Danyelle Ferguson, Josi Kilpack, Shanna Blythe, and Cindy Beck for telling me like it was and helping me improve my writing. Also to the LDS Storymakers for holding awesome conferences, and not only encouraging me along my journey, but showing me how to succeed. I feel as though they all became my friends years before I was officially able to join their ranks.

Thanks to my editor, Heidi Doxey, and to Jennifer Fields for their willingness to help and quick responses when I had a question or concern, and to all of those at Cedar Fort for taking a chance on my book.

I saved the best for last. A huge thanks to my sweetheart, Bill, and my parents for always believing in me and supporting me, even when I wasn't sure I believed in myself anymore. This has been a long process, and I couldn't have done it without them.

ABOUT THE AUTHOR

Heather Justesen was born and raised in the heart of rural Utah. She spent most of her time reading and daydreaming as she grew up, much to some of her teachers' frustration. After attending Snow College, she transferred to Southern Utah University where she met her husband, Bill.

While living in Utah Valley after they both graduated, they foster parented fifteen children, and Heather worked for the newspaper and learned to love gardening. She now lives in her hometown of Fillmore, Utah, where she and her husband own a business, are both active on the local ambulance service, and raise a wild mix of cats, dogs, chickens, geese, ducks, a rabbit, and fish.

This is Heather's first novel with Cedar Fort. To learn more about Heather and her writing, visit her website: www.HeatherJustesen.com or check out her blog: www.HeatherJustesen.blogspot.com.